FRACTURED
Hymns

A.M. Arthur

CHAPTER ONE

August

Ethaniel Shockley waited until the top of the extension ladder was flush to the side of the house and the base secure on the ground before putting his foot on the bottom rung. He double-checked his tool belt, as was his habit before going up, because coming down for a forgotten tool was a pain in the ass. Better to be thorough than waste time.

"You drop your balls somewhere or what, E?" Andy Tolley asked. The skinny Pole from Chicago never missed a chance to give Ethan shit about his insistence on preparedness. Even though Andy had served in the 82nd Infantry, he acted like an unbroken pony—spirited, high-strung and galloping toward disaster.

"At least I brought my balls back with me," Ethan snapped.

Behind Andy, Butch Pelligrino guffawed loudly at the familiar line. The three of them had been roofing houses together for almost two years, and they got along like bread and butter—despite the fact that Butch was former Navy, while Ethan and Andy were both Army. They all three wanted to do their jobs, earn a paycheck, and sleep without having nightmares. Since his return from Afghanistan eight years ago, Ethan had found that a long day's labor in the hot summer sun meant a deep, dreamless sleep.

Winters were more difficult.

"Supervisor said the north end of the roof is rotted, right?" Ethan asked. "The rest is safe to walk on?"

"For the sixth time, yes," Andy said. "They surveyed these roofs yesterday, and this one's mostly fine. The roofs on the two end units are rotted through all around."

"Okay."

Ethan ascended the ladder, carefully placing his feet each time. He had no problem with heights, but sometimes ladders gave him fits. He'd fallen off the barn ladder twice as a kid, and he hated that free-falling feeling. Probably why he'd never bothered with the airborne division. He preferred his feet on a firm, flat surface.

Their company was replacing the roofs on a two-story converted apartment unit. Three bottom units, three top units, and they'd been leaking all winter. The landlord had finally ponied up for an assessment, and the company they worked for got the bid. Ethan, Andy, and Butch were going up to start ripping out the old tar paper so they could look at the structure underneath.

At the top of the ladder, Ethan paused and studied the roof. Big, square patch with little to visibly divide the three units, except some duct tape their boss had placed yesterday. Ethan squinted at the lines. This was where he'd been told to place the ladder so they'd come up on a firm portion of roof, but the whole thing looked warped and sad.

"You gonna make love to it with your eyeballs, or what?" Butch yelled from farther down the ladder.

"At least the monk would be makin' love to somethin'," Andy said.

Ethan removed his hand from the ladder rung long enough to flip them both off, then hoisted one leg over the ledge. The ceiling felt firm enough beneath his right foot, so he climbed off.

So far, so good.

He moved to his right so Andy could get up and over.

"Oh, hey, so's I don't forget," Andy said while Butch climbed up. "Susan is throwing an anniversary party for us next weekend, and she told me to invite anyone I wanted. Since this is mostly going to be her girlfriends, I'm inviting all the men I know."

"Then why are you inviting Butch?" Ethan asked.

Butch took a lighthearted swing at him that Ethan ducked. "Says the guy who couldn't get a piece of snatch if he paid her. You gonna bring a girlfriend around once in a while?"

Ethan ignored the gentle pang of apprehension that always plagued him when his lack of a love life came up in conversations at work. He never brought a girlfriend around, or even talked about one, because he had no interest. And the men he used to scratch the occasional itch were rarely worth a second look.

"I would if I was the girlfriend type," Ethan said, playing up his role as a love-them-and-leave-them ladies' man.

Butch snorted. "You are so full of shit. Just wait, one of these days you'll fall for a pair of big brown eyes and long legs."

He hoped so, as long as they came attached to a dick.

"Whatever, you two," Andy said, "just show up."

"Definitely," Ethan said. He wasn't much of a social butterfly, especially with the guys he worked with. They were all former military, he took great pains to stay firmly in the closet around them. His family, as well. But Andy and Susan had been married for three years and Susan was six months pregnant with their first child. Ethan could suffer a few hours of social niceties in order to wish his work buddy well.

"Let's do this," Butch said.

Ethan walked farther out onto the roof, using his crowbar to test the tar paper with each step. Despite the supervisor's report, something felt off in this section. Too soft. He stopped halfway to the spot where the roof was supposed to be rotted. Instincts that he trusted without question screamed at him to wait. Something wasn't right.

"Guys, hold up a minute," he said.

"What?" Andy kept walking, putting two feet between them before turning around.

Ethan pressed with his left foot. Something snapped. Groaned. His stomach dropped. He glanced back at Butch, whose eyes went wide with alarm. "Back up slow," he said to Butch. "Andy? Really, really slow."

"They told us this was solid," Andy said.

"I know, but it's not."

Ethan shuffled back a few inches, towards Butch. The structure beneath him shuddered and rumbled. Someone's voice squawked over his radio.

The ceiling beneath Andy caved in first, and he was gone in a crash of wood and plaster. Ethan yelled his name.

Butch screamed.

Ethan's world gave out, and he plummeted into darkness.

CHAPTER TWO

October

"Are you sure you don't want to come to church with us, honey?" Mom asked, with expected precision, at nine-thirty on Sunday morning. She was already in her blue floral dress and matching flats, and flanked on either side by his sister-in-law Jillian and niece Sarah.

Ethan looked up from the scrambled eggs he was still choking down at the kitchen table, fork poised to spear some more of the fluffy yellow mess. In the month-plus that he'd been back home to recuperate from his accident, his mother asked the same question every single Sunday on her way out the door.

His answer never changed. "No, thank you, ma'am."

"You know it's an open offer. You might meet some young people your age."

"I know."

"Bye, Uncle Ethan," Sarah said as she followed her mother and Gram out the kitchen door. Sarah was eight and the spitting image of her mother, which Ethan thanked God for every day the thought occurred to him, and he didn't thank God very often.

Other than some DNA, Sarah shared little in common with her father, Ethan's brother Daniel.

Sarah wasn't his daughter, but she was the closest thing Ethan would ever have to one, and he adored her. The only good thing his busted leg had done for him was force him to move home from Pennsylvania to Delaware, where Jillian and Sarah lived with the rest of Ethan's expansive family on two hundred acres of land. Most of the land was for the horse farm they'd been running for three generations. Smaller sections had been handed off to his siblings as they married and settled down, keeping the eldest three Shockley kids tethered to home.

Ethan had been so eager to get away from the stifling horse farm as a teen that he'd enlisted in the Army as soon as he graduated high school—he'd never expected getting away from home to cost him so much of himself.

He shoveled down the last of the cold eggs, along with a glass of orange juice, because he'd promised Mom he would. Eating had become more of a chore than a pleasure since the accident. He never knew what would nauseate him. Sometimes foods he used to love tasted awful for no good reason.

One more side effect of the concussion that had laid him up in the hospital for most of September.

The cast on his right leg, from ankle to above his knee, was the other reason for his long hospital stay. Losing both his mobility and his independence had been the most humiliating time of his life. The decision to move home had also made him a hermit on the farm. The last thing he wanted was (a) sympathetic looks and platitudes, (b) well-meaning questions, or (c) something going wrong in public.

Something like getting dizzy while stepping out of the tub and face-planting on the bathroom floor.

The bruise on his cheek from that incident had almost completely faded.

He leaned on one crutch while he hobbled first his plate and fork, and then his juice glass over to the dishwasher. Putting them in was easy enough. Getting a detergent pod from under the sink required a little extra finesse. Leaning down was like courting a dizzy spell. He stuck his cast-covered leg out to the side, then squatted on his left leg to retrieve the pod. His leg screamed from the stress of standing back up, and he was panting by the time the dishwasher was locked and on.

Sunday mornings were generally quiet around the stables. They didn't open for riders until one o'clock, which gave the family free time to do whatever they wanted. Some of them—Mom, Jillian, Sarah, his brother Caleb and Caleb's fiancée Polly, his sister Abigail's family—attended the Methodist church in town. Dad, Benny, and Benny's two sons went fishing at the pond on the southern edge of the property. Benny's wife Lesley…well, he didn't know what she did on Sundays. Laundry?

Ethan did the same thing he did pretty much every single day: he collected his iPod from its charger on the back kitchen counter, crutched his way out to the front porch, and settled onto the wicker swing with his leg up on a waterproof cushion.

Audiobooks had saved his sanity. He'd always been an avid reader, and he had sixteen boxes of books stored in his parents' attic. Thanks to his concussion, reading printed words for longer than fifteen minutes produced mind-numbing headaches. Even if they'd had high speed internet—which they didn't, because they were in the middle of nowhere—he couldn't have spent more than fifteen or twenty minutes online before getting off, even to play games. More than an hour of television usually ended with a migraine. Coupled with his inability to do anything more physical than hobble a hundred yards from the house to the practice arena, audiobooks were all he had as entertainment.

Earbuds in place, he started his audiobook from the last chapter and lost himself in the narration.

A formation of snow geese flew overhead, migrating elsewhere. This late in October, most of the geese were either gone or had settled into their winter homes. The leaves in the forest surrounding the edges of the horse pasture were a stunning mix of yellows, golds, and reds, and they weren't finished turning yet. It had been an unusually warm autumn so far, but the weather could snap cold anytime.

The family car appeared at the far end of the paved driveway, coming back toward the house. The driveway curved past the main public barn, as well as the smaller private barn—where they housed other people's horses—and the practice arena, before ending in the private family lot. Mom parked her red station wagon in its usual spot.

His three favorite women climbed out of the car, along with a fourth, unexpected face. He didn't know Angel Garrett very well. The young stable hand showed up at the house for dinner most nights because his apartment only had a hot plate, but he always ate in the kitchen instead of the family dining room. He lived on the property, had worked for his parents for three years, and mostly kept to himself. For some reason, seeing Angel get out of his mother's car wearing pressed slacks and a button-up dress shirt surprised him. He wouldn't have pegged the kid as the church-going type.

Then again, what did he actually know about Angel?

Angel said something to Mom, then strolled off toward the garage where his apartment was. Caleb had lived in that tiny apartment before meeting Polly. The two had moved into their own new house on the northwest side of the property last month —an engagement gift from Mom and Dad. Abby had lived in the apartment before that, giving it up for marriage and four kids. Ethan had joined the Army before he could be offered the apartment's moderate amount of privacy. And even if Angel wasn't living there, Ethan could never have managed that long flight of stairs in his present condition.

Mom and Jillian went inside through the kitchen door on the side of the house, but Sarah bounced around to the front porch.

Ethan saw her coming and paused his book. "Hey, chicklet, how was church?"

"It was okay. We didn't have kids' church because the choir sang today. They sang a lot of songs, and then Pastor Jameson talked for a while. He talks to the grownups, though, so I didn't like it much."

"I don't like it much, either. That's why I don't go."

"Mommy says I have to go until I'm fourteen. Then I can choose if I want to go, and I probably won't."

"Why not?"

"You don't go. I'd rather stay here with you."

Ethan wanted to tell her that in six years he might not be here anymore, so she shouldn't use him as an excuse. Instead, he said,

"Well, I think it's good that you go. I know your mommy likes it, and church is good for kids."

Sarah scowled. "Then how come none of my cousins have to go?"

"You know what? You should ask Aunt Abby and Uncle Benny the next time you see them."

"Okay."

His siblings were going to love him for that. Abigail was the eldest of the five Shockley kids, and she had four children of her own, ages fourteen to five, with her husband Mark. They lived in a big house on the north side of the property. A path through the woods connected their home to the main farmhouse, as well as the house where his eldest brother Benny and his family lived. Benny and Lesley's two sons, Doug and Zack, were eight and ten, and they were hell beasts on a good day. Ethan tended to gravitate to the porch when they were inside, because their voices grated on his nerves like sandpaper.

He was a little scared of the offspring that Caleb and Polly were likely to produce.

What had once been a constant barrage of "When are you going to settle down and have kids, Ethan?" had dried up to a mere trickle this past year, and Ethan was glad of it. Mom and Jillian were the only two people in the family who knew he was gay, and they'd subtly gotten the rest to back off.

"What book are you hearing?" Sarah asked.

"*The Three Musketeers* by Alexandre Dumas."

"What's it about?"

"It's about a young man who wants to be a special guard for the king of France, and he ends up having a lot of adventures."

"Adventures like you had?"

Ethan's pulse jumped. Sarah only had a vague idea of what it meant to be in the Army, and he'd explained it as far as "we went overseas to protect innocent people." She didn't need to know anything else until she was older. "Something like that, yeah."

"Neat."

"Sarah!" Jillian's call from inside the house startled them both. "Please come inside and change into your play clothes!"

Sarah giggled, then scampered in through the front door. Ethan un-paused his book.

When his bladder and butt demanded he get up and move around, he left his iPod on the swing and crutched into the downstairs bathroom. He avoided the kitchen, where the sweet scent of cooking hamburgers made his stomach roll unpleasantly. He retreated to the fresh air of the porch, determined to take a short walk. The five steps down from the porch to the front yard took some careful maneuvering, but he managed it without breaking a sweat or having a dizzy spell, so he counted that as a win. Dad had offered several times to build a ramp, but Ethan didn't want him to go to all that trouble. His leg would heal eventually.

His head was another story.

Dad's pickup truck rumbled up the driveway with Dad and Benny in the cab and Ethan's nephews standing up in the back. He waited for the truck to park next to Mom's car, then hobbled over.

"We caught fish," Zack announced. He leapt out of the back with a white pickle bucket in both hands. Water sloshed out, and something inside thrashed. "We caught four fish to eat for lunch."

Ethan checked out the four black crappies. "Nice haul. Who caught them?"

"I did," Zack and Doug said at the same time.

Doug bounced over to join his big brother. "I caught one. That one right there."

Ethan had no idea which fish Doug was pointing at. "That's a nice one, pal. Great job."

"I caught the other three," Zack said, puffing up his chest.

"So that means Dad and Paps were slacking, huh?"

Benny flipped him the bird over his kids' heads. Paps chuckled while he gathered up the poles from the truck bed. William Shockley's four sons looked exactly like him: light brown hair with shades of blond, dark green eyes, long noses, sharp cheekbones. Zack, Doug, and his niece Dana had inherited those looks to a T. Only Abigail and her other three kids had Ruth Shockley's dark brown hair and brown eyes.

"You better get those fish to Gram fast, because she's already cooking hamburgers for lunch," Ethan said.

Doug and Zack raced off with their catch, and moments later the kitchen door slammed.

"How's the leg today, son?" Dad asked. A familiar, repeated question.

"Hurts less than yesterday," was Ethan's canned response. It wasn't always true, but today he could say it honestly.

"Sleep last night?"

"Some."

"Good. Sleep helps bones heal faster."

Ethan didn't know if that was true, but it helped his dad to say it, so he accepted it. Dad never seemed to know what to do with his two youngest sons. Growing up, Ethan had never shown the same interest in horses as his two eldest brothers. Daniel, who was barely a year older, had even less use for the horses, and he'd gotten into a lot of trouble in high school, going so far as to get suspended twice during Ethan's junior year. Daniel had nearly been held back his senior year, but some last minute power-studying with help from Ethan and Jillian—who'd dated Daniel since they were fifteen—had helped him graduate.

Sometimes Ethan missed how close he and Daniel used to be, before high school complicated things. And then Ethan enlisted, Daniel started drinking, and they each ended up in very different kinds of prisons. Daniel's was physical, while Ethan's was emotional.

Benny and Dad carried the fishing equipment into the garage behind the house. Doug and Zack raced back out of the kitchen with their bucket, yelling about cleaning them so Gram could cook them.

Ethan hobbled in the opposite direction. If hamburgers made him queasy, he was pretty sure frying fish would give him dry heaves.

He ended up outside the roofed arena most often used for dressage competitions. Angel was near the middle of the arena, raking out the sand. Even on Sunday, when everyone else took the morning off, the kid was working. Although maybe "kid" was unfair. From a distance he looked eighteen, but Mom said that Angel was twenty-four. Up close—on the few occasions he'd seen Angel up close—Ethan saw the faded scars and worry lines of someone who'd lived hard over a short number of years.

Angel's lean shape blurred out of focus briefly. Ethan blinked a few times, then moved to sit on the first row of built-in bleachers. He'd been standing for too long. His vision cleared after a few minutes off his feet, only to be filled by a sweating bottle of water.

He looked past the bottle at Angel's concerned frown.

"I d-d-didn't open it."

Strange thing to say, but okay. Ethan took the bottle. "Thanks."

"You okay, s-s-sir?"

"Just a little tired." He twisted off the cap. "And you don't have to call me sir. Makes me feel like I'm still in the Army."

"S-s-sorry."

Ethan drank the water in small sips, waiting for each to settle before adding more, until he'd managed about half of the sixteen ounces. His audience hadn't left. "You must be more bored than I am if you're standing there watching me drink water."

Angel's cheeks darkened. "Apologies. Ruth asked me to keep an eye on you when you're about. S-s-says you get d-d-dizzy s-s-spells."

"Oh." Everyone in the family knew about his post-concussive syndrome, so why not the hired help? "Thanks, I guess."

"You're n-n-not mad?"

"Why would I be mad?"

Angel shrugged, clearly out of his element and unsure how to extricate himself from the conversation. He had a bashful cuteness about him, if only he'd smile. His curly brown hair had streaks of gold, likely from time spent in the sun, and his dark brown eyes were haunted with more things than Ethan dared ask about. Another ten pounds on him wouldn't hurt, either.

Twenty-four going on sixty.

"What?" Angel asked. He touched his cheeks like he expected to find something clinging to his tanned skin.

"Nothing. Sorry." He should probably excuse himself, but he was in the unique position of having a conversation with the reticent stable hand. Perfect time to ask a few questions. "Is Angel your real name?"

"N-n-no. It's Matthew."

"Where did Angel come from?"

"My grandmother. She d-d-died when I was ten."

"Oh. Sorry."

Angel shrugged. "It was a long time ago. Cancer."

"Mom had cancer. Breast cancer. She's been in remission for almost five years." After months of chemo, a double mastectomy, and a lot of prayers from a son who rarely saw a reason to speak to God.

"She told me. She's very brave."

"Yeah, she is."

"You took care of her while she was s-s-sick."

Ethan tilted his head up to study Angel more closely. Mom didn't talk about her illness very often, and it surprised him that Angel knew so much about an event that occurred two years before he came to the stables. She obviously liked him. She'd always had a special place in her heart for down-on-their-luck strays. Dad had once said that she insisted they hire Angel, even though he had no experience with horses. Mom used to say you could see someone's heart in their eyes.

He tried to study Angel's eyes more closely, but Angel was looking at the ground.

"Mom needed someone here, and I could take the time off," Ethan said.

"You have s-s-siblings." Angel sounded oddly frustrated.

"They have their own families, and they had to keep the stables running."

"You gave up your life to help her."

"It wasn't much of a life, trust me."

Angel's gaze flickered briefly toward him. "It was very s-s-selfless."

"Family comes first, right?" He glared at his cast. "Maybe if I'd stayed, I wouldn't be such a mess right now."

"You think you're a mess?"

"You don't? My tibia has a spiral fracture that's taking forever to heal. The Post Concussive Syndrome makes getting dressed in the morning an Olympic event and eating a trip to the fifth level of hell. I've not slept a solid night since the accident, and now I'm unloading all my bullshit onto a near stranger. Sorry."

"D-d-don't apologize. I'm a good listener."

"Well, if you're going to listen, can you sit down? You're straining my neck."

Angel perched on the edge of the bleacher next to him, keeping a very deliberate three feet between them. His gaze stayed on the sand, as if looking Ethan in the eye was grounds for termination. Something had happened to this kid to put so much fear into him, and the idea of anyone hurting Angel lit a strange, unexpected burn in Ethan's chest.

"Did you grow up around here?" Ethan asked.

"Hereabouts."

Not much of an answer. The Shockley property was in southern Delaware, which made "hereabouts" pretty much the entire Delmarva peninsula. "You have any family in the area?"

Angel shook his head. "N-n-not alive." He squinted at Ethan, almost making eye contact. "They d-d-didn't tell you about me?"

"Apparently not. Something I should know?"

"Hey, there you are." Benny ambled into the arena, hands deep in the pockets of his cargo pants. "Mom sent me to tell you lunch is almost ready."

Lunch. Another exercise in gag reflex control. "Thanks." To Angel, he asked, "You coming up? They caught some crappies at the pond."

"N-n-no, thank you," Angel said. He retreated from the bleacher and picked up his abandoned rake. "I have work to d-d—finish."

"Thanks for the water."

"You're welcome."

Angel wandered to a different part of the arena and continued to rake out the sand. Ethan stood and tucked the half-empty water bottle into the waist of his sweatpants, and then followed Benny toward the house.

"Making friends with the stray dog?" Benny asked. The comment was unusually cruel, and almost made Ethan stumble. Benny didn't like Angel, that much was clear, but why not? The kid seemed harmless enough.

"Some new stable rule about the owners not being allowed to talk to the hired hands?"

"Mom didn't tell you?"

"Obviously not."

Benny spared a disgusted glance behind him, directed at the arena. "Our so-called Angel? Watch your back around him, bro. He went to prison for killing a guy."

CHAPTER THREE

Angel worked the tines of the rake through the loose sand in a careful forward/back rhythm that helped focus his thoughts. Nothing mattered except preparing the arena for the next round of dressage practice, which was on the schedule for three p.m. He'd meant to finish it last night before bed, but he'd gotten lost in his latest book and forgotten until morning.

The mistake had been both fortuitous and torturous. Fortuitous in that he'd managed an entire conversation with Ethaniel Shockley. Torturous for the exact same reason.

He'd first seen Ethaniel three years ago in the family photos lining the walls of the Shockleys' den. Angel had walked into Pine Creek Methodist Church that Sunday on a whim, needing something more in his life than filling out job applications and avoiding fights at the halfway house. He'd prayed for peace, and in response God sent him Ruth Shockley.

Ruth had struck up a conversation with him after that Sunday's service, claiming she'd heard him singing the hymns in the row ahead of her and had been struck by the beauty of his voice. Angel had never considered his voice anything special, but the compliment endeared the older woman to him. And he'd opened up, surprising both of them with his bluntness. He was on parole, living in a horrible group home, and he needed a job so he could get out of there.

She'd driven him to Shockley Stables for lunch, introduced him to her husband William, and they'd hired him to muck stalls and feed the horses. All in five hours' time.

For three long years in prison, Angel thought God had abandoned him. That Sunday afternoon, over a lunch of pot roast sandwiches, he'd thought maybe God gave a damn again.

Within a week, he'd met all of the Shockley children, the children's respective spouses, and the grandchildren—everyone except Ethaniel, who lived in Pennsylvania and only visited on holidays. Ethaniel, who was handsome and fit and carried a familiar, haunted shadow everywhere he went. Angel was smitten from the moment he saw Ethaniel that first Christmas, admiring him from a distance, and he'd made it his mission to stay far, far away from the youngest Shockley son.

Someone like Ethaniel would never want anyone as damaged and dirty as Angel Garrett, so he took the conversation they'd had and locked it up tight inside of his heart. He'd bring it out later and replay it, maybe pretend Ethaniel was actually his friend, and they were jawing as friends did over silly things like the weather and a couple of crappies.

He'd protect their conversation from spoilage, because sooner or later, Ethaniel would know what he'd done. He'd know and he would look at Angel the way the rest of the Shockley kids looked at him—with disdain and distrust. No one trusted an ex-con, especially one who'd served time for killing a man.

Bless Ruth, William, and the stable manager Russ Hanlon for keeping his other secret.

Angel lost himself in raking the arena, spending far too much time perfecting the smoothness of the ground that would be trodden down and kicked up in only a few hours. This sort of busy work relaxed him. It gave him something to focus on besides the constant soundtrack of regret and pain that screeched through his mind. He finished his task with pleasantly weary arms and a slightly sore back.

Perfect.

He returned the rake to the work shed near the arena. They had a few lessons on the books for today, and he needed to make sure he wasn't needed on-hand for any of them—which meant walking down to the public barn where the office was. He circled behind the private barn in order to keep out of sight of the riders who'd shown up to check on their prize horses. He didn't like speaking to the people who boarded their horses. Not because he disliked them or was afraid of them. He gave very little thought to who they were outside of these acres of land and pasture, so long as they treated their horses good. Mostly he avoided contact in order to avoid The Look.

The Look: *He's the one who killed his momma's boyfriend.*

The Look: *He went away for three years for beating that man to death.*

The Look: *You know someone made that kid their bitch. He probably liked it, too.*

Angel had had enough of The Look.

"Hey! Hey, with the blue shirt!"

The feminine voice startled him into stopping. He'd reached the corner of the private barn and had twenty feet of walking to get to the safety of the other barn, but the voice was speaking to him. He was wearing his blue Shockley Stables polo like he always did when performing official stables tasks, even if he was technically off the clock. A clean white tee was waiting for him on his bed for when he was no longer at work.

Angel turned and blinked at a pair of big brown eyes. He stumbled backward several steps, heart tripping, amazed the girl had gotten so close without him noticing. She was slim, blonde hair pulled back into a thick bun at the nape of her neck, dressed in expensive riding clothes, a hat clutched in one hand. Maybe seventeen, with a cocked hip full of attitude.

With his pulse racing and his personal space invaded, he choked getting the words out. "Can I help you, M-m-miss?"

She couldn't hide The Look: *Oh great, I'm asking questions of a moron.*

"You work here, right?" she asked.

Angel glanced down at his shirt. Maybe he wasn't the moron in the conversation. "Yes."

"Awesome. Do you know where I can find Caleb Shockley? I'm supposed to have a riding lesson, like, five minutes ago, and I can't find anyone."

"D-d-did you check the office?"

"Duh."

"He may s-s-still be at the house. I c-c-can check."

"Great, thanks. I'll be with my horse."

"Your n-n-name?"

"Jennifer Rosen."

Angel walked past Jennifer, adjusting his course to head back to the main house via the driveway. He would have preferred sticking to his less visible routes, but he didn't want to miss Caleb if he passed him. A familiar shape was lounging on the porch swing, eyes closed, earbuds in. Angel's palms went instantly sweaty.

Ethaniel.

He paused at the bottom of the stairs and waited, hating the idea of disturbing the sleeping man. If Angel stood there long enough, maybe Caleb would come outside and save him the task of knocking. Ethaniel looked so peaceful, so relaxed. On the few occasions Angel saw him around the farm, he always seemed agitated. Exhausted.

True peace was a rare thing.

Angel counted to sixty, giving Ethaniel another minute of fleeting peace, but he had a job to do.

He ascended the five wood steps to the porch as quietly as possible. Shuffled across the time-worn boards to the front door and raised his hand to knock.

Pain exploded in his left calf, and then he was on the ground. The back of his head cracked off the wood. He raised both hands over his face, knees curling in tight to protect his midsection, anticipating the next blow, needing to guard his head. Fear and adrenaline surged through him, making his hands shake, but he didn't put them down.

"Jesus Christ. Angel? Shit, I'm sorry. Angel?"

A soft, repentant voice. Not the growl of an enemy or the snarl of a predator. Angel peeked through splayed fingers, still not completely certain who he'd see or what had hit him.

A crutch lay on the porch between him and Ethaniel, who was sitting on the ground near the swing, an arm outstretched in his direction. Ethaniel's face was red, his breath coming in short pants—surprise, pain, he wasn't sure. Angel couldn't make the scene come together.

"Ethan?" Ruth's voice, from inside. "What happened? Did you—oh my."

The screen door squealed open. Angel lowered his hands and blinked up at Ruth, who was looking back and forth between them like she didn't know who to help first. A bit of flour was smeared on the front of her green dress—a faded, casual thing she kept for Sunday only. Every other day of the week she was out in the stables in jeans and a polo, like the rest of her employees.

"My fault, Mom," Ethaniel said.

"What happened?"

Angel hauled himself into a sitting position, then poked at the back of his head. No skin breaks. Thank fuck. "N-n-no, my fault."

"No, it was me." Ethaniel flinched. "I overreacted. I knew someone was close by, but they weren't making much noise. I just...I reacted. I'm sorry I hit you, Angel."

"You hit him?" Ruth glared at her son, then crouched in front of Angel. "Are you bleeding?"

"N-n-no, ma'am," Angel said. "Hit my ankle, is all."

"With the crutch," Ethaniel said.

Lashing out with the crutch had made Ethaniel fall off the swing. "Are you okay, s-s-sir?"

"Well, I definitely embarrassed myself."

"Your leg?"

Ethaniel's eyebrows jumped, like he was surprised by the concern. "Gave it a good jolt, but I think my ass hurts more."

"Well, why don't you both get up off the floor and sit properly," Ruth said. "I'll get you boys some iced tea."

Angel scrambled up. His ankle smarted a bit from the blow, but he'd survived far worse. Ruth had already gone inside, and Ethaniel was staring helplessly at the swing behind him. "Help you?" Angel asked.

"Why not? I'm only the jerk who knocked you onto your ass."

"I've had worse."

Ethaniel's dark green eyes flickered toward him, then away. Angel ignored the odd way that made him feel inside—like Ethaniel was scared of him, but curious at the same time. Angel saw that particular Look less frequently than the others.

He hitched his forearms under Ethaniel's pits. Once Ethaniel got his left leg beneath him, Angel lifted. Ethaniel levered with his good leg, and they got him into the swing. Angel grabbed the chain to steady it while Ethaniel settled his cast on the cushion.

"Thanks," Ethaniel said. "And I am sorry about hitting you like that."

"You were s-s-startled. My fault."

"No, it really was mine. If I'd opened my eyes and looked, instead of reacting like I was back in—" Something darkened his eyes, and he stopped talking.

Afghanistan. War.

Hell.

Angel knew a thing or two about jumping at ghosts.

"I'm not hurt," Angel said.

"Good."

Ruth bustled back onto the porch with two tall glasses of iced tea. "Angel, why don't you sit and rest a minute?"

"Can't, ma'am." He'd had a reason for coming to the house. "Caleb has a lesson. Jennifer Rosen is looking for him."

"Oh that boy." Ruth handed off the teas, then stormed back into the house, hollering for her son.

Ethaniel grunted. "Caleb will be lucky to be on time to his own wedding."

Angel had no response, other than to agree, which might be seen as rude. He wasn't a member of the Shockley family, and he had no reason to think Ethaniel would appreciate jokes at his brother's expense. So he remained silent, cold tea in one hand, his back straight, shoulders tense. He wanted to leave now that his task was finished, but Ruth had given him tea and leaving it untouched definitely *was* rude, and he'd never purposely do something to upset her. She'd only ever been kind to him.

The screen door burst open and Caleb jogged out, down the steps, toward the driveway. Angel watched him go, amused at his fumbling haste, then sipped his tea. Too sweet for him, but this was Ruth's house and her pitcher of iced tea, so he wouldn't complain. Considering his life before coming to Shockley Stables, he had very little to complain about.

"You can sit, you know."

He blinked at Ethaniel, confused by the statement. Of course he could sit. He was fully capable—oh. Ethaniel was pointing at the wicker chair near the swing. "I can't s-s-stay."

"Why not? You aren't working this afternoon, are you?"

"N-n-no."

"You got someplace to be?"

"No."

"Good, then you can keep me company a while. All I do is sit around and listen to audiobooks, so you'll shake up my day a little bit."

"You don't mind?"

Ethaniel smiled, showing off a dimple in his left cheek. "I invited you, didn't I?"

"Your brothers d-d-don't like me n-n-near the house."

"You eat here almost every day."

"And then I go."

His smile dimmed. "Caleb and Benny give you shit?"

"It's their land." Angel could take dirty looks and the occasional insult. Child's play, really. He'd survived worse than two privileged horse breeders and their rude comments. And he might as well make sure Ethaniel had no illusions about Angel's past. "And I'm a convicted killer their mother hired and let live in her garage."

Ethaniel's eyes narrowed over his tea glass. "You in any danger of killing again?"

An angry burn settled in Angel's chest, and he gripped his glass tight enough to make his knuckles ache. "No, sir. N-n-not unless I'm pushed again."

"Pushed." Ethaniel said the word like he was trying it out, unsure what it sounded like on his own tongue. The thoughtfulness confused Angel. "Benny told me you were in jail for killing someone, but not why."

"Prison."

"Sorry?"

"I was in prison. Jail is d-d-different." Most people didn't know that, and a deep shudder tore down his spine. The few weeks he'd spent in jail between his arrest, arraignment and eventual sentencing—the court system moved much faster when you pled guilty—were a holiday at the beach compared to the harsh realities of life in a state prison.

"Okay, prison then," Ethaniel said. "What happened?"

His heart sped up and his brain fumbled. "My mother's boyfriend was beating her. N-n-not for the first time, but this time with a bottle. She was s-s-screaming. Bleeding. I grabbed a bat and hit him. Twice."

The entire experience had lasted only a few minutes, but the build-up had taken months. At first, Angel had kind of liked Shawn. Shawn hadn't been an addict of any kind, unlike Angel's mother, who was on and off heroin, and then meth for years. Shawn had kept her straight for a while. And then Angel turned eighteen, Shawn kicked him out, and his mother started showing up with bruises. A lot of bruises.

Angel had always been thin and underfed—par for his existence as extra baggage when his mother was using, and as another mouth in crowded group homes when she tried rehab again. And again. And again. He possessed no real feelings of love for his mother anymore, but he'd loved her once. Loved her enough to protect her from the man who was beating her on a daily basis.

He'd stopped loving her when she refused to testify in his defense. She was too angry that her lover was dead and she had nowhere to live.

*"Even if you go to prison, you'll have a bed and three meals a day.
What the fuck do I have now, huh? What? What about me?"*

Always, always, it was what about her? Her lack of support
was why he'd pled guilty. He'd done it, after all, and he would do
it again to protect her even though she'd never lifted a finger for
him. In Delaware, manslaughter was a Class B felony that carried
a sentence anywhere from two to twenty-five years. The judge in
his case had been sympathetic enough to Angel's past to give him
a fairly light sentence, considering a man was dead.

A worthless piece of abusive garbage, but still a man.

"You got manslaughter?" Ethaniel asked.

"Yes. S-s-served three years. Finished my parole this s-s-
pring."

"Free man."

"No." Angel shook his head. "N-n-never free."

"I hear you." Ethaniel's voice softened, hinting at the demons
he probably carried from his days in Afghanistan.

Angel could never pretend to understand that sort of pain.

They didn't talk for a while. Angel sipped his tea, hoping to
stomach about half before making his excuses. But the longer he
stood there, the more he wanted to stay. Ethaniel was kind to
him, like Ruth and William and Russ. And Jillian, to some degree,
even though she told him to stay away from Sarah. The others
looked at him like the hired hand he was, and they didn't let him
forget his place.

He didn't want to stay long enough for one of them to shoo
him off.

"I should go." Angel put his glass on the porch railing.

"Sure." Ethaniel put the earbuds back in. "Stop by whenever. I'm here most days."

Angel didn't respond. Ethaniel probably didn't mean it. He was saying it to be polite. He'd already been extraordinarily polite, given their circumstances. Ethaniel owed Angel nothing, not even a conversation.

So why did Angel walk away feeling like he'd done Ethaniel some kind of favor?

Chapter Four

Lashing out at Angel like a paranoid fool was decidedly more embarrassing than any face-plant he'd done since returning home. At least the stumbling and falling over could be blamed on his PCS. He despised excusing asshole behavior with his PTSD, but that's all it had been. He was dozing, he sensed someone close by, and he'd reacted without thinking.

Thank God he hadn't hurt Angel too badly. The kid had been stunned and scared stupid, and that had made Ethan feel like a complete douchebag—especially knowing that he'd done time. The way he'd frozen, hands up, waiting for the next hit, had kicked Ethan in the gut.

He watched Angel until he disappeared around the side of the house, unable to imagine the spooked young man taking a life, much less beating someone to death with a baseball bat.

People surprise themselves when their backs are to the wall. You know that, dickhead.

Yeah, he knew that. Too well.

He left the earbuds in, but didn't turn the book back on. He'd lost track of the story anyway, somewhere between almost napping and attacking Angel. In the five weeks since he'd been home, he'd only lost it like that one other time. Fortunately, it had been on his dad, and he hadn't actually hurt him. Ethan had fallen asleep on the living sofa. Dad thought it was a good idea to wake him up by shaking his shoulder.

They'd both ended up on the ground.

After that, everyone knew not to touch Ethan when he was sleeping. He'd rather they use a fog horn to wake him than to risk him lashing out. He would never forgive himself if he scared Sarah like that. Never.

You are a pathetic mess.

Mom came outside with a plate of brownies. "Oh, Angel left already?"

Ethan pretended he was listening to his book. She leveled the plate at him, and he shook his head. So far, lunch was staying put and he didn't want to tempt fate.

"That poor boy has had such a hard life," she said. Either she didn't believe he was listening to the iPod, or she was talking to herself. "It's not going to get any easier."

Something in her second statement niggled at his curiosity. Things wouldn't get easier because he was a felon? Sure, that would always be a big noose around his neck, but it didn't have to drag him down forever. Unless Angel had another big secret she knew about and hadn't shared with him.

"I didn't know he goes to church with you," Ethan said.

"You'd know if you came once in a while."

"No, thanks."

She smiled indulgently, then bit into a brownie almost absent-mindedly. Chewed. Swallowed. "He sings in the choir. He has a lovely voice. I think it helps settle his soul somewhat."

Ethan had a hard time picturing Angel in front of a church full of strangers, wearing a crimson robe, swaying to the soul power of hymns. "Whatever gets you through the day, right?"

Mom sifted her fingers through his hair like she'd done when he was a child. "What gets you through the day, baby?"

Sadness squeezed his chest. "I don't know. I'm more worried about getting through one hour to the next. A whole day is too big for me."

"Your leg's gonna heal. You won't be on those crutches forever."

"What about the PCS? Dr. Oliver said it could take up to a year or more to right itself. Some of the symptoms might never go away. I can't roof houses if I'm in danger of getting dizzy all the time. I can't even be around the horses by myself."

"So you'll find something new. You have time."

Ethan bit his tongue. He loved his parents for taking him in while he recovered from his accident. He loved that they would do anything for him, including allowing him to live at home for the rest of his life. But Ethan had fought too hard, sacrificed too much of himself, to gain independence. He would not allow a serious concussion to tie him down to this land, not when he'd spent his whole life trying to escape.

"What about music?" Mom asked. "You used to love your guitar. It's in the closet of the guest room. We never sold it."

"I haven't played since I was seventeen."

In truth, the excuse was flimsy. He'd given up his guitar because the Army didn't allow for any practice time. Music had given him a creative outlet as a teenager, when his siblings were busy with the horses. Horses that never seemed particularly fond of Ethan, nor he of them. He'd retreat to the attic and play for hours, building calluses upon calluses, as he taught himself everything from show tunes to rock ballads to his mother's favorite church hymns.

"Some passions never go away, baby. If you ever want the guitar again, one of us can bring it to you."

Fantastic.

Because of his leg, he'd been installed in what had once been Mom's sewing room, the only spare room with a door on the first floor. Her sewing equipment had been moved upstairs to his old bedroom. He hadn't set foot—or crutch—on the second floor since his return. Managing the stairs on crutches, with the added bonus of possibly getting dizzy, kept his ass on the ground floor.

"Thanks, Mom. I'll think about it."

She put the brownie plate on the rail next to Angel's abandoned tea glass, then squatted in front of him. Concern burned in her dark brown eyes—eyes framed with thick worry lines and fatigue. So many more lines than he remembered. "I know you lost two friends in that accident, but you didn't die, Ethaniel Shockley. Please don't ever feel guilty for surviving when Andy and Butch didn't."

Heat in his chest rose into his throat, then his eyes, choking him and stinging them. "Andy was going to be a father. His son will be born any day now. How do I not feel guilty about that?"

Mom clasped his hands in hers, so warm and strong. "I don't know, but I thank God every single day that you're still alive. You have so much love to give, Ethan, I know you do. You're still here for a reason. Please don't shut out an opportunity for joy."

"By playing the guitar again?"

"Maybe. No one knows God's plan, honey. Trust in Him."

You trust in Him. He lost that privilege a long time ago. "Sure, Mom. I trusted in Him when I went up on that roof, and look where it got me."

Despite his angry words and that they'd been said to wound, Mom only smiled. "It got you back home. Not how I would have liked, certainly, but here you are."

"With a broken leg and brain damage."

"As I said, not how I would've liked. But I am glad you're here, especially if Danny gets out soon." Anxiety flittered across his mother's face, there and gone, but not so fast that he didn't see it. She prayed every day for Daniel to be safe in prison and for him to come home to them.

After serving nine years of a fifteen-year sentence for second-degree assault with a deadly weapon, Daniel was up for parole tomorrow. If it was granted, he could be back on the land by Tuesday. Ethan wasn't sure how he felt about that, considering the first and last time he'd visited Daniel in prison—bare weeks after returning home from Afghanistan—Daniel had laid the whole thing on Ethan. Sure, Daniel had a temper, and growing up, Ethan was usually around to help Daniel out of scrapes, or to help him avoid fights altogether. But Ethan had been overseas dealing with his own personal hell. Ethan hadn't needed his big brother accusing him of not being there to stop him from going into an alcoholic rage and beating a guy half to death.

They hadn't spoken since, or even exchanged letters. The only people Daniel contacted regularly were Mom and Jillian. Daniel had never met Sarah face-to-face, only seen pictures.

"Daniel hates me," Ethan said. "And before you say no, he doesn't, he really does. There's a reason we haven't spoken in eight years."

"He was upset, honey. Upset and scared, and he needed someone to blame."

Ethan wasn't going to waste time fighting his mom on this. She always wanted to believe the best about her children. She wanted to believe that Daniel would come home a penitent man and get his life together, maybe even take his place at the stables. She wanted to believe that her family wasn't fatally fractured, and that they would find a way to be whole again.

He wouldn't take that hope away from her.

"Please, give Danny a chance," Mom said. "For me?"

"I will." He didn't hesitate. He'd do anything for her. She had enough worry in her life with his medical issues that he wouldn't heap more on her shoulders.

"Good. I've got a lemon chicken roasting for supper. We'll eat around five-thirty."

Mom's lemon roasted chicken was one of the few things that had yet to turn his stomach since coming home. Mostly he stuck to plain, boiled chicken breasts as his protein source, but lemon chicken was the only really flavorful thing he could actually eat. "Anyone coming over?"

"Benny, Lesley and the boys. Caleb and Polly. Oh, and I invited Angel earlier this morning. He'll be at the table with us."

Ethan quirked a curious eyebrow, but didn't question it. When Angel ate at the house, he took a plate of food and ate in the kitchen, while the rest of the family had their meal in the formal dining room. Including him at the table was rare, usually reserved for holidays, and even then Angel never spoke a word. How she got Angel to agree to eat at the table, he did not know.

The rest of the day passed, one hour at a time, to the cadence of his book's narrator. Benny and his family tumbled into the yard a little after five, which forced Ethan to turn off the book. Doug and Zack decided that the front yard was a great place to pretend to play war. Loudly. Complete with fake machine gun fire. They thought it was cool that Uncle Ethan was a soldier.

They'd seen one too many movies glorifying battle.

Ethan eased off the swing, tucked his iPod into his back pocket, and hobbled into the house. The familiar aroma of lemon and baked chicken greeted him. His stomach didn't turn or flip, which was an excellent sign. Sarah rushed past him to play with her cousins.

Benny and Dad were in the living room watching a football game. Ethan eased into a chair, mostly for the company. The figures on TV moved too fast and in too many directions for him to focus for long.

Lesley passed the living room, heading for the front door. Moments later her voice bellowed for the kids to come inside and wash up. Three sets of feet soon thundered toward the downstairs bathroom. Ethan smiled at the familiar sound. He and his siblings had done that more times than he could count. Getting their hands washed first had become a game for them.

Simpler days. God, I miss those.

Days when his biggest fear was not getting an A on his math test. Days when the simple act of bending over to pick up a piece of trash wasn't an invitation for his smashed brain to rebel and make him faint.

Days when he didn't have to hide who he was from his family, because he hadn't even figured out himself that he was gay. That hadn't happened until tenth grade, and he'd fought it. Fought hard and for a long time. Until his buddies began dying around him and Ethan lost a part of himself after a bombing in Kandahar.

He hauled his damaged ass out of the chair, because he'd take longer to get to the dining room than anyone else. The food was on the table, all of the places set. Lemon chicken, mashed potatoes, string beans, and a bowl of salad. The warring scents were potent, but not overwhelming. Ethan chose a seat at the far end of the table, away from the cluster of serving dishes. Mom had learned that first week to give Ethan some distance from the actual food after him nearly barfing on the table from the overwhelming smells.

Mom came in with Angel behind her. He was a little red-faced—what Ethan could see of his face, because if he looked any harder toward the floor his head would be at a perfect ninety degrees. "Go sit across from Ethan there," she said.

Angel nodded, then slipped over and into the chair directly across from Ethan's. Mom's chair was between theirs, capping one end, while Dad's captained the other. Angel looked extremely uncomfortable being there at all, but at least he was sitting with friendlies.

He was still staring at the table when Benny walked in, so he didn't see the glare leveled at him. Ethan saw it, though, and it set off a slow burn of annoyance. Benny took a seat near Dad's chair. Everyone else filed in, Polly and Caleb scooting in the door at the last minute. Little Doug ended up in the chair next to Angel, and he didn't seem to care. He was eight, and it wasn't likely that Benny had told his boys the full truth about the quiet stable hand who usually took his meals in the kitchen.

Sarah sat next to Ethan, all smiles and joy. Ethan dropped a kiss on the top of her brown head, simply because he could.

Dad said the blessing, then began carving up the chicken. Ethan eagerly accepted a few slices of breast meat, as well as a single scoop of string beans. He always started with small portions so he didn't feel overwhelmed by size or smell. Angel accepted a leg, and a little bit of everything else. The healthy-sized plate of food made Ethan smile around his first bite of chicken.

Lemon burst on his tongue. He chewed slowly, savoring it, not wanting to tempt fate by glutting himself. Small bites, a little at a time, mixed with a string bean here and there. He hated having to be so careful, while the rest of the family ate with little fuss or worry, but he'd rather be slow than end up vomiting.

He became aware of eyes on him, and he glanced up just as Angel looked down at his plate. Had Angel been watching him eat? The thought tempted Ethan to smile. Around him, the family chatted about nonsensical things that he half listened to, most of it related in one way or another to the stables. Ethan wasn't a part of that, so he paid little attention.

Not until Dad spoke up with, "Caleb, would you like to tell me why I fielded an angry call from Lionel Rosen about an hour ago?"

Caleb looked up from his dinner plate. "Who?"

"Lionel Rosen." Dad didn't offer any other hints, leaving his son to suss it out for himself. He was famous for that, teaching his kids to stand on their own two feet and think for themselves. It was good for logic problems, but not so good for an eight year-old with a twisted ankle who couldn't figure out how to get back up on his horse.

Ethan disliked the stables for a reason.

Angel had stopped eating and tilted his head, listening without staring, as though he knew—oh. The reason Angel had come to the house earlier.

"Jennifer's father," Caleb finally said, the penny dropping long after Ethan had figured it out.

"Yes," Dad said.

"I'm sorry, Dad, I forgot her lesson was at one. I honestly thought we'd scheduled her for one-thirty."

Ethan might have believed Caleb if he hadn't glared in Angel's general direction. Protectiveness surged in Ethan's chest, as irrational as it was genuine. Caleb had no reason to blame Angel for this. He'd probably saved their father from an even bigger ass-reaming if Jennifer had been forced to walk to the house to find Caleb. Caleb had screwed up, period.

"I apologized on your behalf," Dad continued. "But he insisted on a new trainer, so Benny will take over Jennifer's lessons."

Caleb squawked, his mouth opening to argue. He snapped it shut fast, which was a very good idea. Their father ran the stables like a four-star general, and his commands were not to be questioned. Ever. Benny gave no response to the new assignment. Caleb was a better rider, but Mr. Rosen was paying the bills and the client got what the client asked for. The stables couldn't afford to lose anyone, or to have their reputation bad-mouthed.

The conversation was over.

Ethan focused on managing three more bites of chicken, taking care to chew each one to mush before swallowing. So far, so good. He tempted fate with two more string beans, and they seemed to do fine. He missed the days when he didn't have to measure every single thing he put into his mouth.

Another bite of chicken down the hatch. A sip of water to moisten his mouth.

Sarah was nattering on about a school art project she had to finish after supper was over, and he always tried to pay attention when she talked. Sometimes listening to conversation while eating led to dizzy spells, because it split his concentration, but he never wanted Sarah to think he wasn't interested.

"—trace our hands, but don't overlap the lines or anything, so it's a really neat pattern. And then we can color all the lines in different markers, but Mrs. Baker wants it to mean something, and I don't know what it's supposed to mean. Can you help me do that, Uncle Ethan?"

He'd missed the first part, but he could clarify with Jillian later. "Sure, chicklet," he replied. "Sounds like fun."

"Yay!" Sarah attacked him with a sideways hug, her little arms looping his waist.

The lovely gesture had the unfortunate side effect of jostling his stomach, which went rolling. Hell. He patted Sarah's back, then gave Jillian a pleading look. Jillian's eyes widened briefly.

"Let him eat," Jillian said, gently tugging Sarah back into her chair.

"Sorry, Mom," Sarah said. Grinning like only a proud child could.

"Excuse me a moment," Ethan said.

Mom handed him his crutches without a word. Elevating made his stomach turn over. All of that lovely chicken was about to make a reappearance. He hobbled into the hall, down to the bathroom and inside, all the while willing his insides to remain patient. To at least give him the dignity of privacy. He flipped the light switch, and the fluorescent glare sent angry signals to his gut.

Most families kept magazines, or extra toilet paper, or scented potpourri on the back of their toilets. His family kept a basin for him, because his leg didn't allow for kneeling in front of the throne. He closed the lid and eased down. Set the crutches against the side of the bathtub, then grabbed the basin.

His stomach flipped, churned. Heaved.

And then the vomiting began.

* * *

Angel discreetly observed the rest of the Shockleys during Ethaniel's abrupt departure from the supper table. Only Ruth and Jillian appeared at all concerned. The kids paid little attention, and the adults were involved in a discussion about a local mayoral candidate that meant nothing to Angel. Had they gotten so used to Ethaniel's condition that they'd stopped worrying when he was hurting?

Something like anger flared in his gut, and he worked to keep his expression calm. They should care, damn it. A near stranger shouldn't care more than his own blood.

He knew that post-concussive syndrome made food a challenge for Ethaniel, and he'd been doing so well with supper—

at least in Angel's opinion. He'd only ever eaten in the same room as Ethaniel a handful of times, and that was all before the accident. This was his first opportunity to watch how Ethaniel carefully cut a piece of chicken into bites no bigger than a quarter, then chewed it with a precision that would make any digestive expert piss themselves with joy. He'd been as silent as Angel, until Sarah engaged him.

The little girl had meant well, but Ethaniel had been fine until that hug.

He winced at the distant, muffled sound of retching. Caused by nothing more offensive than some chicken breast and a gesture of love. Angel currently had control over his body, and he empathized with everything Ethaniel had lost.

"He'll get through it," Ruth whispered, so low he almost missed it.

Angel met her sad eyes. He didn't know how it felt to watch one's child in so much pain, but he saw a lot of it in her eyes. Ruth was an amazing lady. She'd taken in a perfect stranger and given him hope, and he wanted to help her. Soothe her hurts, but he didn't know how. All he could think to do was gently squeeze her hand.

Ruth covered his fingers with her free hand and patted. Her smile said thank you.

Angel dutifully cleaned his plate. He turned down second helpings. Even though it was offered and not asked for, taking extra felt wrong. Greedy. They were doing him a favor by feeding him in the first place. He wasn't family. He didn't belong at this table. He'd never do anything to make Ruth turn him out.

Dinner drew to an end. Benny's family excused themselves first. Ethaniel hadn't returned. Angel doubted he would.

"May I help clear the table?" Angel asked, his first words since walking into the dining room.

"Certainly," Ruth replied.

He collected plates and silverware with extra care, not willing to risk sloshing bits of food or chipping anything. Ruth, bless her, still did the dishes by hand in a two-basin sink, then arranged them in a big wooden drying rack. She filled one basin with hot soapy water. Angel scraped remnants of dinner into the compost bucket, then gently slid the plates into the water.

Slowly but surely the dishes ended up damp and sparkling in the drying rack. Angel fetched the food platters and arranged them on the counter.

"Make sure you fix yourself a plate to take with you," Ruth said, angling her head toward the leftovers.

"There isn't much left, ma'am," he replied. "Will Ethaniel want to try again, d-d-do you think?"

"No, honey, he'll do better with some broth and crackers now."

"Yes, ma'am."

He found a plastic container in the lower cabinet, about the right size for a big sandwich, and put the last of the string beans into it. That bowl went into the sink for Ruth. He picked at the chicken carcass, finding what little meat was left.

"D-d-do you want the bones for s-s-soup?"

Ruth had discovered through trial and error that chicken broth was something Ethaniel could keep down. It wasn't as nutritionally fortified as an actual balanced meal, but it gave him calories. Instead of heaping sodium down his throat with instant broth, Ruth made her own stock with vegetables and chicken bones, then strained it extra carefully before skimming off all the grease.

"Go ahead and stick them in a container in the fridge," Ruth replied. "I can make another batch of broth tomorrow."

He did as asked, then washed his greasy fingers. The potatoes were gone, but the food he had would make a nice little lunch for tomorrow. "Thank you, Ruth."

"You know I hate storing leftovers."

Ruth Code for she wished the whole family would come by for dinner more often, so she could cook big meals the way she enjoyed. She was an old-fashioned woman who truly loved taking care of her family. She'd beaten cancer and been given another chance to keep showing everyone how much she loved them.

Angel couldn't imagine his life right now if she hadn't lived to be in church that Sunday.

Once the dishes were done and the dining table wiped down, Angel collected his leftovers. "Thank you for d-d-dinner," he said. "It was real n-n-nice of you to have me eat with the family."

Rush dried her hands on a dishtowel as she turned to him. "I should insist you eat with us more often. You may be a paid employee, but so are Benny and Caleb. You're family now, Angel."

His heart fluttered at the unexpected declaration. He didn't really know what it meant to have family. His mother had loved her drugs and endless string of boyfriends more than him, and he'd lost his grandmother when he was ten—the only stable, loving person in his life. He'd prayed to God while he served his prison time, prayed for a safe place to live out his days and maybe make a difference to others. God had more than answered his prayers, and Angel often found himself waiting for the other shoe to drop.

It hadn't yet, and now he was being called family. He didn't know what to do with that, so he took those tender feelings, and he held them close. "Thank you, ma'am."

"You go on, then. Get some rest, since you didn't manage to on your day off."

He smiled. She knew everything going on around the property, and it somehow got back that he was raking the arena when he wasn't scheduled. "Good n-n-night."

Her own good night followed him out the back door. The rear of the house had a wide deck with a built-in picnic table and bench off to the left, and a covered barbecue grill on the right. William liked to grill a lot in the summer, the scent filling Angel's nearby apartment with the wonders of sizzling meat and smoke.

He trotted down the back steps and was halfway to his apartment when he realized he hadn't seen Ethaniel again. Disappointment hit him. He should have at least made sure he was all right, since no one else seemed to give a very big damn. Maybe that was unfair, since they dealt with Ethaniel's symptoms on a daily basis, but how could they not be concerned when something as simple as a hug made a man upchuck?

A long staircase built on the side of the garage led up to his second-story apartment, which he never locked because he had nothing of value to protect. The only secret he kept was in the medicine cabinet, and he doubted a thief would recognize the names of his pills. The large, boxy living space had come furnished with a worn floral sofa and a thirty-year-old television set that had a VCR/DVD combo attached, but no hookup to cable. One corner held a dorm-sized refrigerator, a small sink, and a hot plate. The bathroom had a tiny standing shower and barely enough space for one person to maneuver, and his bedroom possessed a twin bed and antique dresser.

For all of its faded colors and slightly musty smell, this little apartment was heaven on earth. It was freedom, and it was privacy. After three years of living, sleeping, eating, showering, and shitting around other men, he treasured his solitude.

Treasured it when he wasn't cursing it, because he was often lonely here. Staying away from people meant he couldn't get hurt again, but it didn't feed the part of him that still craved affection. Love. Someone to one day, maybe, love him back. He wasn't likely to find that at the stables. He wasn't a heroine in a romance novel who was going to stumble upon his Prince Charming while mucking a stall, fall desperately in love, and then be whisked away to a life of luxury. He was the tertiary character who was mentioned twice in passing, and then never seen again.

He glanced at his plank and cinder block bookshelf, which was littered with books from thrift stores and library sales, many of them romance novels. He often wondered what kinds of books Ethaniel listened to every day, but never had the guts to ask.

The leftovers went into the fridge. He brought out a bottle of orange soda, unscrewed the cap, and took two long, satisfying pulls. The carbonation had gone flat after repeated openings, but the taste was the same. Sweet and super-fake-orange and exactly what he remembered. Gramma always had orange soda for him, and a few sips a day was one of his only real indulgences. He'd finish the bottle tomorrow, then open a new one. He rationed it so he didn't spend too much money on such a frivolous thing. And it wouldn't be a treat if he had too much, too often.

Sweet tooth appeased, he dug a wrinkled pack of cigarettes out of the bottom drawer near the sink, as well as a packet of matches.

His other indulgence. Maybe science said nicotine was actually a stimulant and woke your brain up, but a smoke had always served to calm Angel down when his nerves were jumping. He'd started when he was twelve after a kid in one of his many group homes said he was a pussy-ass punk if he didn't smoke. Angel had enough trouble fitting in because of his stutter, and if smoking made him seem tougher than he was, he'd smoke.

Withdrawal had been hell, occurring while in lockup and during all of his lawyer visits and hearings. He'd been a twitchy mess, unable to be as coherent as he probably should have, especially when describing his mom's abuse at her dead boyfriend's hands. At least he'd been relatively even again when he arrived in prison to serve his sentence, and then he'd had a whole host of new problems to crowd his days and nights.

Smoking now was a really stupid thing to do, considering his meds, but it was maybe three a week. The damned things were expensive, way more than he remembered, and he hoped to give it up for real—this time because he chose to. Not because he was incarcerated and the law said no more.

He respected the Shockleys too much to smoke indoors, even next to an open window, so he pulled on a sweatshirt and went outside. The small landing at the top of the stairs had a lovely view of the woods to the west. During the day he could admire the turning leaves in big splotches of yellow, orange, amber, red, and every shade in between. The sun was almost completely down, casting the side yard in shadows.

The faint rumble of the television set drifted from the main house. Caleb's truck was still in the driveway, and muffled voices carried across the lawn. He didn't see anyone outside, so it had to be coming from the front of the house. Maybe the porch. Not one to eavesdrop on private business, he tuned out the sounds and shook a cigarette out of the pack. The match flared brightly, bringing the scent of ozone. He lit the end of the cigarette, shook out the match, and placed it on the railing for safekeeping. The first blast of hot smoke tickled his lungs and throat.

The second made him cough. His blood hummed despite his lungs' unhappy reaction. He allowed the acrid smoke to trickle from his lips in a slow stream, barely visible in the dim light.

"I didn't take you for a smoker."

He nearly dropped the cigarette. He tracked the sound of Ethaniel's voice to the lawn, halfway between the back porch and the base of his stairs. Ethaniel's tone hadn't been accusing, and it was impossible to see his face, so Angel didn't know how to take the comment.

"I d-d-don't s-s-smoke often," Angel replied. "And n-n-never close to the horses or s-s-stables." He sounded defensive and he hadn't meant to come across like that. He didn't imagine Ethaniel was a big fan of smoking, and being caught at it made Angel feel disgusting. Dirty. He stubbed the glowing end out on the bottom of his shoe.

"I didn't imagine you would smoke by the horses." Ethaniel crutched a few steps closer. He was engaging Angel, encouraging another conversation. On purpose.

Angel's heart fluttered. He shoved the half-used cigarette into the pack, then thumped down the stairs. It seemed silly to keep conversing from such a distance, and it wasn't as though Ethaniel was going to attempt the stairs. Ethaniel surprised him further by meeting him at the bottom of the steps.

"I s-s-smoked a lot when I was a teenager," Angel said, as if he owed Ethaniel an explanation. "D-d-don't know why I s-s-started again."

"You couldn't smoke in prison?"

His stomach twisted. He hated talking about prison. Hated. It. But Ethaniel hadn't sounded accusatory, only curious. And he wasn't avoiding him at all costs, like his siblings and their kids. He made an effort. If prison was what it took to keep Ethaniel talking to him, he'd go with it. "N-n-no. You can't in most s-s-state prisons n-n-now."

"Maybe you started smoking again because it was something familiar. Something you could control."

Angel gaped. How had he pulled that out of Angel's head? Maybe Ethaniel needed something like that, too. Something he could control while his body continued to betray him. "You lose a lot of freedom. S-s-simple things you take for granted on the outside." He waved his hand around. "Even fresh air."

Ethaniel nodded slowly, his face a study of shadows in the bad light. "I've always been an outdoorsy person. I think it's why roofing houses fit me so well. When I was laid up in that hospital for a month, stuck in bed with only a window and a bad view of the building next door? It was hell. I can't imagine being stuck inside for three years."

"We had a yard. An hour a day, if the weather was good."

"An hour a day. That fucking sucks." Ethaniel actually seemed upset. Angry on his behalf. Few people ever got angry over him.

Angel didn't know what to do with that. "I really love this job. I can be outside all I want."

"Well, you're not going to get fired for smoking a cigarette once in a while."

He almost corrected Ethaniel's assumption that his previous statement had to do with job security. It was a statement of fact. Being outside, in open spaces, was easier than feeling boxed in. Or trapped. "I kn-n-now. Your parents are really fair. I would n-n-never betray their trust."

"Good. I'd hate to have to start disliking you."

Angel blinked. That almost sounded like…flirting. Certainly Ethaniel wasn't flirting with him. Ethaniel was no more gay than Angel was straight. He was simply being nice, but that didn't mean Angel couldn't flirt back.

Only a little bit. "I think I'd hate that, too."

Ethaniel tilted his head, a gesture of curiosity. "May I ask you something, Angel?"

As long as you don't ask if I'm gay, because I couldn't take it if you saw me differently when I say yes. "Of course."

"Have you ever gotten help for your stutter?"

As far as personal questions went, Angel hadn't expected that one. "My grandmother got a book from the library once. It helped for a while. I only s-s-stuttered bad when I got n-n-nervous or s-s-scared."

"Are you nervous or scared around me?"

"N-n-no." Oh. Angel got it. "It got bad again in prison." Horrifically bad. Every other word had tripped out of his mouth on multiple syllables, making him sound like a perfect moron. Making him sound weak. Making him a target.

"Would you like help mastering it again?"

"What?"

Ethaniel shifted his weight on those crutches, shoulders hunching a little. Embarrassed? "I kind of spent the day listening to an audiobook on stuttering and speech therapy. I can't read words for very long without getting migraines, but I was curious, and I hope I didn't overstep."

"Why would you do that?" Angel was truly flabbergasted. He didn't understand.

"I'm sorry." Ethaniel turned away, frowning. "Forget it. Have a good night, then."

Angel stared at his departing back, confused as to what had suddenly ruined their glorious moment.

CHAPTER FIVE

Ethan hated few things more than he hated vomiting, and he'd done more of it in the last two months than his entire life prior to falling through that roof. After losing all of the food he'd managed to work down during dinner, he had retreated to the front porch to feel sorry for himself in private. He'd said polite good-byes to Benny and the kids when they left.

He'd waited for a headache that never come, and he was sitting in perfect stillness when Caleb burst out the front door with Polly.

"That was fucking humiliating," Caleb said.

"I know, baby, but your father did what he thought was best for the stables," Polly replied.

They moved toward the steps, too involved in each other to notice him.

"He could have done it in private, not in front of everyone. Especially not in front of that stupid kid."

Ethan bristled.

"I can't believe Mom invited an ex-con to sit at the family dinner table," Caleb continued. He was getting his rant on hardcore.

"If Daniel is paroled tomorrow, he'll be an ex-con at the dinner table."

"Daniel's family, and he's not a killer."

"What the hell's your beef with Angel?" Ethan asked, unable to keep quiet any longer.

The pair whipped around.

Caleb glared. "What are you doing, sitting around in the dark?"

Ethan ignored the question. "Why do you hate Angel so much?"

"I'm going to wait in the car," Polly said, wisely slipping away.

"What do you care?" Caleb asked after she'd gone. "You two pals all of a sudden?"

Ethan levered to his feet, not liking the way Caleb was looking down on him. Even leaning forward on the crutches, Ethan was taller than him. "Angel killed a man who was abusing his mother. He paid his debt. Why can't you lay off? It's not his fault you were late for a lesson."

"Forget it." For a moment, Caleb looked genuinely upset. The emotion flashed so quickly Ethan almost missed it in the shadows cast by the porch light. "Just…watch your back, okay?"

"What's going on, Caleb? It's not like you to screw up lesson times."

"Nothing's going on. I'll see you."

He hadn't been able to stop Caleb from storming off the porch to his truck. Something was up with Caleb, but his brother had inherited their father's stubborn streak. Getting him to confide would be a huge challenge, and Ethaniel wasn't likely to succeed. He'd made a mental note to call Polly tomorrow and see if she knew what was going on.

Bored and antsy, he'd decided to take a walk around the yard. Finding Angel smoking a cigarette had surprised him, but that was quickly overshadowed by the delight of having another chance to talk with him. And then what had been a pleasant conversation with Angel turned utterly embarrassing when he decided to bring up the stuttering issue.

"Why would you do that?" Angel asked.

The stunned, almost angry layer to his voice threw Ethan. While he hadn't expected Angel to jump up and down for joy at the idea, he really had not expected him to be so mad. Ethan wanted to help and he'd upset Angel instead.

"I'm sorry." He couldn't stop a frown as he angled to leave. He was an idiot. "Forget it. Have a good night then."

"What?" Angel was suddenly in front of him, eyes wide and…confused. "I d-d-didn't mean to s-s-sound s-s-so harsh. I was s-s—damn it. Surprised."

"Oh. You aren't angry with me for meddling in your business?"

"N-n-no. It was very…thoughtful. N-n-no one has shown much interest in my s-s-stutter, because I d-d-don't talk much."

Hope sprung alive in Ethan. "You can tell me to fuck off, but would you like to improve your stutter? You'd be doing me a favor, too. I don't have much to do around here because my equilibrium is so off, and I'd have something to focus on. I want to help."

Angel smiled, and he was even cuter like that, his face a portrait of light and shadows. "Okay. Let's d-d-do it."

"Great. My schedule is totally open, so we can start whenever's good for you."

"I finish my work by three o'clock most d-d-days. Is tomorrow too s-s—early?"

"No, it's not." A bigger challenge than when they'd do the work hit him. "Where would you feel comfortable doing this? I can't really go up to your apartment. I'd probably get dizzy halfway up the stairs and fall back down the rest of them."

Angel's face twisted in horror. "N-n-no more falling for you ever."

The reaction was both adorable and incredibly sweet. "Okay, so ground floor. Would the house be too uncomfortable? People coming and going?"

He nodded. "The garage? If it gets cold there's a s-s-space heater we can use."

The garage was a good compromise. Not too far from the house and relatively private. "Okay. How about we meet in the garage at three-thirty tomorrow?"

"Okay." Angel smiled again, and Ethan swore he blushed a little, too. "Thank you."

"Don't thank me until I actually do something helpful."

"You care. That's helpful." This time he did blush. "May I ask you a personal question?"

"I guess that's only fair." Curiosity kept Ethan from putting a limit on the topic.

"Is there a medicine you can take for your n-n-nausea?" Angel asked so gently he almost seemed apologetic for prying. Discussions of Ethan's medical issues weren't fun, but they also weren't verboten—unlike Afghanistan.

"My body doesn't get along well with pills, never has. I tried a couple of anti-nausea medications, but they either made it worse or gave me migraines. Ginger ale settles me sometimes, but it doesn't help keep food down if it wants back up."

"I'm s-s-sorry."

"It's not your fault."

"I kn-n-now, but it must really s-s-suck."

"Yeah, it does. I was almost okay at dinner, too." Until Sarah jostled him. He didn't blame her, though. A joyous hug from his niece was worth an empty stomach. He'd also been on his feet for a long time now, and he didn't expect his luck to hold. Vertigo liked to sneak up on him. "Anyway, tomorrow at three-thirty?"

"Yep."

"Cool. Good night, Angel."

"Good n-n-night, s-s-sir."

"Don't sir me. Call me Ethan."

A bashful smile quirked Angel's lips. "Ethan."

"Better."

Ethan hobbled back to the deck, careful on each step going up. His pits ached from the crutches, and his left leg throbbed after not being elevated for so long. At least an hour, thanks to dinner and this conversation.

"Let me know when you want some warm broth," Mom said as he eased inside the house. She was at the kitchen table working on the Sunday paper's crossword.

"Maybe in a bit." He needed to sit for a while and let his body relax before he badgered it with food. And Mom didn't scrimp on the broth. No reconstituted granules for her kids. She made it from scratch.

"All right. Just holler."

Ethan almost left it alone. "Mom, how come you invited Angel to eat supper with the family tonight?"

She turned in her chair, her face a little too innocent. "I invite him every single Sunday to eat with us in the dining room, and he always says no."

"How'd you change his mind tonight?"

"I told him he'd run out of no's, and all he had left was yes."

He could easily imagine her doing that. "I'm glad. He seems lonely."

"Yes, he is. He's got no family besides us, and your brothers excel at giving that poor boy grief. Don't know why when their own flesh and blood is serving time as we speak."

"Caleb and Benny can't see past the word kill. They don't care that one crime was self-defense and the other was intent to harm."

"You care."

"Of course I do. You don't go through a war zone and not see the shades of gray afterward." He instantly wanted to smack himself. He tried to keep his time in the Army out of their conversations. Four years that Mom had spent worrying about one son dying in a foreign country while the other sat through a trial and subsequent conviction and incarceration. He hated reminding her of bad times. "I listened to a book on speech therapy today. I'm going to help Angel with his stutter."

Mom's surprise shifted quickly into delight. "That's wonderful, sweetheart. I offered when he first came to us, but he said no."

"He's pretty fond of no."

"He's a proud young man. He won't take anything he sees as charity."

Ethan couldn't fault a man for that. "He's doing me a favor, too. I need something else to keep me busy."

"Busy is good."

On that sage note, Ethan made his way past the living room where Dad was ensconced in his favorite chair with a glass of whiskey in his fist, then down the hall to his new room. Shelving units were still full of Mom's excessive collection of sewing supplies and patterns. She'd hand-sewn a lot of their clothes when they were small. "Cheaper that way with five young'uns," she'd often say. He had a double bed and his old dresser from upstairs and that was it.

After the accident, he'd broken his lease on his Mechanicsburg apartment and moved all of his stuff into storage. Not that he had much beyond the basic furniture and cooking equipment. Anything of sentimental value was tucked up tight in the attic.

He grabbed his laptop off the dresser and dumped it on the bed so it was close by if he wanted it. Stretching out felt amazing as he finally took pressure off his arms and legs. He arranged himself so he was half propped up against the headboard with a pillow under his cast. The throbbing dulled a bit, and his sloshing stomach settled. He closed his eyes and drifted for a while, not thinking about anything at all.

Until a shy smile and big brown eyes flashed unbidden into his mind. Thick, curly brown hair that looked soft as silk. Pink lips that would stretch—shit!

Ethan jerked awake, face blazing and dick at half-mast. He could *not* have those kinds of thoughts about Angel. The poor kid had been through enough. He didn't need his boss's son perving on him, or featuring him in an X-rated fantasy. The simple truth that he was attracted to Angel hit him in the gut. And it surprised the hell out of him. While he never thought of himself as having a type, on the occasions he went looking to scratch an itch, he tended toward men closer to his age, if not older. Larger builds, muscles.

He'd never found himself interested in someone like Angel. A good six inches shorter than him, almost too slim, who looked much younger than twenty-four if you weren't looking into his eyes. Sad, world-weary eyes that had seen too much and expected little from others. Ethan also saw a hidden fear in them. Signs of a man who was afraid to really let himself be seen, because he'd been hurt too many times.

Ethan saw Angel, and he wanted to know more.

He hauled his laptop closer and booted it up. Waited for the DSL to connect—out here in the sticks, they couldn't get high-speed wireless, and it drove him nuts. His email popped open first. Some spam on penis enlargement pills—*doing fine in that department, thanks*—and cheap airfares. He wouldn't be flying anytime soon, not until the PCS cleared up. Only one new message, from Owen Hart, a friend he'd left behind in Pennsylvania.

He'd met Owen first at a batting cage, then again for a drink in which they discussed the complexities of Owen's love life. Ethan had been attracted to the black-haired, dark-eyed man, and curious about the grief that always seemed to lurk in those eyes.

But Owen had figured out his relationship with his partner, David, and he and Ethan had stayed friends, mostly emailing each other goofy photos, memes, or internet jokes. Owen had even visited him a few times while Ethan was in the hospital.

Ethan liked having Owen as a lifeline to the world outside of Shockley Stables.

Instead of anything silly, Owen had typed out a short message.

Hey E—
Just wanted to drop a line and say hey.
Hey.
Things are pretty quiet out here in Central PA. Which is saying something, considering I have a teenage son. Michael's settling into high school with amazing speed, and he's already talking about this girl named Allie. I'm not ready for him to be talking about girls. Dear gods.

How is everything in Bumfuck, Delaware? Your PCS getting any better? Need a friend to come and take you out for something other than rubbing down horses? A good rubdown for yourself? Drop me a line anytime.
—O

Ethan read the brief note twice, mostly to memorize the words and enjoy the act of actually reading for a change. He hated that he couldn't do it for long, and he still had some internet research to get to, so a reply would have to wait until tomorrow. He was glad to hear that freshly-fifteen year-old

Michael was adjusting well to his new high school. No mention of David, though.

He opened up a search engine and typed in "Matthew Garrett manslaughter conviction", and hit enter.

The slow connection took a moment to bring results. He ended up clicking on several different articles, less interested in the specifics of Angel's case than in information on the man himself. Passed between his drug-addict mother Susan Garrett, his maternal grandmother until her death fourteen years ago, and several group foster homes. Kicked out by his mother's boyfriend, Shawn Lawrence, when he turned eighteen. For a few months, Angel noticed his mother frequently sporting bruises. The day he went to confront Lawrence, he found the man beating Susan with a vodka bottle. In several different articles, Angel was quoted as having said to police, "She's been hit too many times, suffered too much. Seeing someone who says he loves her making her bleed like that...I lost it. In that moment, I'd have done anything to save her more hurt."

Angel had grabbed a baseball bat from the coat closet and hit Lawrence in the head twice. The first "to drop the bastard" and the second "to keep his ass down." He hadn't intended to kill, but that had been the result.

Ethan blinked as the words began to swim. A dull throb set in his temples. He'd read too long, but he didn't want to stop. Angel had gone to jail for protecting a woman who'd treated him terribly for most of his life. A woman who had, according to all the articles, given a sworn statement to police condemning Angel. She'd stood up against her own son for a man who fed her meth and beat her with glass bottles.

Dear God in heaven, how betrayed Angel must have felt.

Angel went to prison, served three years, and had spent the last three hiding out at Shockley Stables, living a quiet, probably lonely life. Ethan's heart ached for the young man who'd survived so much in such a short amount of time.

He ignored his approaching headache and searched a bit longer, finding more rehashes of the same information. Until he came across an op-ed piece from a small college paper, in which the author argued that Angel should have received a suspended sentence and community service. He'd been defending his mother, acting in self-defense, and, according to the writer, had been thrown under the bus because he was poor, his mother and the victim were drug addicts, and even suggested the state-appointed defense attorney did a spectacularly shitty job by allowing Angel to plead guilty, instead of fighting it.

Ethan bookmarked that link to read in-depth another day, because the throb had become an insistent slam against his skull. He shut the laptop and sank into his pillows, frustrated that twenty minutes of surfing and reading had turned into a nightmare that wanted to smash his brain against his skull. He closed his eyes and contemplated the energy needed to reach for the bottle of acetaminophen he kept on the table near the bed that served as his nightstand. Too much effort, since he didn't have any water and hated swallowing pills dry.

The gentle knock on his door was a godsend. "Ready for that broth?" Mom asked.

"Sure." He opened his eyes, a little alarmed that his vision was blurry. "Can you bring me some water, please?" He hated asking, and he'd only do it with his mother. Being waited on by his father or brothers?

No, thank you.

She took another step inside, a frown creasing her forehead. "Headache?"

"Yeah."

"Too much computer?"

Busted. "Yeah." She was going to ask what had him so fascinated, so he saved her the trouble. "I was curious about Angel."

"Oh?" Mom moved closer, the blurry action making his stomach roll. "Anything in particular about him?"

"Mostly him personally. His background and what led to the arrest. It looks so awful on paper. His own mother turned against him."

"Angel's had a hard life. He didn't have the love and support that you and your siblings have. When I first met Angel that day in church, I saw a boy with so much love to give and no outlet for it. And a boy who truly deserved a second chance."

"I'm glad."

"So am I. I'll be right back with that water and some migraine pills."

He closed his eyes against the fuzzy lines of his room, imagining that his brain really was leaking out of his ears. At times like these, when the simplest task left him nauseated and in pain, he couldn't stop a stray flash of regret. Regret that Andy—a married man with a baby on the way—had died while Ethan—single, gay, and already messed up by time spent in a war zone—had survived.

Sometimes he really thought God had let the wrong man live.

Chapter Six

The house phone rang around ten a.m. the next morning. Ethan was on his swing, listening intently to his audiobook on speech therapy, while keeping one ear open for the telephone. Mom had stayed around the house, instead of going out to the stables with Dad, and she only let it ring once before snatching it up.

Ethan paused his book, his stomach curling into unpleasant knots that had nothing to do with the scrambled eggs he'd kept down for breakfast. He strained to hear something, anything, but Mom must have been in the kitchen when she answered the phone. Several long minutes passed, an eternity of time while he waited for the results of the parole board hearing. Waited to see Mom upset or overjoyed, depending on the news she received.

He gave up on doing nothing and hauled ass onto his crutches. The change in elevation made his head spin around twice before he righted himself. Footsteps charged toward the front door, and then Mom burst through. Color stained both cheeks. Her eyes were wide, glittering with tears. The expression was one of utter shock, and he had no idea which news she'd gotten.

"Well?" he asked.

"Tomorrow."

"We'll know tomorrow?"

Mom shook her head, now smiling. "My boy's coming home tomorrow. Danny got parole!"

Her joy at her son's release was the only emotion Ethan felt at the announcement. He allowed her strangling hug, gave her a squeeze back as best he could, so grateful to see her this happy. This relieved. He waited it out, until she bounded down the steps and ran off toward the barns to give everyone the good news, running like he'd never seen her run before.

Daniel was getting released tomorrow.

Ethan thumped down in the wicker chair, waiting for his tumultuous emotions to calm and settle on something. Anything. He was happy for his parents, who were getting a son back. He was happy for Daniel, who was getting out of nine years of hell. He was happy for Caleb and Benny and Abby, who were all getting their brother back. He was happy for Jillian, who was getting her husband, and for Sarah, who would finally meet her father.

He felt nothing for himself.

"Get out. Get out, you fucking pussy, and stay the fuck out of my life."

The last words Daniel had spoken to him over the phone in that prison visitation stall. A final denouncement from a brother he'd once been closer to than anyone else in the world. Ethan had sent a few birthday cards over the years, mostly to remind Daniel that Ethan still cared, but he never heard anything back. Daniel never asked about him when Mom or Jillian visited. Daniel hadn't even bothered with a phone call after Ethan nearly died falling through that roof.

He didn't know if he should be happy or scared or apathetic. All he felt on that porch, on a chilly morning in mid-October, was numb.

The numbness lasted throughout the day. Family members came and went as they heard the news. His nieces and nephews were all at school and would learn their long-lost uncle was on his way home after the bus dropped them off. Benny and Caleb came up with Mom and Dad for lunch. Ethan avoided a conversation by way of an upset stomach. He hated lying but he couldn't pretend to feel something he didn't, even when his brothers looked so happy.

Abby swung by around two. She owned a small tapas-style restaurant in Bethany Beach that was getting rave reviews, so she pretty much made her own hours. Abby was the perfect picture of their mother twenty years ago—thick chestnut hair, big brown eyes. She always had on something stylish, and she clomped onto the porch in shiny silver heels, a black pencil skirt, and a matching silver jacket over a black shirt.

"Hey, gimpy," she said.

"Hey, squirt." She might be seven years older, but she was also twelve inches shorter. "I guess Mom called?"

"Yes, she did." Abby leaned against the porch rail and crossed her arms. "Why are you hiding out here?"

"I'm always out here. It's my spot."

"Yeah, but everyone else is inside being all supportive and happy for Daniel."

Ethan studied his sister, aware of the flat line of her lips and the dullness in her eyes. "Aren't you happy for Daniel?"

She shrugged. "I'm happy for Mom and Dad. Daniel getting locked up was tough on them, especially with you overseas. I think Mom's long overdue for having all of her chicks under one roof again."

Truth.

"You don't look too thrilled about the news, either," Abby added.

"We haven't spoken in eight years. I'm pretty sure he hates my guts."

"Do you hate him back?"

"No. I never hated him. But he needed to blame someone for his mistakes, and I was a convenient target."

Her gaze flickered toward the front door. "Is Jillian here?"

"No, I think she works until four today."

"I wonder how she's going to take this. I mean, I know Daniel's her husband and they've been together since high school, but they were married all of a year before he went away. They're both different people, you know? And Sarah. What's she going to say? She's only ever seen pictures of her father."

"I know all of this, Abs."

"I know you know, I'm just talking it out. I do that all the time at work. It drives my chefs crazy."

"I bet."

She blew a raspberry, and he laughed. He and Abby hadn't been particularly close growing up, and they chatted amiably at all family get-togethers, but he had truly enjoyed seeing her more often this past month. She worked hard, balancing time at the restaurant with her own family—a husband and four kids, and bless her for pulling it off. He looked forward to the day when he could visit her restaurant and enjoy the exotic food for himself.

"How's your head?" she asked.

"Not much improvement."

"The leg?"

He tapped his knuckles on the cast. "Attached."

"Good. Well, I guess I should go inside and be happy for our parents and their wayward son."

"I thought I was the wayward son."

"Nah, you're the prodigal son."

He preferred wayward. Prodigal implied he belonged here and never should have left.

Frustrated and antsy, Ethan hauled up to his feet and maneuvered his way to the yard. He considered going down to one of the barns to look at the horses, but the distance down meant distance back. Uphill. No thank you. He turned to the right and the west-facing side of the house. About a dozen yards away, near a small cluster of birch trees, was the little-used screen house Dad's father had built more than sixty years ago. The structure was twelve feet by fifteen feet, with a solid roof, and four walls that were made of screen panels to allow in natural light and air, and to keep out the bugs. One wall had a long, built-in bench and connected table. The folding outdoor chairs that usually lined the other side of the table were closed and neatly stacked for the winter.

Growing up, they'd had countless summer picnics and birthday parties out here. He didn't know how often his parents still used it. Not much, judging by the layer of dust on the table and bench. The floor was a pile of stones over packed earth, and they made a difficult surface for his crutches. He gazed around the little room, phantom scents of barbecue and corn on the cob lingering, old memories poking.

If it hadn't been October and going into cold weather, he probably would have moved in here, instead of the house. Or at least spent his days out here, rather than on the front porch.

He hauled one of the folding chairs out, a little alarmed by the way the nylon fabric creaked when he sat. He'd angled himself to face the far western woods and the gorgeous view of the turning leaves. The property truly was beautiful in a way he'd never appreciated until now.

Sitting upright wasn't as comfortable for his leg, so Ethan got another folding chair out and set it opposite him, so he could elevate the cast. Some of the ache dissolved.

He'd somehow forgotten his iPod, and he had no energy left to fetch it, so he gazed at the leaves, counting how many different shades of red, yellow, gold and orange he could see, some still mixed with green. He was up to thirty-nine distinct colors when the back of his neck prickled with unease—a sense of being watched that he'd developed in the Army and that had never deserted him. He looked over his shoulder, toward the screen house's door.

Angel stood there, hands deep in his jeans pockets.

"Hey," Ethan said, surprised to see him of all people. Pleased, too, if the soft tug in his heart was any indication. And then it hit him. "Shit, what time is it?"

"Almost four." Angel's shoulders hunched. "I wasn't s-s-sure if I s-s-should look for you, and then I couldn't think where to look. You're always on the porch."

"I needed a break. I'm sorry, I got totally lost in thought."

"It's okay. I mean, if you d-d-don't want to d-d-do the lessons, I get it."

"No, it's not about that." His neck was starting to hurt. "Come in, please."

Angel did, wary in a way that Ethan didn't like. He circled around so he was in front of Ethan's prop chair, still hunched forward, unhappy.

"I still want to do the lessons, I promise," Ethan said. "I'm just…distracted. I really am sorry I lost track of time."

"N-n-no problem. I heard about D-D-Daniel. It's good n-n-news."

"Mom is beside herself with relief."

Angel tilted his head. "You d-d-don't s-s-sound happy."

"The last time Daniel and I spoke, he told me to get the fuck out of his life and stay out. He blames me for his arrest, and we haven't spoken in eight years."

"But you weren't even here when he was arrested. You d-d-didn't beat up that guy. He d-d-did."

Ethan snorted. "Yes, well a logical person would see it that way. Daniel has never taken responsibility for his own actions, not even when we were kids. It was always someone else's fault that he failed the test, or that he got caught stealing. He was never to blame, he was always someone else's victim."

If they were lucky, maybe prison had finally taught Daniel something about consequences.

* * *

Lord Almighty, when had Ethaniel gotten so bitter? Angel's heart hurt listening to the older man talk about Daniel. Angel knew the type. He'd met more than one on the inside—the consummate victim, always being shat upon by life and others. Angel had avoided those guys whenever possible. The attitude didn't help in the real world, and it absolutely did not help as a prisoner. Every single man was behind bars for a reason. Consequences for an action taken.

Even actions taken in defense of others.

Angel wanted to say the right thing to Ethaniel, something that would make him feel better. Or at least feel a little less bad. Ethaniel had enough to deal with. He didn't need his brother's bullshit, too.

"Prison changes people," Angel said. "Maybe your brother will be a better man."

Ethaniel stared at him with his mesmerizing green eyes, which sparkled like emerald fire in the afternoon light. "Do you think prison made you a better man, Angel?"

His gut tightened. He kept his hands deep in his pockets so Ethaniel didn't see them trembling. He hated talking about prison. Sometimes people asked out of morbid curiosity, only wanting to know the worst of the worst so they could leer at the details the same way people slowed down to stare at a traffic accident. Sometimes people asked because they wanted to make sure he wasn't apt to repeat history or to lash out in violence over a perceived slight.

Ethaniel seemed to be asking for another reason: reassurance. Reassurance that maybe Daniel wasn't still the same selfish, bitter man he sounded like. Angel wanted to give him that hope, but he also didn't want to lie. Not to Ethaniel. Not ever.

"It made me a d-d-different man than I was before," Angel said. "N-n-not as quick to judge people or to get mad. I value life more than I d-d-did before prison. I d-d-don't want to hurt anyone ever again. I'd rather d-d-die than go back."

Something flashed in Ethaniel's eyes. Something like grief, maybe even understanding. "I felt like that after I left the Army. I didn't want to see another soul hurt and bleeding, even dead because of me." Ethaniel flinched and looked at his lap. "Shit, I don't talk about this stuff."

"Me either." Angel swallowed down his nerves and took a leap of faith. "Maybe we both just n-n-needed s-s-someone who'll unders-s-stand."

Ethaniel lifted his head, surprise arching his slim eyebrows. "Maybe so. For years I worked construction jobs around other vets. They were some of my best friends. We didn't have to talk about the past, because we all knew it. We all knew the terror and the regret and the nightmares. I guess that was enough for a while."

"But you d-d-don't have that here."

"No one else here has been to war. It's not unspoken with them. They don't know, so they ask questions, but I can't tell them about it. I don't want them to know what kind of hell that was. My family doesn't need that stain on their souls."

Angel's chest tightened with emotions he didn't understand. He drew his hands out of his pockets, unsure what he was doing with them. He wanted to reach out for Ethaniel, to offer reassurance in his touch, but he didn't know if Ethaniel would accept it or recoil. Some men reacted badly to other men touching them. Angel had been burned enough times to be wary of offering his touch unrequested. So he curled his fingers in the legs of his jeans.

Grief surrounded Ethaniel, a crushing thing that Angel wanted to make go away. And he knew he had to offer up a small part of himself to do so. "I'm already s–s–stained," Angel said. "My s–s–soul. N–n–nothing you tell me can make it worse, I promise."

After a moment's pause, Ethaniel said, "Can you sit, please? I'm getting dizzy."

The invitation made his pulse flutter. Angel opened a dusty lawn chair, then cast about for the best location. He chose to sit on Ethaniel's left side, near his knee, close enough for a private conversation without invading his personal space. It might not be the speech therapy they'd planned, but they were talking, and Angel was overjoyed with the attention.

"Do you ever leave the farm?" Ethaniel asked.

"Yes."

"Besides church and helping out with shopping."

He squirmed a bit. "I helped William pick up a pony last s–s–summer."

"But you don't go out and, I don't know, hang out with people?" Ethaniel's tone was polite, curious, no demanding edge to it.

Angel still felt like a reclusive fool. "N–n–no, n–n–not really."

"Don't you get lonely?"

"All the time." He'd been lonely his entire life. Loneliness was as familiar to him as an old, fuzzy blanket. Sometimes it suffocated him, but it also kept him safe.

Ethaniel studied him like he was a puzzle whose pieces didn't quite line up. "So why not go out and find company? You're young and cute. Girls would fall all over each other to be with you."

You're young and cute. The compliments buzzed pleasantly over Angel's skin. He rarely saw himself as anything other than a burden, so the outside perspective on his looks buoyed his waning self-confidence. He'd once looked at himself in the mirror and seen a boy who was decent-looking, maybe a little too skinny, and the whole "twink" thing had worked for him for a while. He'd given his first blow job when he was fifteen, then popped his anal cherry four months later in the backseat of a much older man's Hummer.

It had hurt like hell, because he hadn't told the trick it was his first time. He'd wanted the experience. He'd wanted something to make him feel older, stronger, more in control of his life. He'd been put back into a group home, and nothing about that situation was within his flimsy control—not the boys who beat him up because of his stutter, or the frequency with which his food was stolen. Something about sex had freed him, and having sex with men finally made him feel real.

Not like the one time he'd had sex with a woman. A girl, really, only a few years older than him. Fourteen at the time, he and his mother had been living with a douche named Donald, who fed her addictions and had wild parties at the house. Donald insisted Angel have sex with the girl "to prove he was a real man." Desperate for an adult's approval, he did, only to find out afterward that the girl had only volunteered in exchange for drugs. He also found out Donald had pimped out his mother to his drug-addled pals.

So Angel had called the police on Donald, which got Donald arrested and sent away. His mother beat the hell out of him, then got sent to rehab again. For three years, until his arrest, Angel had sex as often as he could find a willing participant. Then sex became a survival game, and he hadn't sought it out once since his release.

"Angel?" Ethaniel's hand covered his knee, startling him out of his own head. The concern in Ethaniel's eyes made his pulse flutter with nerves. And want.

"I'm s-s-sorry, I got lost in thought."

"I noticed. Where'd you go?"

He steeled himself for a bad reaction to his truth. "Losing my virginity. I was fourteen."

"Jesus." Ethaniel blinked hard. "That's young."

Angel shrugged. "I've made worse mistakes." That particular mistake got a miserable waste of space off the streets and proved to Angel that he was never going to be into women. "What about you? Your first time?"

Ethaniel's gaze flickered away. His cheeks darkened. "Seventeen."

He couldn't figure out the embarrassment. Seventeen wasn't very old. But the reaction was endearing. Ethaniel shifted in his chair, one hand sliding across his lap. Angel's own cheeks pinked up. Had Ethaniel tried to casually adjust himself? Was their conversation—what the hell was their conversation now?

* * *

Ethan berated himself for allowing his thoughts to wander off the rails while Angel had lost himself inside of his own head. For a few precious seconds, Angel had looked so sad, so in need of affection, that it had taken all of his strength to stay put and not tug him into a hug. And then when Angel admitted to what he'd been thinking about, Ethan's own imagination had returned to last night's thoughts.

Thoughts of Angel's pretty lips opening to take his dick. New thoughts of Angel naked with someone else, in the throes of innocent, naked fumbling with a girl his own age, had morphed into a boy, and the whole tangled mess in his head had sent blood the wrong way. Then Angel asked how old he was when he lost his virginity, and images of fucking his neighbor Walter Blythe in the bed of his father's pickup when they were both seventeen played out in vivid color—one of his favorite pre-war memories. He was half-hard before he could shut off the porn in his head, and damn it all, Angel noticed him trying to cover the new swell in his jeans.

Angel's eyes widened and his nostrils flared—not the disgusted reaction that Ethan had anticipated. Hell, Angel even swallowed.

Would he swallow?

Dear Lord, he was not going there. Not at all.

An awkward tension sprang to life, thickening the chilly air between them. Ethan couldn't make himself admit his first partner was a guy, or that he was gay. Maybe he could shake off the half-stiffy as a reaction to remembering his first time having sex, and Angel wouldn't question the gender of the person. But Angel's reaction to his unexpected erection made him wonder...

Angel squared his shoulders, some kind of determination in his posture. "My first time with a guy, I was fifteen."

Ethan stared, stunned stupid by the blunt admission. And from Angel Garrett, who until yesterday morning, had been a silent enigma with whom he occasionally exchanged a greeting. Angel had gifted him with a truth and a secret, and Ethan was terrified of fumbling and hurting this precious friendship they were cultivating. He was also terrified of trusting his own truth to someone until he was absolutely sure about what he'd heard.

"You're gay?" Ethan asked.

"Yes." His whole body tensed up, defensive. "The girl—I didn't want to have sex with her. And it felt wrong the whole time. With guys it feels right."

Part of that statement struck Ethan as wrong. And alarming. "You didn't want to have sex with the girl? Angel, were you—"

"It's not what you think, and I don't want to talk about it. It's a small thing now, compared to so much else that's happened."

Ethan wanted to demand that story, to hear why he'd had sex when he wasn't into it, but Angel had put his foot down. He had a scary determination about him now, a spine of steel that wasn't going to bend to anything Ethan demanded. And he hadn't stuttered once in the last few sentences.

He kept that observation to himself. If Angel was made aware, he might start again.

"Thank you for telling me your truth," Ethan said instead.

"Your parents and Russ know I'm gay, but no one else. Didn't want to give your brothers another reason to hate me."

He had no idea how his brothers would react to learning Angel was gay. He was more worried about their reactions when they found out Ethan was, too. Sooner or later, the truth would come out. He was tired of living a lie and not being himself with his family. He also didn't want to risk losing them. His family was all he had.

"Benny and Caleb don't hate you. I doubt they have a truly hateful bone in their bodies." They weren't like Daniel. They took care of their women, did their jobs, and they didn't blame others for their mistakes. Maybe last night Caleb had tried shifting the blame for his lateness to Angel, but that wasn't usual behavior for Caleb. Something else had prompted that, and Ethan had forgotten to call Polly to see what was up.

"They're lucky to have you sticking up for them, Ethan. Don't know if I'd believe that coming from anyone else."

Ethan smiled, grateful for the trust Angel had in him and his character judgment.

"May I ask you s-s-something?" Angel said. The stutter was back, which meant his nerves of steel had buckled.

"Of course."

"You're always s-s-single when I s-s-see you."

"That's not a question."

"Why are you? You're gorgeous." Angel's cheeks darkened, and he looked away.

The compliment burned hard in Ethan's gut, pushing his waning arousal back on track to full readiness. "Relationships are difficult for me to maintain. I have so much crap rolling around in my head, and being with me means a lot of baggage. Most people don't have the patience to deal with it."

"What kind of crap?"

"Nightmares, the kind you wake up from screaming, sometimes trying to hit. To defend yourself. A car backfires and I freak out, feel like I'm back in a war zone. A certain smell does it, too. Ozone. And copper, because it's so close to blood." He was rambling, and he needed to stop. Angel didn't need this shit dumped on him. "Sorry."

"D-d-don't apologize. I asked."

"Anyway, all that crap makes it hard to keep a boyfriend around."

Angel startled, and Ethan realized what he'd said. *Damn it to hell, anyway, for letting your guard down.* Angel's eyes widened in surprise, and his gaze flickered once to Ethan's lap. Then he shook himself, like a wet dog, and his lips curved in a kind smile.

"I'm guessing your family d-d-doesn't kn-n-now?" Angel asked.

"My mother does, and Jillian. A friend I left behind in Pennsylvania, and now you."

"Thank you for trusting me." Angel's expression went slack, a little distant, and then he chuckled.

"What?" Ethan asked, more curious than alarmed. He liked the sound of Angel's laughter, and it struck him that he'd never heard it before. Soft and melodic, like he was singing it instead of feeling it.

"I was thinking about Ruth. Her trying so hard to get us talking and friendly now makes more sense. We do have stuff in common that we don't have with anyone else on the farm."

Ethan's eyebrows jumped. "You think my mother is trying to hook us up?"

"Oh no, I mean us being friends. Talking like this. I don't think she'd try to hook us up. Not that way."

He saw a challenge in that statement—a challenge that his inner alpha, the rebellious side which insisted he leave home and join the Army, decided to meet. "If we're both as cute as the other one says we are, then why not?"

Angel hesitated, his lips parting to answer, then pressing tight. Like he was considering his words. "Most mothers don't want their sons dating an ex-con."

"You've met my Mom, right? Her own son is a soon-to-be ex-con."

"That's different. Daniel is blood."

Ethan wanted to get into Angel's head and find the real hesitation. It was more than what Ethan's mother may or may not want for him. Something more personal, but they weren't the best of friends, and it wasn't his place to poke. "How about we meet halfway, and agree to get to know each other. Friends or more, we take each day as it comes."

Angel's lips quirked into a shy smile. "Deal."

Outside voices drifted to the screen house from the driveway. A pack of kids, Ethan's nieces and nephews, came up the drive in a cluster, heading for the front porch. Someone had probably texted one of the older kids and ordered everyone to Gram and Paps's house after school. Time to tell everyone that Uncle Danny was coming home tomorrow.

"How do you think Sarah will take the news?" Angel asked.

Ethan loosed a heavy sigh. "I don't know. She knows he exists. She's seen pictures, but he's never been a part of her life outside of letters and cards. She doesn't know him. Hell, I've been more of a father to that precious angel than Daniel ever could." More bitterness coated his words, and he wasn't ashamed at his lack of self-censor this time. Angel wouldn't judge him.

"She adores you. I see it whenever she looks at you. Anyone can."

"But I'm not her father. She has to get to know her real dad."

"Ethan, as someone who never knew his father, and who lived through a revolving door of his mother's boyfriends, it takes more than a sperm donation to make someone a dad. You gotta be there when it matters. You gotta show them that you love them."

Wise words from an old soul. Ethan couldn't recall a single time when his father said "I love you," but he knew that he was loved. Love shone through in everything William Shockley did for his children—food, clothing, land, homes, careers, unerring support. He'd gone back and forth from Delaware to Pennsylvania every couple of days during the month that Ethan spent in the hospital, being there for his wife and son as often as possible.

Ethan had been in the room when Jillian gave birth. He'd been there for eight birthdays. He'd helped Sarah build her first snowman. He'd taken her to Hershey's Chocolate World last summer, a month before his accident. He'd give his life for that little girl.

"Sarah's never wanted for love," Ethan said. "I don't want Daniel to break her heart."

"You think he's likely to?"

"I think the odds aren't in his favor. Daniel's bull-headed and isn't much of a planner. He'll want Sarah to love him right away, to accept him. Same with Jillian. He'll get mad if they pull away, and he'll find a way to blame me for it."

Angel scowled. Ethan didn't like that dark look on his pretty face. Not even a little bit.

"I should get back to the house," Ethan said. "Jillian will be home from work soon."

"Of course."

His ass hurt a little from sitting so long on an uncomfortable chair. Angel folded the chairs and arranged them back in their pile.

"Sorry we didn't get to any kind of actual speech therapy stuff."

"It's okay."

"Although I guess you could say we made progress." Ethan winked. "You've not stuttered much for the last few minutes we've been talking."

Angel's eyebrows nearly hit his hairline. The small smile became a cheek-shattering grin. "You're right. Thank you."

"I don't know if it was because of me, but you're welcome."

"We'll have to test it next time we talk."

* * *

Angel followed Ethaniel halfway, before angling toward his apartment. Learning he had not stuttered for part of their conversation had floored him, and he knew deep inside that it was because of Ethaniel. The stutter came from nerves and a sense of not being in control of his environment. With Ethaniel, he felt perfectly safe. In control. Protected.

"You need somebody in your life who's your safe place, Angel, dear. Somebody you can count on always. I hope you find it."

A snippet of conversation from over two years ago, when Ruth told him about her battle with breast cancer. Her family and her husband had been her safe place and support system. Angel hadn't understood such a mystical thing. He hadn't believed it could happen for him. And then Ethaniel had admitted he was gay, and it had rocked Angel to his core.

Now he saw hope in front of him. Hope shaped like Ethaniel Shockley.

CHAPTER SEVEN

Sarah had a class field trip which Ethan had completely forgotten about until Mom reminded him. It explained why Sarah wasn't with her group of cousins, and why Jillian drove up with her in the backseat a little after five. The rest of the family had been informed of the news and gradually dispersed to their respective homes. Mark came by to collect his four kids so Abby could stay and be an extra shoulder to lean on.

Ethan wasn't sure if Abby's shoulder was for Jillian, Mom, or him.

Sarah barreled into the living room and nearly leapt into Ethan's lap. He was sitting on one end of the sofa, his cast propped on a stool. Mom and Dad filled the rest of the sofa, Abby in an armchair.

"I saw a shark today," Sarah announced as she wedged herself firmly between him and her grandmother. "We went to the aquarium in Bally-Ballit—"

"Baltimore?" Ethan said.

"Yeah! I saw a shark and a whale and all kinds of fish."

"That sounds like a fun day."

Jillian hovered near the entrance of the living room, arms crossed, her eyes downcast. She'd heard the news, apparently. This was about breaking it gently to Sarah.

"You'll have to tell me all about it after dinner," Ethan said.

"I can't tell you now?"

"Right now we need to talk about something as a family, okay? Something very important."

Sarah frowned, her lips puckering up. She looked around at the adults in the room. "What are we talking about?"

"Sarah, honey." Jillian came forward a few steps, distress all over her face. "You know how your daddy is living away from here, because he did a bad thing, and that we're waiting for him to be allowed to come home?"

"Uh huh."

"Well, he's coming home."

"Why?"

Jillian worried her lower lip with her teeth.

"You remember how last summer you broke the kitchen window with a softball?" Ethan asked, trying to make prison punishment make sense in her young mind. "And you remember how mad Gram was?"

"Yes."

"Well, you did something bad and you were punished for it by not being allowed to play ball for two weeks. Once the punishment was over, you could play ball again. It's like that with your daddy. His punishment for his bad thing is over, so he can come back to you and your mommy."

Sarah twisted her fingers in her lap, thinking. Ethan glanced at Jillian, whose grateful smile told him he'd done a good job. The tension in the room was suffocating.

"Is he going to live here with us?" Sarah finally asked.

"Yes, honey, he is," Jillian said. "This is your daddy's home, too. We'll see him tomorrow."

She tensed up. "Tomorrow?"

"I know it's soon, but I'm sure he's super excited to get here and finally meet you. It's been so long." Jillian knelt in front of them. "I know you've never met your daddy, and you don't have to love him right away. But I do need you to be kind to him, okay? Be his friend?"

Sarah twisted to look at Ethan, her eyes bright. "Do I have to be his friend?"

"Yes, you do, chicklet." Ethan ruffled her hair. "It'll be okay, I promise."

She seemed to take his word for it, even though she didn't relax. "Okay. Will you be there, Uncle Ethan?"

"Of course I will."

"Good."

He ached for her confusion and fear. She had to meet a man she didn't know, whom she'd been told was an important person in her life. Angel's words about what being a father meant drifted back to him. Wise words from someone who'd never had one—just like Sarah.

Only that wasn't completely true. She'd always had her grandfather, her other uncles, and Ethan. Daniel's only claim to Sarah right now was biological, and Sarah was a wary kid. He'd have to earn her trust and love.

Ethan prayed that Daniel could be patient enough to do so.

* * *

Angel once again found himself seated at the family dining table to enjoy a healthy serving of pot roast and vegetables. Ruth insisted that he'd run out of excuses to eat in the kitchen, and this time he didn't argue. She was determined to include him, now more than ever. And he wasn't about to turn down a chance to see Ethaniel.

The family was clustered near one end of the long table, since it was only himself, Ethaniel, Ruth, William, Jillian and Sarah. Ethaniel was seated farthest from the food, Sarah right next to him, so Angel took a seat across from him. He returned Ethaniel's smile, his pulse jumping a bit. After their conversation in the screen house, Angel wasn't entirely sure how to act around Ethaniel in front of the family. They were friends, yes, but was that okay? He was still a hired hand.

A hired hand perversely interested in his boss's son, and now that he knew Ethaniel was gay, his crush felt less…intrusive. He'd tried hard to think of something else, anything else, for the last hour, and failed miserably. He needed to shut down his feelings before they got any stronger. Yes, Ruth was pushing them into being friends. Angel was certain that he and Ethaniel could help each other, be an ear to bend when they needed it.

No way in hell was Ruth trying to push them together romantically. He hadn't been able to articulate his certainty to Ethaniel, because he didn't want Ethaniel to ever know that secret. He'd have to explain everything, and Ethaniel had enough of his own ugly in his head. He didn't need Angel's too.

Ruth was engaged in a one-sided conversation with herself, mostly preparations for Daniel's return. Buying his favorite food, getting him some modern clothes and deodorant and a toothbrush. Jillian and Sarah lived in two of the three extra upstairs bedrooms, and the third was currently used as storage. Would Daniel move in with Jillian, or would they sleep apart for a while?

When Angel had got out of prison, he'd wanted nothing more than to be left alone. Not an easy thing when you're thrust into sharing a room at a halfway house with a guy on parole for armed robbery who finds every opportunity to touch you "accidentally." Angel hadn't wanted physical contact. He'd wanted distance.

But he imagined his time in prison was far different from Daniel's. In the family photos around the house, Daniel had seemed as tall as Ethaniel, his muscles bulkier. He had a cocky smile that dared folks to challenge him. If anyone inside had taken him down, Angel imagined he went down fighting and came back up swinging.

Warm fingers tapped the top of his hand, which was curled around his fork, unmoving. He followed the fingers to the owner's face. Ethaniel gazed at him, eyebrows furrowed. Silently asking if he was okay.

Angel smiled and used his fork to spear a lump of carrot, noting Ethaniel's own plate. Steamed veggies, no sauce, no meat. Barely touched.

Ethaniel withdrew his hand, and Angel missed the touch. He liked Ethaniel's touches, fleeting though they were. They were comforting, tender. Not bruising or cruel or angry.

After supper, Angel volunteered to help Ruth clear the table. It was the least he could do, and they worked in a quiet peace.

Ruth hummed some hymn under her breath, happier than he'd ever seen her.

"Saw you and Ethan talking in the screen house earlier," Ruth said as she settled the last pot in the drying rack.

Angel glanced around, but they were alone in the kitchen. Still, he pitched his voice low. "I told him my truth, and he told me his."

Her grin widened. "That's lovely, dear. I'm so glad. He doesn't have anyone to talk to about things, and he certainly wouldn't talk to me about..." She mouthed the words "gay things."

He forgave the awkward phrasing because she sounded so secretive and adorable. She accepted everything about her children without a second thought. Ethaniel was so lucky. He wanted to ask if friendship was her only motivation, but Jillian entered the room.

"Angel, can I talk to you?" Jillian asked.

The question floored him. They'd never had a direct conversation before. "Of course."

He followed her out the back door to the porch. The chilly fall air made him wish for his sweatshirt, so he folded his arms over his middle.

Jillian paced a little bit. "I don't know what to expect from Daniel tomorrow."

She wants advice. I can do this. Show I'm useful for more than mucking stalls and leading horses.

"I d-d-don't either. Prison affects everyone d-d-differently. But you n-n-need to be patient with him. Really patient."

"I can do that."

"He's lived with rules and s-s-structure for a long time. He might want routines. He might get confused. He might be n-n-nervous or short tempered. And d-d-don't s-s-sneak up on him. Ever."

"Okay. I just...I don't know how I'm supposed to act tomorrow."

Angel had no answer for her, so he listened.

"Daniel and I have been together since we were fifteen. We loved each other so much, even though he's always had a temper. We got married because I had a pregnancy scare. I miscarried early, and then I got pregnant with Sarah. A week after that, Daniel got drunk and got into that fight, and then he was in prison, and I'm not the same woman he knew." She spun in a circle, as though her answers were in the air someplace. Her eyes glistened. "I don't know if I still love him."

His heart ached for Jillian's pain. "It's been n-n-nine years. N-n-no one will blame you if you d-d-don't. You grew up. You're a mother."

"I promised him I'd wait. I said I'd wait until he got out so we could try again, but I said that before he was sentenced. We didn't think it would be for so long, but it was his second offense, his victim nearly died, so the judge threw the book at him. I don't know if I want Daniel anymore. Sarah deserves to know her father, though, right?"

"S-s-sarah can s-s-still kn-n-now her father without you being with him."

"But where would I go? I don't have any family around here to help me."

Angel stared. Was she crazy? "You have family right here. Ruth won't s-s-send you away if you d-d-divorce her s-s-son. They all love you." He still couldn't believe she was confiding all of this in him, and not to Ethaniel or Ruth. Then again, he had a unique perspective on an ex-con's mindset.

"I love it here." Jillian's voice was raspy, softer. "It's a great environment for Sarah, and she loves being outdoors. She has all kinds of cousins to play with."

"Want my advice?"

"Yes, please."

"Take it one d-d-day at a time. One. Too many will overwhelm you. Trust me, I kn-n-now."

Jillian stared at him for a moment. "You two were in the same prison."

"Yes."

"Did you know him?"

Angel shook his head. "I was in a d-d-different c-c-cell block."

"Oh. Was it as awful as it is on TV?"

His insides got a little watery. He didn't want to sugarcoat the realities of prison life, because her husband was coming back after nine years of it. But she didn't need to know everything. She didn't need to know what weapons could be made out of if you were creative enough. That you could walk into your cell on any given day and find a gift on your rock-hard pillow in the shape of a pile of fresh feces. That some of the guards were more erratic and violent than the prisoners. That once you put on those white linen clothes and got a number, you were no longer a person.

You were a thing to be ordered around, fed, and occasionally beat on for no good reason.

Jillian didn't need to know those things.

"It can be violent," Angel said. "People get hurt. People fight. You toughen up fast." Or in his case, find someone to protect him from the other predators. It was all a survival game, and Angel wasn't ashamed of anything he'd done in order to get through it and get out. The things he was ashamed of were the ones out of his control.

"A few years ago, our scheduled visit was cancelled because he got into a fight." Jillian wiped her eyes. "I couldn't see him for a month."

Angel didn't doubt that. Infractions meant a month in the hole—a cinderblock room with no window, a slot in the door for a food tray, and no contact with anyone except the trustee who delivered meals twice a day. You pissed and shit in a hole in the floor, and all you had for company was a blanket. No bed. No chair. No TV. Nothing but yourself and all the time in the world.

He'd only spent one out of thirty-eight months in the hole, and the experience still occasionally haunted his nightmares. He'd almost gone crazy in that little room, sent there for doing nothing more serious than lining up for breakfast too slowly, because he'd spent the previous night vomiting up his dinner. His stomach had taken days to right itself, and they hadn't allowed him supplies to clean up the two messes he'd made on the floor.

No, Jillian didn't need to know that.

"They take away privileges like phone and visits when you break the rules," Angel said.

"That's what Daniel said."

"Be patient with him. And be kind. It's all you can d-d-do while he acclimates. He has to figure things out too."

"You're right." She sniffled and wiped her eyes again. "Thank you."

"You're welcome."

She went back inside. Angel lingered a moment, unsure if he should go in and say good night to Ethaniel. He peeked in the window. Ruth was having an animated discussion with William and Jillian, and he didn't want to intrude. They had a son to welcome home.

Angel went back to his apartment. Alone.

* * *

Ethan didn't sleep for shit that night. Whenever his racing mind managed to calm enough for him to nod off, his thoughts were filled with naughty images of Angel. Images that left him half-hard all night long, culminating in morning wood he couldn't make go away. The green numbers of his alarm clock taunted him with a six and a ten. Too early, but he was awake and likely to stay that way.

He slowly hobbled down the hall to the bathroom. He was the only one who showered down here, so they left his stool in the tub. The modified shower head was set to shoulder height when he was sitting. He went through the motions of wrapping his cast in plastic, taping it down, and then easing into his chair.

Once he turned the water on, mostly to mask the noise, he palmed some shampoo and grasped his hard cock. The shock of his own hand on his erection stunned him. He hadn't whacked off since the accident. Hell, he hadn't really gotten hard until recently, and it occurred to him he didn't know how the PCS would be affected by an orgasm. Would he shoot himself into a fainting spell?

Nothing would be mortifying than being found passed out in the shower with his own spunk stuck to his chest.

He stroked himself lightly, and the little sparks of pleasure that tickled up his spine told him the risk was worth it. He closed his eyes as he dragged his palm over the crown, then back down the length in a tight, slick grip. Need burned in his gut, spreading out, waking him up. He thought of Angel and his musical laughter. The way he smiled. So pretty.

He stroked harder, faster, fucking his own fist, needing to get off right the hell now. It had been months. Even before the accident, he'd had a sexual dry spell. Sharing one super-hot kiss with Owen Hart didn't count, because neither of them had gone further that night. At least, not with each other. He didn't know what Owen had gotten up to when he went in search of his complicated other half.

His orgasm boiled closer and closer, tightening his muscles, making his strokes stutter. Angel. His Angel. Yes, that felt right. The rightness shot through him, and his release followed. He swallowed a moan and stroked himself through it, drawing out the shocks of pleasure coursing down his spine, making his thighs tremble.

When it was over and Ethan resumed regular showering, he didn't know whether to laugh or cry. He'd made Angel the star of his jerk-off session, and he had no idea how Angel might feel about that. Flattered? Horrified? Intrigued?

He hoped intrigued. He didn't know why Angel thought they were meant to be friends only, rather than lovers, but he was more determined than ever to find out.

Mom and Dad were in the kitchen eating breakfast when he finally managed to get out there, dried and dressed. She immediately went about making his regular meal of scrambled eggs and orange juice. His stomach didn't roil at the scents of scrapple and syrup, so he counted that as a win. Jillian and Sarah shuffled in a little later, neither of them dressed.

"I took the day off," Jillian said before Ethan could ask. "And Sarah isn't going to school today."

"That makes good sense," Mom said. "Today's a big day. Paps and me are driving up in a little while. I figure if we don't hit traffic, we'll be home around lunch, but I'm not sure how long everything takes."

The drive up north would take a little over an hour, plus the same time back. Longer if Daniel wanted to stop somewhere. Before prison he'd been addicted to Burger King's original chicken sandwich, and he might insist on stopping for his first in almost a decade. Ethan could imagine the childlike glee on his brother's face while biting into it.

"I've got my cell phone on me," Dad said. "We'll call when we're about thirty minutes out, so you can be ready. Caleb and Benny want to be here, so call your brothers."

"What about Abby?" Ethan asked.

"She's at the restaurant doing financials. Said she'll swing by before supper."

Mom's nervous excitement filled the kitchen to the brim, almost choking Ethan. He ate as quickly as he dared, then escaped to the porch. It was chillier this morning than it had been for a while, so he hobbled back inside for a wool blanket from the trunk in the living room. He wrapped it around his shoulders, then settled in with his speech therapy book.

He waved later on when Dad drove the station wagon down the lane toward the main road. He thought he spotted Angel a few times, ducking in and out of the barns and arena, but with the distance he couldn't be sure. The morning passed. Jillian carried out a tray of broth and crackers for lunch, because that was all he thought his nervous stomach could manage today. Every hour brought Daniel closer to them. Every hour brought them all closer to potential disaster and heartbreak.

Around one, the house line rang and Ethan didn't have to ask. Jillian stayed inside a while, and then Caleb and Benny were racing up the lane from the barns. They joked and shoved each other like they were teenagers again, afraid of nothing and no one. Ethan envied them the ease with which they moved through their lives.

Sarah came out with Jillian, and she immediately situated herself behind Ethan, between his swing and the wall of the house. Jillian hovered nearby, arms crossed, shivering. Ethan levered onto a single crutch. She slid against his chest, accepting the one-armed embrace. Sarah scooted up and wrapped her skinny arms around both of their waists, her face pressed into Jillian's stomach. Caleb and Benny watched them with what he could only describe as tolerance, as though they didn't understand what all the fuss was about, or why Sarah was quaking against them.

Ethan almost asked where Lesley and Polly were, but at the same time, he knew. This was a family moment, and they'd be by later tonight to say hello. Mom had already announced a big family dinner for next Sunday as a welcome home to Daniel, the date giving everyone time to plan. And giving Daniel time to adjust before he was surrounded by people.

The station wagon finally trundled into view. Jillian stiffened. Caleb and Benny tumbled off the porch and into the yard, like excited puppies about to piddle on the carpet. Nothing else described the pair. Ethan waited with Jillian and Sarah, taking his cues from them. Sarah didn't turn to look. She waited, eyes scrunched shut. Ethan ached for her fear.

Dad finally parked and turned off the engine. He and Mom got out first, both of them smiling. The rear passenger door opened. A perfectly smooth head appeared, shaved clean and shiny, and Ethan stared. Gaped a little as Daniel stood straight, as familiar as he was a perfect stranger. Even from a distance, the angles were sharper, harsher, and his nose had a new bend in the bridge from being broken at least once.

Daniel's laser stare went straight for their trio on the porch, and Ethan shivered.

"Danny, my boy!" Benny whooped and went right in for a hug. Daniel hugged him back, then Caleb, slapping their backs and bumping fists like they were all teenagers. For a moment, the old Daniel was there, smiling and carefree. The spell broke the instant Daniel's eyes found them again, and he went quiet.

"Come on," Ethan whispered. Sarah shook her head. "You can stay up here for a minute longer, okay? But you have to say hello."

Sarah retreated behind the porch swing again. Ethan squeezed Jillian's shoulder, then let her go so he could hobble down the porch steps with his crutches. She didn't follow him.

Daniel met him in the yard, halfway between the car and the porch. His frosty stare looked Ethan up and down once. "You're still alive," he said.

"Looks that way."

And like that, he was dismissed. Daniel sidestepped him, that coldness softening. "Jilly?" Hope colored his angry tone.

"Hey," she said.

Ethan angled so he could watch them both. Jillian took the stairs slowly, wide eyes filling with tears as she neared her husband. He'd shaved his head and hardened his body, and Ethan swore he saw ink peeking out of the collar of his t-shirt, but he was Daniel Shockley, and he was real. A sting of relief reminded Ethan why this was a good thing. Maybe Daniel still hated him, and maybe things with his wife and daughter would never be perfect, but Daniel was free.

He had a second chance to make things right.

Daniel opened his arms. Jillian stepped into them. His touch seemed gentle at first, hesitant, as if unwilling to startle. Then his grip tightened by degrees. Ethan watched, determined to step in if Jillian showed any signs of distress, but she didn't. She let Daniel crush her in his arms, smell her hair, skim her back and shoulders.

"Fuck, girl, I've missed you," he said. "Missed you every fucking day."

Jillian didn't answer, and that's when Ethan realized she was crying. Silently sobbing into Daniel's shoulder. Ethan glanced up at Sarah, who hadn't moved from her hiding place. He waved her forward. She shook her head.

Everyone hung around a bit awkwardly until Daniel released Jillian. He held her at arm's length, studying her, so much love in his eyes that Ethan couldn't believe he was the same man who'd so coldly dismissed his own brother only minutes ago. Ethan wasn't jealous. Daniel had made his feelings clear years ago.

"You are the most fucking gorgeous thing I've ever seen," Daniel said.

Mom was going to give him lip about the language later, Ethan was certain, but right now she was smiling indulgently. Too happy to have Daniel home to care he was dropping f-bombs left and right in front of Sarah.

Jillian seemed uncertain how to respond, so she smiled.

Daniel finally broke eye contact, his gaze landing on the porch. "Oh fuck me, is that her?"

"She's really nervous," Jillian said. "Sarah, can you come on down and say hi to your daddy?"

Ethan tracked her careful movements, each slow step drawing her out of the safety of the porch. She stopped at the top of the steps, hands clutched tight to her middle. Jillian had dressed her up in a pretty pink top and purple jeans, and she looked so much like her mother it was uncanny. Right down to the identical nervous expression.

"Hi," Sarah said.

"Hey, baby girl." Daniel sounded out of breath. Ethan had no idea how it felt to see one's child for the first time in his entire life, and to find not a baby but an eight-year-old girl with opinions of her own.

Sarah cast a helpless look at Ethan, who wanted to scoop her up and tell her it would be okay. He held still, not wanting to intrude unless absolutely necessary.

"You're so pretty, Sarah," Daniel said. "You look exactly like your mom."

"Thank you."

Daniel took a direct step toward her. Sarah's eyes flashed wide, and she bolted. Off the porch and around to hide behind Ethan, little fingers grasping his belt. The icy glare Daniel leveled at him sent his stomach plummeting to the ground. Perfect. Daniel could blame this on him, too.

"Give her time, honey," Jillian said. "She has to get to know you."

"How's that going to fucking happen if she runs from me?"

"Let her come to you when she's ready. And don't forget, the last photo she saw of you, you had hair."

He scraped his fingers over his bald scalp. "I wanted a new look."

"It's definitely a look," Caleb said. "Where'd you park your Harley, dude?"

Daniel flipped him off.

"Jillian, dear, why don't you take Danny inside and help him settle in," Mom said. "I have to get supper started, and the boys need to get back to work."

"Gimpy, too?" Daniel asked, nodding at Ethan.

Ethan bristled.

"Ethan's still recuperating and he's got a long way to go yet," Mom said.

* * *

Ethan ended up spending the rest of the afternoon in the screen house with Sarah, both of them in thick jackets. Sarah carefully colored page after page in a Doc McStuffins book, while Ethan alternated between his audiobook and coloring with Sarah. As the hours stretched closer to evening, Ethan's dread of dinner set in hard and fast.

"Ethan?" Angel's voice called out. He was still a dozen feet from the screen house, making a steady line for them.

"Hey, Angel."

He stopped outside the door. "Hi, S-s-sarah."

"Hi, Mr. Garrett," Sarah said. The formality was probably her mother's doing, so Sarah didn't think Angel was a friend.

To Ethan, he said, "Your mother s-s-sent me to tell you d-d-dinner will be ready in half an hour." The message gave him plenty of time to hobble up to the house.

"Thanks," Ethan said. "Sarah, you want to take your things back up and get them put away before supper?"

"Okay." She gathered her crayons and coloring book, and then took off for the house. She slowed her pace halfway there, as if remembering the stranger in her home.

"How is she?" Angel asked. He came inside the screen porch, still dressed in his Shockley Stables fleece.

"Terrified. Then again, Daniel shaved his head and bulked up, so he's got this weird too-pale Vin Diesel thing going on."

Angel chuckled, then quickly sobered. "How are you d-d-doing?"

Ethan shrugged. "Well, he still hates me for the past, and now I think he hates me more because Sarah hid behind me instead of letting Daniel hug her."

"Ouch."

"Yeah."

"She'll come around."

"Maybe, but Daniel has never been known for his patience. I'm afraid he'll push Sarah, and then get angry when she doesn't respond the way he wants. He has to let their relationship grow organically, or it's going to fail."

Angel's eyes softened, and Ethan understood—his words referred as much to him and Angel as they did to Daniel and Sarah. It had to grow organically, slowly, as it had been growing for the last few days.

"You can't change D-d-daniel, Ethan. But you can be there for S-s-sarah. And Jillian."

"I know. Thanks."

"For what?"

"Reminding me. And being my friend."

Angel smiled. "It's n-n-no hardship. Trust me."

Ethan stood and crutched over to where Angel stood by the door. The sun was going down, and they were pretty far from the house. Far enough not to fear being seen this close to him. Part of him longed to be closer. To put his hands on someone who wasn't related by blood or marriage, like he had yesterday. But not on the dirty denim covering a knee.

On skin.

"I do trust you, Angel," he said. "Do you trust me?"

"Yes." No hesitation.

Good. "Then I'd like to ask you something."

Angel's Adam's apple bobbed. "Okay."

He held Angel's dark brown eyes as he said, "May I touch your face?"

* * *

Angel's breath caught, stunned into silence by the straightforward but overwhelming question. That Ethaniel had asked permission to do something so simple was amazing and intensely considerate. Ethaniel wanted to touch him, but he didn't want to surprise or startle, or to take liberties.

He blinked hard, making sure he was awake and aware. Other than the occasional hug or pat from Ruth, no one besides Ethaniel had touched him with intent in years. He hadn't given it much thought before, but now Angel *craved* touch. His skin begged for it.

"Yes," Angel said. "You may."

Ethaniel shifted his weight to his left side, freeing his right hand from the crutch handle. It rose, and while Angel wanted to track the progress of those fingers, he couldn't stop watching Ethaniel's face. Intense green eyes studied him as though he was a precious mystery worth solving, taking in every detail, every tic of muscle. Heat ghosted near Angel's cheek, a shadow of a touch.

Angel's pulse quickened. His breath came shorter. Anticipation curled deep in his gut, a burning warmth that lit him up. No contact yet, and already he wanted to fly to the moon.

Work-roughened skin—a thumb, maybe—brushed the arch of Angel's left cheekbone. Angel gasped. Heat flared in Ethaniel's eyes. Eyes burning with something Angel couldn't name. He was too scared of losing it to name it, so he remained still and *experienced* this.

The thumb traced a soft line across his cheekbone, back to the top of his ear. Stopped. Descended along his jaw, around to his chin. The path left scorching skin behind. Skin awake and aware and needing more. The thumb became two fingers, and they danced the same path. Angel pressed into the touch, needing more. Ethaniel's palm cupped his cheek, fingers splayed, an electric touch that zinged through Angel's heart.

How could something this simple be more powerful than the best orgasm of his life? The contact was far from sexual, and yet Angel felt naked. Seen. The only person on Earth who mattered to Ethaniel. Only this skin on skin connection mattered. Ethaniel's thumb circled in slowly widening arcs, until its path nearly touched Angel's nose. His chin trembled. He was desperate for Ethaniel to meet his gaze, but those gleaming emeralds remained fixed on his explorations.

Ethaniel was a beautiful man, but he had never looked more exquisite than in that moment, in a shadowed screen house, lightly stroking Angel's face.

Blood pulsed in Angel's dick, awakening desire long ago forgotten, smashed beneath the heavy boots of the justice system. He was getting hard for the first time in a long while, and from someone else's touch. A touch he craved. His body screamed for more. He was safe. He was with Ethaniel. He could have more and not fear losing part of himself. All Angel had to do was lean forward and kiss him.

Now, more than touch, Angel longed to taste Ethaniel. And more than ever, that was a very, very bad idea.

He pressed into Ethaniel's palm, pulse racing, mouth dry. He angled his head. Ethaniel drew closer, his attention elsewhere. Below Angel's eyes. On his lips.

Oh dear Lord, was he going to—?

"Hey, numb nuts! Dinner!" Caleb's voice carried down from the house, shattering the moment into tiny, frozen pieces.

Ethaniel pulled back, straightening, his hand falling away. "On my way," he shouted back.

Angel flinched. His cheek was cold. "Thank you," he said, surprised at the rasp in his voice.

"For what?"

"This. It was lovely." And he really hoped the deepening shadows of dusk were hiding the bulge in his jeans. He was grateful for the bulky fleece, but tugging it lower would only draw attention to the problem. Hopefully the walk to the garage would take care of his unexpected erection.

"Thank you for indulging me," Ethaniel said. "I think maybe we both needed that."

Angel could think of quite a few things he needed, but he would never, ever ask for. Not from Ethaniel. "Yeah."

"You coming up for supper?"

"No. Ruth is saving me a plate. Your family needs to be alone with your brother tonight."

"You know Mom considers you family now."

"I know." And he loved her for it. "I'll see you tomorrow, Ethan."

"Sure. Maybe we'll actually get some speech therapy in."

Angel grinned. "Maybe."

He watched Ethaniel go, mesmerized by the sure way he took the path back to the house. Moving with strength and ease and a confidence that Angel swore hadn't been there a few days ago. He didn't dare hope that it had anything to do with himself.

CHAPTER EIGHT

Ethan used the trek back to the house to get his racing pulse under control. He'd known that touching Angel was going to rile him up a little, but he hadn't expected it to light a fire deep in his belly. A consuming fire that wanted the younger man in a way he hadn't wanted someone in a long damned time. Angel was everything he didn't think he liked: younger, smaller, almost fragile, with demons in his eyes that did constant battle with hope. Ethan wanted to protect him from those demons as badly as he'd wanted to bend him over the picnic table and fuck him senseless.

And dear God, he wanted to throttle his brother for interrupting what would have been a mind-blowing kiss. A kiss he planned to follow up on as soon as possible. Angel had been as aroused as Ethan, and Ethan wasn't letting this go.

His fractured leg was pounding by the time he made it into the house, and the discomfort killed any lingering effects of his tactile exploration. Pain was better than a bucket of ice water. The interior of the house was thick with the greasy scent of fried pork chops. Daniel's favorite.

Ethan's stomach rolled. He thudded down the hallway to the dining room, where everyone else had settled around the table: his parents, Caleb and Polly, Benny, Daniel, Jillian, and Sarah.

Another face surprised him because he hadn't noticed the extra car outside. Pastor Alan Jameson from Mom's church. He knew the man from Christmas Eve services. Pastor Jameson had stopped by once when Ethan first came home to offer a blessing. Ethan had struggled to be polite.

"Ethaniel, it's nice to see you," Jameson said. He stood up long enough to shake Ethan's hand.

"You too, Pastor." Ethan settled at his usual end of the table, eager to stretch his cast out a bit.

Daniel ignored him completely. Next to him, Jillian was subdued, her cheeks a little flushed.

"Now that we're here," Dad said, "I was hoping Pastor Jameson could say the blessing."

Ethan dutifully bowed his head, keeping his eyes open. A small act of rebellion against a man who believed in the version of God who hated gays and said to condemn them. Ethan preferred the God who spoke through Jesus when Jesus said to love your neighbor. Not that he and God had ever had the best of relationships. Not since Afghanistan.

"Dear heavenly Father," Jameson said, "We sit humbly before You and offer our thanks to You. We thank You for the many blessings You have bestowed upon this family, Your servants in all things. We thank You for allowing Daniel to return to the fold, and we ask for Your blessings upon him and his wife and child. We thank You for the food on this table, and the roof over our heads. In Your name we pray. Amen."

A chorus of "Amen" rose around the table. Ethan stayed silent.

Ethan contemplated one of the juicy, browned pork chops while the others were served. Mom made the absolute best pan-fried pork chops. Daniel used to request them for every birthday dinner, and Mom had stopped making them (according to Caleb) after Daniel was locked up. Mom had also thrown together a pan of baked macaroni and cheese, garlic string beans, and a bowl of canned pears. All of Daniel's favorite foods.

Mom excused herself to the kitchen, then returned with a small plate for Ethan. Steamed string beans, sans garlic, two of the pear halves, and half a boiled chicken breast.

"Thanks, Mom," Ethan said.

"You on some kind of fag diet?" Daniel asked.

Conversation at the table ground to a halt as everyone stared at them. Ethan met his brother's hostile stare, and a chill blasted through him. "No. Post concussive syndrome."

"What the fu—heck's that?"

He knew damned well what it was. Mom said she'd explained his accident to Daniel during a phone call last month. And Ethan's patience was stretched thin. "I fell through a roof and hit my head. I eat too much, or anything that's too rich or fatty, and I get sick. I stand up too fast, I could pass out. Reading gives me migraines. It's a real treat, believe me."

Daniel grunted, then tackled his dinner. Ethan indulged in one more glare—the fag diet remark still stung—before cutting into his own food. Sarah had been installed on Jillian's left, between her and Caleb, and Ethan hated that she was so far away from him. She almost always sat next to him at meals. She ate with laser focus, as if nothing in the world mattered more than the precise way in which she cut her pork and speared her macaroni.

No one talked about anything more mundane than the stables. Not that Ethan was surprised. "What was it like in prison?" wasn't exactly proper dinnertime conversation. All anyone had to do was look at the hard, angry man wearing Daniel's skin and they'd have their answer.

Ethan concentrated on his dinner, on small bites and careful chewing, and he finished his entire plate long after the others had moved on to cherry pie for dessert. He wouldn't be able to stomach that gooey sweetness anyway, so he didn't mind. After that, all of the men except Ethan excused themselves to the living room to watch television. Jillian helped Mom clean up. Ethan removed himself to the kitchen table to observe the women he loved so much, wishing the entire time he could be more useful to them. Sarah sat across from him with her missed schoolwork, dropped off by one of her cousins earlier.

Angel knocked on the back door as they were finishing the last of the dishes. Ethan waved him in, grinning at the sight of him. Angel smiled back, his cheeks staining pink.

Mom pulled a covered plate out of the oven and plunked it down at the seat next to Ethan. "Eat up, honey."

Maybe not the best of plans as the mixed scents of the pork and cheese made Ethan's stomach tighten, but he appreciated the gesture. Angel slid into the chair next to him. Sarah shot him a shy smile, then returned to her sheet of math problems.

"Is that Pastor Jameson's van outside?" Angel whispered.

"Yeah, he's in the living room," Ethan replied softly. "Guess he wanted to bless the wayward son."

"Think the blessing took?"

"Time will tell."

Angel ate, while Ethan relaxed into the very simple pleasure of having Angel by his side. He liked it. He couldn't explain why, but he did. Mom was smiling to beat the devil while she finished the last of the dishes. Jillian simply looked tired. Worn out already, and her husband had only been home a few hours.

Daniel stalked into the kitchen—stalked was really the only way Ethan could describe the menacing way Daniel moved now, shoulders back, tense and ready to fight—and aimed for the fridge. "Dad says there's a six pack in here," he said to no one in particular.

"Won't drinking violate your parole?" Jillian asked.

"Only if someone tattles to my P.O." Daniel was angled away from Ethan, but his accusatory tone was impossible to miss.

Jillian sighed but didn't respond.

"Bottom shelf," Mom said.

Daniel pulled out a six pack of Budweiser. Halfway back, he noticed Angel and stopped. "Who the hell are you?"

"Daniel," Mom said, voice tight. "Manners."

Daniel didn't amend his question. Angel stared at him like a mouse cornered by a cat. Eyes big. Silent.

"Angel Garrett," Ethan replied. "He works for the stables."

"The kid you gave my apartment to?"

"It's the family's apartment," Mom said. "I told you about Angel, dear. He's part of the family, and I expect you to treat him as such."

Daniel's cold stare flickered to Ethan. Maybe not the best stated request from Mom, but she still had hope that Daniel would forgive Ethan. Then Daniel looked at Angel again, and something in his eyes made Ethan uncomfortable. He couldn't describe it, not really, but Angel sank deeper into his chair, eyes on his plate. The instinct to protect Angel roared to life from deep inside of Ethan, and he bristled. Sat up straighter.

As if sensing the change, Daniel's gaze swiveled back to Ethan. Their eyes met, and without even meaning to, Ethan realized he'd issued a challenge.

Shit.

Daniel grunted, then left with his beer.

Sarah whimpered. Her head was down, but Ethan saw her lip trembling. He covered her little hand with his, and her head popped up. Tears streaked her cheeks, and his heart broke for her. "Why's he so mad?" she whispered.

Ethan didn't know how to explain it, so he opened his arms. Sarah scampered around the table and climbed onto his lap. He held her tight, ignoring his unhappy stomach, and focused on Sarah. On her shaking limbs and soft cries, and the wetness soaking his shirt collar. He shushed her and stroked her hair. "It'll be okay," he said. "It'll be okay."

* * *

Angel didn't register Sarah moving onto Ethaniel's lap right away. His lizard brain was screaming at him to get the hell out of that kitchen and hide, to do anything he could to make himself unnoticeable. But Daniel had noticed him, and for a long, devastating moment, Angel had seen a version of The Look he hadn't seen since prison.

The Look: *You'll give it up to save yourself a beating, because you're a weak little bitch.*

He'd never expected to see that Look on the outside, and certainly not from a member of the Shockley family, and avoiding Daniel Shockley had become his new priority in life. His belly ached with it, because only a few minutes ago, his top priority had been touching Ethaniel again.

Movement clued him in before Ruth squatted by his chair. "You don't let Daniel get to you, honey," she said. "He'll come around."

Angel's heart slammed into his ribs. He didn't want Daniel to come around. He didn't want Daniel anywhere near him. But he couldn't say that to Ruth, so he nodded his understanding. He tried to finish his supper, but his stomach was in knots and the house too confining. He needed out.

Jillian extricated Sarah from Ethaniel, and the pair went off. Ruth left the kitchen, too.

"I should go," Angel said. Nothing else came to mind.

Ethaniel picked up Sarah's abandoned pencil and twirled it around in his fingers. "If you want."

He didn't want to go, but staying was playing with fire. "I have to." Sitting this close to Ethaniel, it took all of Angel's strength not to reach out and touch him. To grab his hand and still those idling fingers. To touch his face the way Ethaniel had touched his. They had no privacy in this house, and even looking at Ethaniel courted danger.

Ethaniel twisted his upper body to face him, his expression thoughtful. "Give me five minutes?"

"To do what?"

"Wait here."

Completely stumped, Angel did as Ethaniel asked. He remained at the table, listening to the rumble of voices from the living room. The occasional bout of laughter. Ethaniel returned after a long five minutes—probably closer to ten, but he was on crutches—with something tucked into the waistband of his jeans. He handed it off to Angel, grinning.

Angel accepted the walkie-talkie. It wasn't new, and it reminded him of a child's toy. He stared at it, not understanding.

"Keep it on channel two," Ethaniel said. "We used them a lot when we were kids, because no one around here had cell phones."

"Oh. Thanks."

"I've got the other one."

"Oh!" Angel laughed to cover his idiocy. Ethaniel wanted to be able to talk to him outside of their infrequent stolen moments. The thought warmed his heart. "Thank you."

"I'm going to go make nice with the pastor for a while, then probably turn in for the night. Around eight-thirty."

"Okay. Eight-thirty."

It was the oddest non-date that Angel had ever planned, and as he walked through the cold night to his apartment with the walkie in hand, he'd never looked forward to anything more in his life.

* * *

Ethan hadn't been in the living room for five minutes before Pastor Jameson asked, "So son, when will I see you sitting with my flock on Sunday?"

He hated the word flock. It made him think of seagulls circling a bucket of spilled fries on the boardwalk, all screeching and flapping and annoying. "God and I have our own understanding," Ethan replied.

Jameson arched one eyebrow. "I see."

"I expect you'll see him a few Sundays from now," Mom said with a devilish twinkle in her eyes. "That's the next choir performance, isn't it?"

"Yes, it is."

Ethan stared at his mother until he understood her point. Angel was in the choir. He would suffer through the ritual of putting on a suit and going to church in order to hear Angel sing.

"I didn't realize Ethan was a fan of recitals," Jameson said.

"I've always loved music," Ethan said. "I played the guitar a lot when I was a teenager. Might take it up again." He hadn't realized he'd made a conscious decision about that until he said it. He needed something besides audiobooks to occupy his time, especially with winter coming. Music was a good distraction, as long as it didn't react badly with his PCS. Reading the sheet music might give him a migraine.

"A soldier, a roofer, and now a musician," Daniel said. "Ever gonna settle on a career path, little brother?"

"What? Like you did?" Ethan regretted the barb the instant it passed his lips, but Daniel had been back for less than a day and he was already tired of the insults. Tired of being the focus of Daniel's anger. He'd been trampled on enough in his life, and he wasn't letting Daniel get away with it anymore.

Daniel tensed, poised to retort.

"Boys," Dad said.

That ended that. Only Dad could cut off an argument with a single word.

Jameson left a little after eight. Jillian came down and asked Daniel if he wanted to come upstairs while she read Sarah a bedtime story. Ethan watched him go, curious if Sarah had requested him, or if Jillian had coaxed her into agreeing.

Around eight-twenty, he excused himself for the night. His room was far enough from the living room, with the bathroom between them, that he didn't worry about anyone overhearing his conversation with Angel. He locked his door—not something he usually did, in case he had some sort of emergency—then carefully skinned out of his pants and flannel shirt. He crawled into bed in his boxers and undershirt. The other walkie was beneath his pillow. He turned it on, listening to the faint crackle of static.

The numbers on his clock flipped to eight-thirty. He pressed the button and said, "Angel?" Released.

A moment later, the static cleared. "I'm here."

Ethan grinned. "Hey."

"Hi." Pause. "How was family time?"

"Only slightly painful. Pastor Jameson asked when he'd finally see me in church."

"What did you s-s-say?"

The faint stutter only widened Ethan's grin. Angel was nervous, and that fact was ten kinds of adorable. "Not much, because Mom volunteered me to attend the choir's next recital." When Angel didn't comment, he added, "I assume you'll be singing?"

"Yes."

"Good, then I'll go."

"Because of me?"

"Yes." He imagined Angel was blushing.

"You d-d-don't like church." Not a question.

"No. And it's not just that a lot of churches preach against gays. From what I've read, some are pretty progressive and inclusive."

"Then what?"

Ethan considered his words. "I grew up believing that if you loved God enough and prayed hard enough, He'd answer your prayers. I prayed a lot while I was in the Army, and my buddies still got blown to pieces." Screams and concussive blasts ricocheted through his mind, and he blinked hard against the sting of tears. "The only time He answered my prayer was when Mom beat her cancer, and you can bet it was because she had a whole church full of people doing the praying. It had nothing to do with me."

"I can respect that."

Angel's simple comment said so much about the younger man's character, and it made Ethan curious. "How come you like church so much?"

"I'd n-n-never gone to church a d-d-day in my life until I walked into Pine Creek Methodist looking for something. Anything. I was stuck in that halfway house until I got a job, and no one likes to hire ex-cons. S-s-so I figured why not give God a try. Pine Creek was the closest church. I met your mother that day. If it wasn't a sign from God, then I don't know what is."

"Do you think God forgave you for killing Shawn Lawrence?"

The walkie stayed quiet for so long that Ethan feared he'd overstepped. Then, "No. God only forgives if we're truly sorry for our sins, and I'm not sorry I killed Shawn. Not one bit." The vehemence in Angel's voice matched his words, and Ethan wished he was in the same room as Angel so he could offer some kind of comfort.

"God hasn't forgiven me for killing Shawn," Angel said. "But I think he's forgiven me a lot of other sins. I've done a lot of shit I'm not proud of to survive this long."

Ethan fought the urge to ask about those things, because he didn't want to push Angel too far. They'd both put conditions on their friendship. Ethan didn't talk about Afghanistan. Angel didn't talk about prison. Or at least they didn't ask each other about those things. Voluntary information was still on the table.

I'll show you mine if you show me yours didn't always work, but it was worth a shot.

"So have I," Ethan said. "Done shit I'm not proud of. When you and four buddies are pinned down in a stone building with mortars going off in every direction, and someone's rushing at you with what looks like a bomb in their hands, you do what it takes to survive that moment."

You shoot the person rushing you in the face first, then suss out if they were really a threat.

It was them or her, and he chose them. He always would.

In this hellhole, the only thing you had was the guy next to you. Beside you. Watching your back.

So he shot her.

Smoke filled his nostrils and choked him. Yells and screams echoed in his ears. He tasted blood on his tongue. Walls shook.

Bits of stone fell. The harsh chatter of rapid gunfire. Burning motor oil.

Mikey shrieked as a mortar tore through a wall and peppered his back with shrapnel.

Oh God. No.

Ethan tried to roll away, but a weight on his right leg pinned him down. His gun was gone. The enemy was encroaching on their position, so close, and he couldn't run. His buddies wouldn't leave him behind. They'd die trying to save him, and he didn't want anyone else to die today. He thrashed. Hit his head with something metal in his hand, but what good would a radio do against a platoon of enemy soldiers?

He was alone, and he was going to die here.

Not alone. His neck hairs prickled. Someone was nearby. Saying his name. How did the enemy know his name?

Cold air tickled his face and bare arms.

"Ethan? Please, it's Angel, come back to me."

The soothing voice penetrated. The stone building shattered in the same moment someone touched his shoulder. He grabbed the wrist with his opposite hand and yanked. Rolled. Something thick around his torso stopped the roll from turning into a pin, and he found himself tangled up in a blanket with a smaller body trapped beneath his.

Big brown eyes blinked up at him, full of surprise when he expected fear.

Angel.

Angel in the war?

No, Angel was in his bedroom. Ethan had him flat on his back, on his bed, and Angel wasn't scared. The position wasn't doing Ethan's right leg any favors, but he couldn't seem to move. How had he gone from that debris-filled house to being in bed with Angel?

Flashback.

Shit.

"Ethan?" So soft. Tentative.

Ethan rolled away, onto his back and sat against the headboard. Sweat broke out across his face and chest, despite the cold air seeping in through his wide open window. Angel pushed into a crouching position near his knees.

"Are you okay?" Angel whispered.

"What happened?"

"You were talking about doing things to survive, and then you made this noise. You stayed on the line, said something about being left behind, and then you must have let go of the button." Angel swallowed hard. "You didn't answer me when I called back, so I ran over here. Your window doesn't have a screen on it, and I got it open from the outside."

As the story sank in, Angel's appearance finally registered. He was shoeless, dressed in cotton boxers, a white tee, and nothing else. And his teeth were chattering. "Jesus Christ, Angel, come here." He held up the blanket.

Angel hesitated briefly, before the cold in the room forced him into action. He leapt off the bed, and at first Ethan feared he would leave the way he came. Instead, Angel shut the window again, then crawled beneath the blanket. Icy toes brushed Ethan's thigh. Ethan slid lower, then tugged Angel snug against him and tucked the blanket around Angel's shoulders. The position left Angel no choice but to rest his cheek on Ethan's shoulder.

The cold skin made Ethan shiver. He held Angel while his body warmed, utterly content in a way he hadn't been in a long time. Stiff at first, Angel relaxed against him, until his steady breathing matched Ethan's. A hand skimmed out and rested lightly over Ethan's heart.

"I'm glad you're okay," Angel said.

"So to speak."

"D-d-do you have flashbacks like that a lot?"

"Had them more when I first left the Army. I got counseling. Working with other vets helped. They got bad again after the accident."

"I'm s-s-sorry."

"It is what it is."

"I can't begin to imagine what all that was like for you."

Ethan traced small circles on Angel's bicep. "You must have fought battles of your own in prison."

Angel exhaled harshly. "Probably not as many as I should have fought." He didn't elaborate, so Ethan left it alone. For now.

He was far too content to simply hold Angel. To feel the heat of another male body pressed closely to his. He inhaled the faint scents of shampoo and sweat, and the barest hint of cigarette smoke.

Angel chuckled, the soft sound a rumble against Ethan's chest.

"What?" Ethan asked.

"It's silly. I was just thinking I feel like a teenager who sneaked into his boyfriend's bedroom after curfew."

Ethan laughed, even while his heart twisted sharply at the word boyfriend. "You do that a lot in your wild teen years?"

"A few times. You?"

"Never snuck into a bedroom. Snuck out to fool around in a truck bed a few times."

"I blew a guy in the back of a VW bus once."

"Now that sounds like an interesting story."

"Not really, as far as hookups go. Most interesting thing about it was he'd parked outside a Kmart in broad daylight. Half the fun was the idea of getting caught."

Ethan was fascinated by this light-hearted, risk-taking version of Angel. The man he knew was so careful, so guarded. Pre-prison Angel had quite the adventurous streak. "Did you? Get caught?"

"No." His slight body shivered. "Not for public sex, anyway."

Right. Without thinking it through, Ethan let his left hand come up to sift through Angel's hair. As soft as he'd imagined. And thick. Angel leaned into the touch and made a sound not unlike a cat's purr. "This okay?" Ethan asked, barely a whisper.

"Yes." The breathy way Angel replied sent signals to Ethan's dick.

Wake up and join the party signals.

Angel's fingers traced along his collarbone, back and forth, a hypnotic action that wanted to lull Ethan to sleep. He focused on the gentle pressure, hoping to ignore his slowly thickening cock. Flat on his back like this, the erection wouldn't stay hidden for long, and he couldn't exactly roll onto his side thanks to the damned cast.

And why hide it? He was attracted to Angel, and he could make an educated guess Angel felt the same. Fooling around with the stable hand in his parents' house might not be the best plan ever, but Ethan was exhausted of being alone. He hoped Angel was, too. He'd never know if he didn't try.

Heart pounding, Ethan tugged gently on Angel's hair. Angel raised his head, angling to look at Ethan. Their gazes locked, and something zinged through Ethan's bloodstream. Sharp and heady and unlike anything he'd ever experienced from something as simple as a look. Angel's eyes widened, as if he'd felt it too. And maybe he had. Ethan glanced at Angel's full lips, so curious what they felt like. Curious what Angel tasted like.

When he met Angel's eyes again, they were wide and shiny. Anxious.

Angel licked his lips. "Ethan, I—"

Ethan pressed the tip of his finger to Angel's lips. "May I?"

A full-body shudder later, Angel twisted onto his stomach, half his body curled around Ethan's. A stiffening cock pressed into his hip. Angel skated his fingers across Ethan's cheek, into his hair, and then a hot mouth covered his.

Sensations exploded all around him, and Ethan embraced the whirlwind. Warm lips teasing. Gentle fingers massaging. Arousal flooded his body. He needed more. Needed to touch. He slanted his head and parted his lips. Angel didn't deepen the kiss the way he needed, so Ethan helped him out. He thrust his tongue into Angel's mouth, and Angel gasped. Ethan tasted orange soda and tobacco and something else, less identifiable. He tasted Angel, and he was amazing.

Ethan trailed his fingers down Angel's back, hard enough that Angel arched into the touch. He gripped Angel's hips and tugged until Angel was straddling his waist, knees on either side of his hips, his hard cock pressed firmly to Ethan's stomach, and oh yeah, that was good. Still kissing him, Ethan rubbed his hands along Angel's back, across soft cotton to rest his palms on Angel's ass. As much as he wanted to feel Angel's bare skin, he didn't want to push him too far. He could gladly make out like this all night long, and Angel seemed in no hurry to stop.

Angel's tongue lashed at Ethan's, finally getting into the game. Ethan retreated, allowing Angel to steal into his mouth. To explore and taste, and to take a little control. Angel jerked his hips once, twice, which had the added benefit of brushing his boxer-clad ass against the tip of Ethan's straining erection. The most delicious kind of teasing, and oh my Lord, the idea of shoving off their clothes and sliding Angel backward onto his cock—*shit.*

Ethan groaned into Angel's mouth, his hands gripping Angel's hips to hold him still. His waist was narrow, hips the perfect size for Ethan to hold comfortably in his large, work-roughened hands. Everything about Angel was smaller, more delicate than any guy Ethan had been with since he was a teenager. He sought out men he could manhandle in bed, be rough with without worrying if he'd hurt them. Men who could fuck him through the mattress when the need arose.

Everything about Angel was wrong. So why did Ethan feel like he'd found something irreplaceable and perfect?

They stayed that way for a long time, kissing and touching and existing in a wonderful moment of peace. Peace that couldn't last forever. Angel pulled away first, sitting up on Ethan's stomach, his lips shiny and swollen. Eyes soft-lidded and full of wonder. He pressed his palms flat over Ethan's pecs, as if he needed the support to keep from collapsing. Ethan squeezed his hips, and Angel smiled.

"This is definitely a first for me," Angel said.

"What is?"

"Making out with the boss's son, in his bed, with the boss in the same house."

Ethan chuckled. He wasn't a teenager anymore, but the idea of secretly making out under his parents' roof had its appeal. He felt young again, even though he was still a month from thirty and nothing close to old. Not chronologically, anyway. "First for me, too."

"Making out with the hired help?"

"Making out with someone like you."

Angel stiffened. "S-s-someone like me?"

Oh hell, he'd stepped in it. "I don't mean prison, I swear. I don't care about that. It's in your past."

"Then what d-d-did you mean?" Angel was nervous and stuttering again, but he hadn't climbed off or moved away, which Ethan took as a sign that he hadn't totally blown this.

"I'm not usually attracted to guys who are, uh, smaller than me. Shorter, I mean. I've always gone after guys my size, sometimes taller. Muscular." He was pretty sure he sounded like a total asshole.

"What's s-s-so s-s-special about me, then, that you'd break pattern? Convenience?"

"Fuck no." Ethan feathered his fingertips through Angel's hair, loving the way Angel leaned into the caress. "I talked to you. Got to know you. Did I fantasize just now about fucking you until we both passed out from exhaustion? Yes." Angel shivered. "But I also could have kissed you like that all night and been satisfied."

A shadow settled in Angel's eyes, shrouding his entire body. Making him seem to shrink. His attention dropped to Ethan's chest, and Ethan didn't like that. What had he said wrong?

"Talk to me, Angel." He slid his hands from Angel's hips and let them rest lightly on his thighs. "Please."

Angel released a long, shuddering breath. "I like our friendship, and I don't want to screw it up. You're the only real friend I've had in years."

The grief-stricken truth in Angel's words twisted like a knife in Ethan's heart. "I like our friendship, too. And I won't push you into anything, I promise." *God, don't make me promise to be friends.* Now that he knew what Angel's kisses were like, he didn't think he could go back.

"You deserve better than me, Ethan."

"What?" He tucked a finger beneath Angel's chin and forced him to raise his head. Angel didn't meet his eyes, but whatever. "You've met me, right? In the last three days, I've hit you with my crutch, had a flashback, and thrown up at dinner. I'm a mess." Still no eye contact. "Maybe you deserve better than *me.*"

Angel's brown eyes flashed with anger, finally meeting his. "Don't say that."

"It's true. My leg will heal, but there's no guarantee what will happen with the concussion symptoms. I could be like this for the rest of my life."

"Dizzy spells and barfing don't make you who you are. You were a great guy long before your accident. I just wish I'd been able to tell you that before." Angel blushed, but he didn't look away again.

Ethan traced slow circles on Angel's thighs. Thin but muscular, from long days on his feet, with a light sprinkling of hair. "Thank you. I can't believe I never paid attention to you before now. All those times I was home and you were here."

"I made sure to stay out of your way."

"Why?"

Angel's cheeks darkened. "I've had a crush on you since I first saw a picture of you in the den."

Ethan grinned. "Yeah?"

He shrugged, and that miserable shadow returned. "Doesn't change anything."

"Sure it does. You like me. I like you. We're both unique messes, and maybe we aren't meant for anyone except each other." Ethan had never seen serendipity in the timing of his accident, or the injuries that had forced him back to the family home. Not until this moment. "You said yourself God meant for you to be here. Maybe I'm supposed to be here, too."

"I thought you didn't believe in God."

"No, I believe. We don't talk to each other much, that's all."

Angel was quiet for a long time, lost in his own thoughts, and the only thing that kept Ethan from squirming was the fact that Angel was still hard. The evidence lay hot on his stomach, pressed against slightly bunched boxers in a way that looked uncomfortable. Ethan didn't let himself stare or imagine, and he tried not to think about his own persistent hard-on. He'd told Angel what he wanted.

Minutes stretched into an eternity of silence.

"What are you thinking?" Ethan asked when he could no longer stand it.

"Studying."

"Studying what?"

"The way you're looking at me right now. Hopeful and kind. I want to remember it."

Ethan's gut twisted. "Why do you think I'll stop looking at you like this?"

"I know you will."

"Look, Angel, I'm not naïve. I've heard the stories of what goes on in prisons, and even if you tell me about it, it won't change anything." Other than ignite a burning need to find and punish every man who'd ever caused Angel pain. But he would never blame Angel for doing what he had to do to survive, while surrounded by hundreds of men who were twice his size, many of them violent offenders.

Angel made a pained noise, almost a sob. "It's not about that. Not really."

"Then tell me. What is it you think you can say that will make me look at you differently?"

"I'm HIV positive."

CHAPTER NINE

By Saturday morning, Ethan was ready to climb out of his own skin. He hadn't been able to concentrate on his audiobooks for shit, and he loathed the idea of sitting in the swing doing nothing. It had rained on Thursday and Friday, a cold wintery rain that kept him locked up inside the house with a snarly Daniel and his annoying habit of blasting the volume on the television when no one but Ethan was home.

Three whole days apart, and it was slowly killing him. Three days since Angel dropped his bombshell, then immediately fled his room through the window. Ethan hadn't been able to absorb the news, much less react, before the chance was taken away. He had given Angel Wednesday, because he'd needed time to think. Time to reconcile the idea of kind, considerate Angel carrying such a thing inside of his body.

Time to do research online, headache or no, and realize that living with a positive partner wasn't as difficult as he'd initially thought. And while the news did change things, it didn't change how he felt about Angel. The tug in his heart when he thought the man's name, or pictured his shy smile. All of Angel's previous hesitation made sense, and the only unanswered question that made Ethan's chest tighten with rage was how Angel had been infected.

Angel hadn't come to the house for dinner Wednesday, and he didn't answer the walkie-talkie, so Ethan had planned to seek him out the next day.

Then rain happened. Two solid days of rain that ended in a lot of cancelled lessons and appointments, which meant family in and out of the house. Other people Daniel could talk to while he ignored Ethan.

But after three days of silence from Angel, Ethan couldn't take it any longer. The yard was soaked, but he was determined to track down his friend. Mom noticed his agitation over breakfast, because she did the breakfast dishes slower than normal while he choked down his plate of eggs. Everyone else was finished and gone by the time she pounced.

"What's going on, baby?" Wiping her hands on a dishtowel, she plunked down in the kitchen chair opposite him.

He considered her for a moment. Her silver hair and gentle smile. The near constant fatigue that seemed to plague her, likely due to stress over all of the different hats she wore: mother, grandmother, business owner, cook, caregiver, worrier. He hated that some of that stress was his fault. But in front of that fatigue and stress was love and patience.

She knew.

Angel didn't seem the type to take a job in which he could be injured, without warning his new bosses about certain precautions that needed to be taken. One kick from a spooked horse, and he could be bleeding, and their stable manager Russ would need to know how to handle it.

"Did Angel tell you when you hired him?" he asked.

Mom frowned, puzzled. "About what?" She glanced around the kitchen, then lowered her voice. "That he's gay? Yes, he told me. I don't really know why, but he did. I suppose he felt it would have a bearing on our wanting him here."

He hadn't meant that, but hearing Mom knew and didn't care from the start that Angel was gay did relieve a small amount of the burden weighing on his heart. "Not that. Mom, he told me he's positive."

Her eyebrows arched impossibly high. "When?"

"Tuesday night."

"That was quite brave of him."

Ethan grunted. "Yeah, well, he told me, then he ran off and he's been avoiding me ever since."

This time she looked surprised. "Really? That seems unlike him."

"It's pissing me off. I want to talk to him, but it's not like I can go schlepping around in the rain to find him, and he hasn't been to the house."

"I'd noticed that, yes." Mom twisted the dishtowel around her left hand.

"And you didn't answer my question."

"Oh? Oh. Yes, your father and I both knew when we hired him. He told us when I offered him the job, and he agreed that it was best for us to tell Russ."

"Does anyone else know?"

"I'm not sure, honey. We all three promised Angel we'd keep it our secret, unless something happened that required us to inform someone."

"What about the stables? Your insurance?"

"Our insurance is fine, don't you worry about that. We added extra first aid kits to the barns and sheds, and Angel knows how to handle himself if he gets cut. The only danger we're in is if something happens in front of a client, and they get bled on, but Angel is rarely around any of the riders so the odds of a problem are practically non-existent."

A snippet of an old conversation whispered back to him. Two Christmases ago. Benny had been talking about the stables, and Angel's name had come up. At that point, Angel had been working there for over a year, and Ethan had offhandedly asked if Angel was interested in becoming a trainer, or working with the horses one day.

"Something more interesting than mucking stalls," Ethan had said.

"Mom says he likes what he does," Benny replied. *"Says he's not a real sociable type."*

And the conversation had switched to a billing issue with one of their new boarders. Benny had the attention span of a gnat on caffeine. It amazed Ethan that he could sit still long enough to ever catch a fish on his weekly Sunday outings. Of course, his boys always came home bragging they'd caught the fish.

"Caleb and Benny don't know?" Ethan asked.

"Not as far as I'm aware, and until the day they're named as owners of this stable, it's no business of theirs." Mom's passionate defense of Angel's privacy helped Ethan's resolve, but something else niggled at him.

"Mom, may I ask you something?"

"Something else, you mean?"

He nodded. "Yes."

"Of course, honey."

"If you knew Angel was"—he couldn't help it, he checked to make sure they were still alone—"positive, why have you been pushing us together?"

"Ethaniel Ezekiel Shockley, what sort of question is that?"

He stared at his mother and her slowly reddening cheeks, unsure if the question had been rhetorical or not. Her behavior lately had been sweet, but a little odd, even for her. "It's an honest one. I can't imagine it's the dream of most moms to see their negative son with a positive guy."

Her brown eyes glimmered, and for a moment, he thought she was going to burst into tears. Instead, she reached out and clasped his hand. "You're right, it's not what I dreamed for you when you were a baby. But you, my Ethaniel, have never chosen the easy road, not even when you were a boy. You insisted we take the training wheels off your bike before you were ready."

"I sprained my wrist and scraped both knees up good falling off that thing." He'd been a headstrong kid, positive of what he wanted out of life, and it was to be challenged. To be more than a horse trainer in rural Delaware and to make his life matter. It had taken him to basic training in North Carolina, and then overseas to foreign countries. Now he was reaping the rewards of his old adventurous self, wiling away his days doing nothing more rewarding than not getting dizzy once an hour.

"You joined the Army, even though your father and I begged you to stay," Mom continued. "When you came home, you moved away. The day you came out to me, I honestly wasn't as surprised as I should have been. It fit with you."

Ethan frowned. "I didn't make a choice to be gay."

"I know, honey, and I didn't mean it that way. I only meant that it isn't an easy life, a man loving men, and you'll face even more challenges because of it than your brothers."

He thought he was seeing her point now, and it was pissing him off. "You think choosing Angel is par for the course when it comes to my life? Another rough road to barrel down at top speed?"

"No, goodness, no." She kept fiddling with that dishtowel, and he wanted to rip it out of her hands. "This is coming out all wrong. You're stronger than your brothers; you always have been. It's something inside of you that you don't even see. You take licks, you get knocked down, and you get back up again. You keep moving forward, and you drive the people who love you to do the same.

"When I got sick, baby, you were the one who held me together. Your father, bless him, he tried but he was scared. Your brothers wanted to pretend it wasn't happening. Abby had the restaurant and her four kids. Your strength got me through it."

Her words dumbfounded him. Ethan had never felt strong. He kept moving forward because the only other option was to curl up and die, and that wasn't an option, damn it. After his medical discharge, PTSD could have turned him toward alcohol or illegal drugs, but he hadn't wanted to wander through life in a fog. He didn't want to muddle his mind with prescriptions. As hard as it had been, he wanted to live because his buddies hadn't. Every day he woke up, he honored them. Every day he lived now, he also honored Andy and Butch.

"You're saying I'm strong enough to handle the challenges of being with Angel," Ethan said, once he'd turned the words over in his mind to make sure they were right. He didn't want to misunderstand her again. "I can do it because it's who I am."

"Yes, honey." Mom squeezed his hand tighter. "And because you both have a lot of love in your hearts. You deserve to share it with someone who can love you back with as much joy and gratitude."

He'd never considered falling in love something to be grateful for, but he and Angel were special cases. They both came with steamer trunk-sized baggage that would sink most ships within moments.

The memory of Angel in his bed, pressed against his body, so warm and alive and lovely, rocketed through his brain. He wanted that again. He wanted it every single night, for as long as life allowed, but his needs weren't the only considerations on the table. More was at stake than Mom's approval or Angel's consent.

"What will Dad think?"

Mom huffed. "Your father is quite fond of Angel, and he's never said a cross word to me about him. But that's a far cry from finding out he's with your own son, whom you didn't know was gay too."

Ethan snorted. "No kidding." He scrubbed his free hand through his hair, noticing how long it had gotten. It shagged past his ears now, when it used to stay moderately close to his scalp. "I should tell him, shouldn't I? That I'm gay. Before he finds out another way."

"I think that would be wise, but it has to be your decision. Do it for the right reason."

"Angel's the right reason." The words popped out without thought, and Ethan felt the truth of them in his bones. He'd come out for Angel, if Angel wanted to be with him.

First he had to talk to the stubborn mule.

* * *

A little after three in the afternoon, Angel trudged up the staircase to his apartment, too worn out to think of anything more taxing than face-planting into bed and sleeping until tomorrow. After two days of rain and little activity other than his daily mucking and feeding duties, this morning had been ball-busting busy at the stables. Riders wanting to take their horses out, postponed lessons reporting in. Angel's day had started at four-thirty, and he was wiped.

The extra stress of Ethan's Look after Tuesday night's bombshell hadn't helped. Bolting afterward hadn't been his best moment ever—in fact, he ranked it up there amongst his most cowardly—but he hadn't known what else to do. Ethan had been stricken, pale, like he'd been punched in the gut and told his junk was being removed. It was an entirely new Look, and it had broken Angel.

So he ran. And he'd avoided Ethan on Wednesday, needing to give both of them time and space. He'd turned off the walkie-talkie, and he stayed away from the main house. Two days of rain had been a convenient excuse. After all, he didn't have to deal with the consequences of his admission if he never faced Ethan again.

Right?

Wrong. Consequences always caught up to you. Angel knew that better than anyone.

A square piece of notepaper was taped to his apartment door. Scribbled black ink. *Garage 4:00. Please? E.*

Ethan had made contact. Angel's insides quaked with fear. He had less than an hour to either barricade himself inside and disappoint Ethan, or find his balls and go downstairs to talk.

He owed Ethan a conversation. Maybe not an explanation—Ethan would no doubt ask how long, how did it happen?—but a conversation. If nothing else, it would give Ethan a chance to let him down easy. Politely.

Angel went straight to his bathroom and took a shower. No need to stink of manure and horse sweat while being dumped by someone he wasn't even dating. Hell, they'd only been speaking to each other for a week. Afterward, he found a clean pair of jeans and a thick wool sweater that he tugged on over an undershirt. He didn't bother shaving. Two days of stubble didn't show much on his cheeks or chin, despite having dark hair.

He considered making a quick cheese sandwich to settle his uneasy stomach, but nerves might make him barf it back up. Better to do this on an empty stomach. He paced the floor, keeping one eye on the microwave clock, not allowing himself to look out the window and see if Ethan had arrived yet.

At 3:58 he put his boots on.

At 3:59 he tromped downstairs.

The two-car garage hadn't held actual vehicles in decades. It was crowded with tools and old bicycles and various other things moved from the barns or the house over the years. Cardboard boxes, trash bags, pieces of furniture. No real order to the mess.

Angel let himself in the side door, and was met by a waft of warm air and the hum of the space heater. Two chairs had been set together in the middle of the cement floor, one an old rocker and the other a wicker thing with a sagging seat.

Ethaniel stood in the middle of it all, leaning on his crutches, scowling at him. "I thought you'd bailed."

Angel blinked, taken aback by the accusation. "It's only now four."

"Yeah, and your note said to meet you here at three-fifty. Weird time, but hey, I was here five minutes early."

What on earth was Ethaniel yammering about? "What n-n-note?"

"The note you passed to me through my mother, like we're in middle school. Garage. Three-fifty. I want to talk. Please. A."

The setup settled into place, and Angel nearly rolled his eyes. "Ruth gave that to you?"

"Yes."

"Ethan, I didn't send that n-n-note, but I d-d-did find a similar one taped to my d-d-door that said to meet you here at four." Damn stutter.

Ethaniel's shoulders jolted. "You what?"

"Your mother s-s-set us up."

His mouth opened, like he wanted to argue. A bark of laughter came out instead. "She did, didn't she?" Mystery solved, Ethaniel eased into the wicker chair, which creaked ominously beneath his weight. "Ugh, that's better."

"Why didn't you sit before?"

"I did. I thought you stood me up, and I was about to leave."

"Oh." Angel crossed his arms. "I didn't stand you up, since I didn't invite you and my note said four. I can't believe Ruth did that."

"I can."

"How come?"

Ethaniel settled his crutches on the ground by his chair and stretched his long legs out. "Because we talked some this morning. I vented about how you were avoiding me and I really wanted to talk to you. Looks like she made it happen."

Angel's heart gave a little twist. "I'd really only meant to avoid you for one day. Then the rain became a good excuse to keep my distance a while longer." Now why had he admitted that? Oh yeah, because being around Ethaniel was like swallowing a truth serum. Honesty tumbled right out of his mouth.

"Why did you run?"

Asking for clarification would only insult them both. "The look on your face."

Ethaniel flinched and hung his head.

"I get a lot of looks from people, especially since I've been out of prison," Angel continued, clearly not letting up on the Truth Word Vomit. "Usually people recognize me as the guy who went to prison for killing someone. Your look was different. It scared me, and I couldn't stay there and wait for you to be disgusted or disappointed, or whatever. I needed to get out."

"Angel, I was surprised." Ethaniel shook his head as he lifted it. "No, there aren't enough letters in the word surprised. Of all the things I thought you'd say, that wasn't it. I didn't know how to react, and I understand you needing space. But cutting me off for three, almost four days? I was ready to talk to you the next day."

"I'm sorry."

"Don't be sorry. Can you please sit, though? This is straining my neck, and I don't want to get dizzy before I get this out."

Yeah, it would suck to get dizzy before he could call it off for good. Angel perched on the edge of the old pine rocking chair, alarmed when the runners squealed. He clasped his hands in his lap, waiting for the killing blow.

"Look, Angel, I'd be lying if I said that you being positive doesn't change things," Ethaniel said, his tone both kind and neutral, and it made Angel want to cry.

It changed everything. "I know."

"I've been doing a lot of thinking, trying to look at this from all angles. I like having all information present, and I like knowing all of my options before I make a decision. Army training kicking in, I guess."

"Okay." A weight settled over his heart, smashing it down. He nearly told Ethaniel that it was okay, he didn't have to say it— only he did. Angel had to hear it.

"So I have two questions for you."

Angel blinked hard. "Um, okay." *How'd you get it?* People always wanted to know how. Ruth hadn't asked, but William had, and he'd been truthful. He'd tell Ethaniel, too, if that was his question. All of it.

"First question. When we were making out in my bed, you started hesitating as things got more intense."

"I would have s-s-stopped." Ethaniel didn't need to ask the question. Angel anticipated that one, because it was something that Angel would have wondered, too, even if he trusted the guy. "I would have s-s-stopped before anything got too messy or d-d-dangerous, I s-s-swear. I've got no cuts on my mouth, and my gums hardly ever bleed unless I brush them too hard. We were okay, and I would have s-s-stopped."

He kind of had, ending the long make out session before he gave into his body's need to be skin on skin with Ethaniel. He would never put Ethaniel in danger.

"I believe you," Ethaniel said. Expression still frustratingly neutral. "I expected you to say that, and I hope you don't think I'm some kind of asshole for asking."

"What? Of course n-n-not. I'm s-s-surprised you don't hate me for not s-s-speaking up s-s-s—damn it. Sooner."

Finally some emotion flickered in his eyes. Something like sadness. "I can't hate you for wanting your privacy, especially not with something so personal."

Angel swallowed against a surge of emotion, grateful beyond words that Ethaniel wasn't crucifying him for this whole mess. "What's your other question?"

Ethaniel's mask of control cracked a little more, allowing a flash of grief and fear. "The HIV. Were you born with it?"

His crushed heart broke into even more pieces. His eyes burned. "No." Ethaniel flinched at his answer, and Angel wanted to sob. He might as well have punched Ethaniel in the nuts.

Ethaniel stared down at his clenched hands, not speaking. His profile was pinched, lips pressed tight, while he worked through his thoughts. Did whatever he needed with the new information. Maybe he was cementing his decision to call it off, fitting Angel's answers into his pre-constructed reasons. He might as well give Ethaniel as much ammunition as he needed to shoot him down.

"Aren't you going to ask?"

"Huh?" Ethaniel blinked at him. "Ask what?"

"How I got it?"

Ethaniel's lips parted, and Angel swore his skin got three shades lighter. His green eyes flashed with genuine pain. "No."

Angel's brain screeched to a mental halt. "N-n-no?" People always wanted to know, didn't they? They wanted the gruesome details, because nothing fascinated human beings more than the misery of their neighbor. The titillation.

"No. If you want to tell me, that's one thing, but I'll never ask you to."

Well, I'll be damned. "Thank you." A small part of Angel wanted to tell, but the rest of him was glad not to relive that today.

"Thank you for being honest with me."

"I owe you at least that much, Ethan."

"I'm not keeping score. You don't owe me anything. But I'm still going to ask you for a favor."

Don't get weird around me once I've ended things? Accept that it's better this way and have a fulfilling life? Get the hell out of my parents' garage and off their land?

The latter was unlikely, but at this point, he expected nothing. Not even friendship.

"Be patient with me," Ethaniel said.

Angel frowned, not understanding what he meant. "Be patient with you?"

"Yes."

"Patient while you…think of the favor?"

"What?" Ethaniel made a surprised noise, not quite a laugh. "No, that is my favor. Be patient with me."

"I d-d-don't understand."

Ethaniel studied him for several long moments that only made Angel feel foolish. Like he was missing something very important in their conversation. He wanted to bolt, to get far away from that feeling, but he was too damned confused by what was happening. He needed Ethaniel to explain things in a way that made sense. He scrubbed both hands over his face, through his hair, needing to do something with them before they started shaking with nerves.

"Oh hell." Ethaniel's eyebrows arched up. "Angel, before when I said that you being positive changes things, I didn't mean I was ending this. I don't want this, whatever it is between us, I don't want it to be over."

The weight crushing Angel's heart eased up, which let it gallop all over the place. Hope seeped in, buoying his courage. "You d-d-don't?"

"No. Not at any moment during all the thinking I've done these last few days did I want to go back to the way things were. I meant what I said on Tuesday, that maybe we're both too messed up to be with anyone else, and I still feel that way. You being positive doesn't change how I feel about you, but there are things I had to research a little bit. Things I may still have questions about in the future."

"Oh." The importance of Ethaniel's words sank in, heating him from the inside out. "You aren't dumping me."

"No. Exactly the opposite. I want a chance to figure us out, to see if we can work."

Hope and joy flirted with each other, not quite giving themselves over to Angel. "Are you sure? Ethan, HIV isn't something that goes away. It's always going to be there, a third person in our bed all the time. There are things we'll probably never be able to do."

"Maybe, maybe not." Ethaniel sank into his chair and the wicker gave an ominous creak. "To be frank, I used to entertain a dream of falling in love, maybe marrying the man I adore more than life itself, and having a fulfilling, monogamous relationship. I always looked at ditching condoms and going bare as the greatest display of love and trust possible."

Angel's skin prickled with grief he had yet to truly acknowledge. He'd accepted years ago that if he ever chose to be with someone again, he would need to be forever vigilant. He would never know what it was like to go bare with someone he loved—not unless that person decided to try PrEP and take the risks that went along with the preventative meds. Every aspect of sex had to be reevaluated and protected against infection, and he'd decided it wasn't worth it. Being alone was easier than living with the gnawing fear that something could still go wrong.

He'd shatter completely if he ever infected someone.

He'd curl up and die if he infected Ethaniel. Cold seeped into his bones despite the space heater.

"But we grow up and our dreams change," Ethaniel said, oblivious to Angel's thoughts. "When I was eighteen, I imagined a career in the Army, seeing the world, and here I sit, leg in a cast and my brain scrambled in more ways than one."

"You dream bigger than this farm, and I can't see past the tree lines." Angel couldn't imagine leaving the safety of these lovely acres, and Ethaniel had thought of nothing else since he was a boy. He wanted Ethaniel, but he was terrified of being left behind one day when he was no longer enough.

"Right now I can't seem to dream bigger than being able to eat a cheeseburger and fries again without throwing up. I've stopped taking things for granted, Angel, because none of us are guaranteed to have tomorrow. I should have learned that in Afghanistan, but it took falling through a roof to really understand. I don't want to keep wishing for things I might never have when something potentially really good is right in front of me."

Angel's heart kicked. He wanted so badly to believe Ethaniel, to jump on the chance for happiness and ride it into the sunset. But this wasn't a movie with a promised happily ever after. He wasn't asking for a commitment from Ethaniel, not really, but he was getting one anyway. Navigating ultra-safe sex wasn't for everyone, but Ethaniel was saying that he was all in for trying.

"Even though we'll never be able to ditch condoms?" Angel asked.

"We could one day, if all the studies about PrEP are true."

Angel had done his own research and spoken with doctors. He knew which behaviors were riskiest and which carried almost no risk. But Ethaniel wasn't on anything right now, he'd admitted to not doing well with medications, condoms weren't foolproof, and the idea of an accident horrified him—not only during sex but also down at the stables, if he wasn't vigilant at all times. Maybe he would never deliberately infect someone, but he would still feel responsible.

"I take multiple pills a day," Angel said. "And they have side effects. If I'm not careful I could get really sick, really fast. One of my meds could turn against me and stick me in the hospital."

"I understand all that. I live in my own medical reality too, you know."

"Well, this is my reality, Ethan. I don't ever want to risk you. I would die if I infected anyone else, especially you." He was babbling now, caught in some odd place between anger and fear.

"Angel, come here," Ethaniel said. He beckoned with one hand, his smile warm and engaging. So Angel went, sliding gently onto Ethaniel's lap. He flinched when the chair squealed again. Ethaniel's hands rested on his lower back. "I'm not asking to jump into the sack right this second, but I'm glad we're being honest with each other."

"I think that was me trying to scare you off."

"Why do you want to scare me off?"

Angel released a long, deep breath, then leaned into Ethaniel, settling comfortably with his head on Ethaniel's shoulder. He liked being held this way, feeling protected and wanted. "Habit, I guess. I keep people at arm's length, and I don't get hurt. Some of the stable hands think I'm retarded because I stutter and don't talk to them, and I'm fine with it because then they won't ask about my past, or pity me if they find things out. Being alone is easier."

"The problem with being alone is that you get so damned lonely."

"I know." He tilted his head so his nose brushed the skin of Ethaniel's neck, and he inhaled the soap-clean scent of him. Absorbed the heat of him. "Can I ask you something?"

Ethaniel chuckled, the sound rumbling through his chest and into Angel's. "That's only fair, I think. In fact, you get two questions, since I got two earlier."

"Have you ever been in love?"

"No." He answered quickly, no hesitation. "I've been in lust a few times, but I've never let myself get close enough to someone to fall in love. I didn't want to saddle them with my baggage."

The answer surprised Angel more than it should have. Ethaniel was almost thirty years old, and he'd never been in love? Lord. "Me either." He pressed his nose harder into Ethaniel's neck, and Ethaniel fidgeted beneath him.

Angel tried to shift his weight a bit, thinking Ethaniel was uncomfortable, but strong hands gripped his waist and held him still. And Angel figured out the reason Ethaniel was adjusting himself. He was hard.

CHAPTER TEN

The very simple fact that he was getting hard from something as average as holding Angel in his lap cemented Ethan's decision to try. His body responded to Angel's proximity in a way that surprised and delighted him, and his brain responded to Angel with amusement and joy. He might have a heavenly host of good reasons to step back and not get involved, but he'd be damned if he could think of a single one while Angel was nuzzling his neck like that.

"So, um, what's your second question?" Ethan asked.

Angel was quiet for a few beats. "You said you researched a little bit. What did you research?"

The answer seemed pretty obvious to Ethan, and maybe it was also obvious to Angel. Maybe he simply needed to hear it. "Other than the basics of the virus and safe sex, I was curious about negative men living with positive partners. I even found a chat room that I liked the idea of, but I can't spend that much time online."

"What about your family?"

"Well, my mother is obviously on our side."

Angel made a snuffling sound that was suspiciously close to a chuckle. "Yeah, that's pretty obvious. But your father and brothers?"

The idea of coming out to his father made his insides twist into a painful little ball. William Shockley went to church twice a year, on Christmas Eve and Easter morning, and he voted his conscience in every election. He tended to avoid political debates in the house. His only hot button topic was animal cruelty, and he donated to various rescue organizations every month. He also loved his children unconditionally, even when he was being hard on them.

None of that gave Ethan a single clue as to how he'd take finding out Ethan was gay. Oh yeah, and that he was interested in their HIV-positive stable hand.

"I have to come out to him," Ethan said. "I don't know how I'm going to do it, but I have to. It has to come from me."

"There's no rush." Angel raised his head, those big brown eyes shiny and hopeful. "I want you, more than I've wanted someone my whole life, and the other night? It was so intense. But your leg and the concussion. I'm scared I'll do something wrong and hurt you."

Ethan brushed the pad of his thumb across Angel's cheek. Angel leaned into the touch, his eyelids drooping. God, that was sexy, and Ethan's dick pulsed. "I won't lie to you. I'm a little worried about how the PCS will affect sex. I haven't, um"—*okay, yes, embarrassing, but get over it if you ever want to get naked with this man*—"I've only had one orgasm since the accident. I jerked off in the shower the other day, but it was really fast and I'm worried that I might pass out during real sex, or something idiotic like that."

A wicked gleam appeared in Angel's eyes, and Ethan's heart trilled. Was this the spirited, pre-prison Angel peeking through?

"What if we conducted an experiment in a controlled environment?" Angel asked.

"I'm intrigued."

"Do you always go to bed at eight-thirty?"

"Eight-thirty or nine, usually."

"What about your parents?"

"On Saturdays? About ten, I guess."

"Think you can stay up later than them?"

Ethan grinned. "Depends on the reason."

Angel sucked his lower lip into his mouth, and the adorableness of it socked Ethan in the gut. "What do you say I sneak in your window about ten-thirty, and we conduct our experiment?"

"I'd say it's a date."

Angel laughed out loud, musical and delightful. "You know, a week ago I was terrified to even speak to you, and now I'm sneaking in your bedroom window with the express purpose of making you come."

The somewhat dirty words sent another pulse of want into Ethan's cock. "Amazing what changes in a week." He tried to shift his weight a little, to make sure Angel knew how hard he was making him, but all he did was pay attention to the new throbbing in his leg. He'd been sitting for too long without it propped up. The damned thing should be out of a cast in another few weeks.

His discomfort must have shown on his face, because Angel scrambled off his lap, leaving Ethan chilly from lack of body heat. "Was I hurting you?"

"No, it wasn't you. My damned leg. I need to move around a bit, then get it up on something."

"Of course."

"Will you be at the dinner table?"

"No." Angel shoved his hands into his jeans pockets. "I don't want to intrude for a while."

"No one thinks of it as an intrusion."

"Sure they do. Especially Daniel." Angel's whole body seemed to flinch at that name, and Ethan didn't like it. Especially after Ethan had practically dared Daniel to mess with Angel.

"Has he bothered you?"

"No, I haven't seen him since the other night in the kitchen."

"If he gives you a hard time, I want you to tell me."

Indignation flared in Angel's eyes. "I can handle myself, Ethan."

"I'm not implying you can't." Angel had the work-muscled arms and shoulders of a seasoned stable hand, but Ethan had no idea if he'd ever actually been taught self-defense. And he was nowhere near as capable as Ethan in a fight. "Daniel doesn't get to be an asshole to you because he hates me, okay?"

"Fair enough." He handed Ethan his crutches, then hovered while Ethan levered to a somewhat upright position. "See you tonight then."

"Definitely."

Angel hesitated before leaning in and brushing lips over Ethan's. He pulled away before Ethan could grab him and deepen the kiss. Probably for the best, because Ethan needed his damned hard-on to go away before he could go back to the house. He watched Angel leave, practically giddy from the positive direction their conversation had taken. Walking into the garage, he hadn't known what to expect from Angel.

And now ten-thirty couldn't come soon enough.

* * *

Angel had never been a bigger nervous wreck in his life.

Forget losing his virginity. Forget facing his first night in a new group home. Hell, forget his first night in fucking prison. He had actually found his balls, looked Ethaniel in the eye, and said—in so many words—that he was sneaking in his bedroom window tonight to blow him.

He paced the length of his apartment, alternately glaring at the slow-moving clock and wishing time would stop for a little while. But the minutes were inching closer to ten-thirty, and he couldn't calm down.

Angel didn't discount his skills at giving head. Lord knew he'd had the practice. No, he was terrified because this was Ethaniel, and he'd crushed on him from afar for so long because he'd never imagined he'd actually have him. He was terrified because this was real. This was happening. And while he'd read dozens of articles on safe sex practices, it was his first time since being infected that he was having any kind of sexual contact with another man.

He'd half-expected their talk about condoms and medical science to have scared Ethaniel out of the idea of sex, but it hadn't. He'd almost seemed…determined.

Not that they had a single condom between them, ensuring things wouldn't go too far too fast.

Fear warred with hope, stirring up doubt. Maybe Ethaniel was playing along for a little while to spare Angel's feelings. Maybe he wanted a little physical release while he healed, and once he was able to move back to Pennsylvania, he'd dump Angel's ass and go. He didn't seem keen on staying in Delaware.

Or maybe Ethaniel truly was the miracle that Angel had prayed for every week at church. Maybe the tertiary character who only appeared in a few chapters was truly getting his chance at meeting his hero and finding a happy ending. Or at least a happily for now.

He could live with happily for now.

The lights inside of the Shockley home went off one by one, until every window was dark. The pole lamp thirty feet from the house cast a yellow glow on the front yard, and a few barn lights twinkled in the distance, keeping the property from being completely black beneath the ocean of stars overhead. Ethaniel's bedroom window was on the opposite side of the house, but Angel knew he was awake. Waiting. Anticipating. Probably as anxious as Angel for a lot of the same reasons.

Angel had spent the first year of his prison time in gen pop, doing anything he could to survive, and the last two years in an isolated cell block coping with being positive. For five years now he'd lived with it, and for five years he'd looked in the mirror and seen someone dirty. Someone with poisoned blood who'd never find a man who could look past all of his filth and find Matthew Garrett deep down, waiting to be loved.

Ethaniel had done just that, and Angel still didn't believe it was real.

At 10:25 he put on his boots.

At 10:27 he began a silent, stealthy trek downstairs and across the side yard to the main house. The yard was eerily silent, except for the occasional creak of a distant cricket. Even they would go silent soon as the weather slipped deeper into the chill of autumn, and the eventual freeze of winter. The first snow would make clandestine meetings like this difficult to hide.

Lord, he hoped they were still stealing time together once it snowed. He had no illusions of them being open about their relationship. They hadn't even defined it to each other, much less the rest of Ethaniel's family.

At least they had Ruth on their side.

He stuck to the shadows as often as they presented themselves, hiding his advancement across the yard to the far side of the house. Faint, golden light slitted through a break in the curtains covering Ethaniel's window. A window left cracked open at the bottom, giving Angel's fingers easier access. The old wood creaked softly, and he lifted it only enough for him to slither inside.

Ethaniel watched him from the bed, propped against several pillows, his cast set up on another. He'd covered the lamp with a swath of fabric of some sort, dimming the light enough so they could see each other, but not alert the entire house. Angel shut the window, then took a moment to study Ethaniel. Bare chest pale and lean, with a smattering of scars from his fall. He wore flannel pants and socks but nothing else, and his lazy smile did funny things to Angel's belly.

"Hey," Angel said. Very smooth.

"You're too far away." Ethaniel patted the coverlet beneath him. "Come here."

As he toed off his boots and shucked his winter coat, it occurred to Angel that he'd never done this before. All of the sex of his wild childhood had been hard and fast, usually in the backseat of a car, bent over a couch, or sure, a few times in a bed. But it had never been about seduction. It had never been about pleasing his partner and going slow, making sure they both really felt something.

It had never been *special*.

Ethaniel looked at him with a strength of desire so powerful that it made Angel's knees weak and his heart pound. It pounded so loudly he was afraid they'd hear him upstairs, despite the layers of wood, plaster and carpeting between them.

And then Ethaniel's desire fractured a tiny bit. "Are you changing your mind?"

Angel blinked hard. "What? No. I'm s-s-sorry."

"If it helps, I'm a little nervous, too."

He bit back a sharp peel of laughter. "It does, actually." Fully dressed, Angel climbed onto the bed. It creaked lightly under his added weight, but nothing that couldn't be Ethaniel himself moving around. He scooted forward until he was kneeling next to Ethaniel's good leg. The frayed hem of the left side of the pants stopped just above the cast. "Are all of your clothes like this?"

"A lot of them. Sweats and elastic waistbands are the easiest things to deal with right now. I hate this fucking cast."

Angel traced light fingertips over the yellowing plaster. "I love it. Do you know why?"

"Tell me." True curiosity coated those two words.

He looked Ethaniel in his lovely green eyes and said, "Because it means you lived. You're alive now, here with your family. With me."

Ethaniel's gaze shuttered, and he looked at his lap. "Sometimes I wish I hadn't lived. Sometimes it's too damned hard."

"Look who you're telling. I don't have PCS or a fractured leg, but my life up until the last three years has been one nightmare after another. I wake up every day grateful to be alive, even though my loneliness eats me up inside. I wake up every day knowing that this could be the day one of my meds reacts badly, or I get horse kicked and it's lights out. I know it's hard to get up every day and fight your own body, Ethan, but think of all the people here who'd miss you if you were gone."

When Ethaniel looked up, his eyes were bright and kind of wet. "I lived while my buddies died overseas. I lived while my two closest friends died in that collapse." He raised a hand and brushed gentle knuckles across Angel's cheekbone, a treasured touch that Angel felt in his bones. "I don't know what I'd do if I lost you too, just when I've found you."

Angel cupped Ethaniel's hand and turned it, pressing that rough palm against his cheek. The heat of his skin seeped into Angel's heart and soul, warming him inside and out. "We can't predict the future, Ethan. No sense in trying. All we really have is this moment. Right now. Past is gone. The future isn't here."

Finally Ethaniel smiled. An honest to goodness smile that drove away the fear and the guilt. "You're right." He worried his lower lip with his teeth. "I really want to kiss you."

"Yeah?" Angel swung one leg over Ethaniel's hips and lowered himself to sit on his upper belly. Ethaniel grasped his waist. Angel tensed for a fraction of a moment at the unexpected touch, then relaxed as the familiar scents of Ethaniel drifted over him—sweat and soap and an earthier fragrance of the man himself. "This okay?"

"This is perfect."

In this position there was no hiding the fact that Angel's dick was getting into things, and if he reached behind, he was sure he'd find Ethaniel's flannel pants starting to tent. That's what he was there for, anyhow. A controlled experiment.

Angel threaded his fingers through Ethaniel's hair, delighting in the thick softness. He loved the streaks of lighter brown mixed in with the darker locks—evidence of a man who spent a lot of time in the sun. He scraped light fingertips over the stubble on Ethaniel's cheeks, enjoying the rasp of it against his skin. Ethaniel watched him silently as he played and explored Ethaniel's face and neck. Discovering small scars and imperfections and even a mole behind his right ear. Tiny little pieces of the man he'd admired and wanted from a distance for so long, and now they were together. In bed.

He brushed his lips across Ethaniel's forehead. The rough exhale against his throat made Angel grin. He rubbed his thickening cock on Ethaniel's belly. The strong hands on his hips pushed him back a bit, until his ass bumped Ethaniel's erection. Angel swallowed a groan. He wanted to play, to tease, to get Ethaniel so worked up he begged to come.

Not this time.

Angel wanted so many things, but the very last thing he wanted to do was to hurt Ethaniel by pushing too far and engaging his PCS.

"Kiss me," Ethaniel whispered. "Please, Angel."

The first press of lips burned hot and hard through Angel's belly, lighting him up inside in a way that both scared and enthralled him. Gentle went out the window, and then he knew only the rough slide of their mouths, the hard thrust of tongues. Ethaniel's hands were everywhere at once—kneading his hips, rubbing his back, cupping his ass, raking through his hair.

Angel never stopped touching him. Hair, face, shoulders, bare chest, arms. He wanted to taste every inch of the man beneath him, but he couldn't stop kissing him. He didn't want to. Their kisses were something to exist inside of forever, a safe place unlike anything Angel had ever known.

Ethaniel squeezed his ass. Angel pushed into his touch, loving the brazenness of it, and knowing in his heart that nothing they did tonight was going to hurt. Nothing was going to make Angel feel ashamed or dirty. Everything about being with Ethaniel was beautiful and right, and it was only the two of them in bed in that moment.

Angel trailed hungry kisses down Ethaniel's throat, laving the skin with his tongue, loving the sharper taste behind Ethaniel's ear. Down over his collarbones to a nipple that begged for attention. Ethaniel pressed a hand over his own mouth to stifle the wonderful sounds Angel's nips and licks were dragging out of him. He paid equal attention to the other nipple before investigating the coarse hair surrounding Ethaniel's navel.

Ethaniel's hip bones were sharp, his stomach a bit concave, testament to the weight he'd lost since food became his enemy.

He was kneeling over Ethaniel's legs, bodily contact gone now that he'd risen up to keep pressure off the cast. His dick pressed hard and painful against his jeans, and Ethaniel's flannel pants were impressively tented. He glanced up the long, lean length of Ethaniel's body and met his simmering gaze.

Ethaniel licked his kiss-swollen lips, leaving them shiny and oh so inviting. He was watching him so nakedly, his soul flayed open for Angel. Angel wasn't sure what to do with that kind of trust, except hold it close and do his best to be worthy of it.

Anxiety wormed into Angel's belly, unexpected and unwanted. He'd lost count of the number of blow jobs he'd given in his lifetime, and even without a condom the chance of infecting Ethaniel was pretty much zero. But pretty much zero wasn't absolutely zero, and probably a hand job was a better idea.

"Angel?"

He blinked hard. "Ethan?"

"Don't overthink it," Ethaniel said. "I've got nothing to give you, and unless there's something else you haven't mentioned, you going down on me is an acceptable risk."

Angel traced the shape of Ethaniel's abs, unable to maintain eye contact while his insides were wobbling all over the place. "It's a silly fear, isn't it? I mean, I've kissed you all over, and I know it's not in my saliva, but I'd die if I did something to hurt you."

"Hey." Ethaniel cupped his cheek and tilted his head up. Angel couldn't raise his gaze past Ethaniel's chin. "You won't."

"How do you know that?"

"Faith."

"In God?"

"In you, Angel. My precious Angel, fallen from heaven."

Angel's heart tripped. The heat and genuine emotion in Ethaniel's eyes burned into his core, and Angel fell. He fell hard and fast, and he wasn't entirely sure it was rational, but yes. He was falling in love with Ethaniel Shockley.

He couldn't say it, so he kissed Ethaniel instead, putting all of his tangled emotions into the steady press of lips and gentle glide of his tongue. He kissed Ethaniel until he couldn't breathe and he was one more lick from coming in his jeans. He pulled away, grabbed the waistband of Ethaniel's pants, and said, "Lift up."

* * *

Ethan raised his hips as ordered, stunned silent by the ferocity of Angel's last kiss. Somehow both gentle and rough, sweet and claiming, and dear God, but it had turned Ethan's crank hard. Cloth whispered down, brushing sensitive skin, until the elastic waistband was below his ass, freeing his cock and balls to the cool air.

Angel loomed above him on all fours, fully clothed and yet somehow the embodiment of sex. His curly hair hung over his forehead, partially hiding his eyes as he studied Ethan's erection. His pubes were a little wild, because who the hell had he had to trim them for? Angel hesitated for so long that Ethan's nerves got the better of him.

"What's wrong?" Ethan asked.

"Nothing." Angel looked up, his brown eyes impish. "Planning my attack."

Ethan snorted back surprised laughter. "You make sucking cock sound like a tactical mission."

"It's been a long time since I've done this for a guy I genuinely wanted to please. I want to do it right."

His heart ached with the meaning behind Angel's words, and for the things he'd left unsaid. He wanted to find and hurt every person who'd ever tormented Angel, ever left him feeling vulnerable and ashamed. He wanted to battle Angel's demons and make the world safe for them both to live in peace. Together.

"It's you, Angel," he said. "If we're together, it won't be wrong."

Those must have been the right words, because Angel smiled. A blinding smile that lit up his entire face and chased away his hesitation. His warm palm caressed the length of Ethan's cock, from root to tip, and Ethan hissed out a breath. Someone else— and not a medical professional—was touching his dick for the first time in too damned long.

And then Angel leaned over and sucked him into wet heat so tight and amazing that Ethan almost screamed. He stifled the sound, barely kept a lid on it, because Angel's mouth was on his cock and nothing had ever felt better. He pulled off, though, and Ethan kind of wanted to cry for the loss.

Angel winked, then tugged his sweatshirt off. He tossed it at Ethan's chest. "Here, cover your mouth with that."

Ethan did, bunching the fabric over his mouth. Fabric that smelled like Angel, and that sent happy signals to his dick and balls. Angel took him in again, his hands rolling Ethan's nuts while his mouth worked his cock. Ethan tried to watch, but holy fuck, it felt so good. He closed his eyes and relaxed into the pillows, trusting Angel to get him there. He fell into the steady strokes and licks, and the gentle press against his taint. His balls drew up tight, warning him of his release, and it was going to be over too soon.

Tingles of not-quite-pain raced behind his eyes. He ignored them and focused on Angel. On the pleasure Angel was giving his broken body. On the absolute care Angel was taking with him. On the soft, joyful sounds Angel himself was making.

He moved the sweatshirt long enough to gasp, "Getting close."

Angel groaned, the sound echoing in Ethan's cock and balls. Long, hard pulls back and a slow glide forward mimicked fucking so perfectly that Ethan's hips twitched with the urge to thrust. God, what would it feel like to fuck Angel for real? To bury to the hilt in his body and urge them both to climax?

The mental image of Angel naked and kneeling on his bed, while Ethan fucked him from behind tipped him into orgasm. Words fled, so he pushed at Angel's head. Angel pulled back, a hand replacing his mouth. Ethan jerked his hips and came, hot come streaking across Angel's hand and wrist. Angel worked him until it all became too much and Ethan told him so.

"Holy shit." Ethan dropped the sweatshirt and tugged Angel up until their foreheads pressed together. Angel's hot breath puffed over his nose and mouth. "Fuck, Angel."

"Yeah?"

"That was so good."

Angel pulled back, dark eyes studying him. "How's your head?"

"Good." Except for those few moments of pain, he was fine. No dizziness, so nausea. "Really good."

"I'm glad." Angel grabbed some tissues off the bedside table and cleaned them both up. He dabbed at a spot on Ethan's pants, then tucked his softening dick back in. Once Ethan was taken care of, he stretched out on the bed next to him, his head pillowed on Ethan's shoulder.

Ethan curled an arm around Angel's back, fingers resting on his hip. "What about you?"

"I'm good."

He chuckled. "Yes, you are. You are very good. You've also got to be hard as a rock. Want some help with it?"

Angel shivered, then pulled the hand on his hip around to press against his crotch. The lack of an erection surprised Ethan until he felt the damp fabric. "I came while I was sucking you," Angel said. "Couldn't help it."

"I'll take that as a huge-ass compliment."

"I loved doing that for you, Ethan. So much."

"One of these days I'd like to return the favor."

Angel raised his head, eyes wide. "Are you sure?"

"Of course I'm sure." He cupped Angel's cheek in his palm. "Once I can get my hands on some supplies, I'd like us to do more. If you want that."

"You want to fuck me?"

"Honestly? No." Before Angel could flinch or run, Ethan smiled and said, "I'd much rather make love to you."

Angel melted against him, turning his head to press a kiss to Ethan's chest. "I like that answer. I want to make love to you, too."

"Good." He sifted his fingers through Angel's hair. "Stay with me?"

"I shouldn't. What if someone sees me leave in the morning?"

"I'll set an early alarm. You'll be able to sneak back and shower before work."

Angel hesitated, then sighed softly. "Okay."

"Excellent." He dragged Angel up for a gentle kiss. "Thank you."

"You're welcome."

Ethan set the alarm clock, then tucked Angel against him. He fell asleep as content as he'd been in his life, and for the first time in months, didn't dream at all.

CHAPTER ELEVEN

Thank God for discreet packaging.

Ordering condoms and lube online had been the easy part for Ethan. Trusting that the box the materials arrived in truly was discreet was what had given him fits for the four days it took to arrive. The return address said Fulfillment Center, and the box was plain brown. Mom handed it over without a word or strange look.

Ethan hid it under his bed.

Daniel's first week home came and went without fanfare. He was still openly hostile to Ethan, so Ethan continued his tactic of careful avoidance as much as possible. Sarah still stuck close to him, and Jillian seemed to dim a bit more each day. She was clearly unhappy with Daniel being back in her life, but she refused to talk about it when Ethan asked.

The best part of Ethan's days were the afternoons he spent with Angel in the garage, going over stuttering exercises and making out in between. Angel hadn't climbed in his bedroom window again since that first time, and that was okay. It had been left unsaid, but they were both waiting for the special delivery.

Ethan crutched his way to the garage on Thursday afternoon, almost giddy with the news that the supplies had finally arrived. Bum leg or not, he wanted to make love to Angel so badly he could think of little else. He constantly lost track of his audiobooks, and he'd woken up almost every morning with wood.

Angel was already in the garage, the space heater cranked up. Mom had helped them procure two sturdier, more comfortable chairs for their lessons. Ethan closed the door, then stopped short at an unexpected addition to the patchwork classroom. His guitar case was leaning against the chair he usually sat in.

"What's that doing here?" Ethan asked.

Angel's cheeks pinked. "Um, I asked Ruth for it."

Curiosity kept his irritation firmly at bay. "Why?"

"I was hoping you would play for me."

"I haven't played in over a decade."

Angel ducked his head but maintained eye contact. "Please?"

He stared at the case with his beloved instrument tucked inside. Music had been his escape during high school. Something he'd turned to out of loneliness and the need for a creative outlet on the farm. He sank into his chair, and Angel took his crutches. He even propped Ethan's leg up on another chair.

Ethan lifted the case and balanced it on his lap. Unlatched the locks and raised the lid. Shiny cedar and mahogany gleamed at him in the dim light. He lifted the Washburn acoustic guitar from its velvet bed, admiring the simple beauty of the instrument. It was perfect for finger picking, which was his favorite way to play, but he had a few plastic picks tucked away for certain songs.

Angel took the case away for him. Ethan balanced the guitar on his thigh and strummed the strings. Used the tuners to fix the sound on several of them.

"I taught myself to play using Mom's hymnals," Ethan said. "Sometimes I would play for her, and she'd sing along." He'd played those hymns on the radio over and over while she was sick, because they seemed to bring her peace.

He wanted to play for her again.

But more than that, he wanted to play for Angel.

"What's your favorite hymn?" Ethan asked.

Angel smiled, no hesitation in his answer. "'Cleanse Me'."

Ethan closed his eyes and thought back. He knew it, but he was having trouble getting all of the pieces. The soft sound of humming startled him into opening his eyes again. Still smiling, Angel hummed the opening verse and the chorus, enough to refresh Ethan on the song. He picked it out on the strings, testing it, and then settled in to play.

The music washed over him, and on the second verse, the prettiest voice Ethan had ever heard began to sing.

"*I praise thee, Lord, for cleansing me from sin.*" Angel's voice was clear and strong as he drew out the lyrics.

"*Fill me with fire where once I burned with shame.*"

So perfect. So Angel.

He played it twice so Angel could sing the entire song to him, and the beauty of the moment filled Ethan's eyes with grateful tears. Now he understood how the sound of a boy singing in the next church pew had so captured his mother's attention. She'd heard an angel singing and she'd brought him home.

She'd brought him to Ethan.

"Do you know 'How Great Thou Art'?" Angel asked.

"Of course."

His Angel sang that song, as well as "Nearer My God, To Thee," "Just As I Am," and "The Old Rugged Cross." Each sound that broke from Angel's throat lifted Ethan up and carried him away. Up to the heavens where he could fly. No broken leg, no smashed brain, not a problem between them. Only beauty and joy and peace.

Angel's hand came to rest over his thigh and squeezed. Ethan blinked at him, the spell of the music fading away. A tear spilled down his cheek, and Angel wiped it away with his thumb.

"You okay?" Angel asked.

"Yeah." He swiped at his damp cheeks. "Feeling emotional, I guess. Your voice is amazing. I mean it. You were born to sing songs like this."

"I love to sing. It gives me hope, you know? That there really is love and happiness to be found in the world."

"I hear that in your voice. It gives me hope, too."

"I'm glad." Angel pressed a kiss to his temple. "You play beautifully, Ethan. Thank you for playing for me."

"Thank you for singing for me."

A swirl of cold air wrapped around Ethan's ankles in time with the swing of the garage door. Angel jumped back, his hand falling away. Daniel filled the doorway, a nasty expression on his face.

"If you two pussies are done praisin' the Lord," he snarled, "Mom says dinner's almost ready."

Ethan's chest tightened. Hitting Daniel with the guitar might feel good for a minute, but then he'd have to buy a new one, and that would suck. He talked himself out of violence and flipped Daniel off. "Thanks for the message. Go away."

Daniel muttered something as he pulled the door shut on his way out.

"Prick." Ethan focused in on Angel, whose entire body was strung up tight. He hadn't spoken or looked at Daniel, but damn it if he wasn't still afraid. "Hey, you with me?"

Angel nodded.

"Angel." He cupped the smaller man's chin and tilted his face up. "Don't let Daniel ruin our afternoon. Our music was beautiful, and not even his perpetual bad mood can shit on that, okay?"

Slowly Angel relaxed, until the tension in his shoulders and face softened into weariness. "I hate how he makes me feel."

"How does he make you feel?"

"Vulnerable." Angel swallowed hard, gaze darting around the room. "Like I'm back in prison and he's sizing me up. He's not like your family, Ethan, he's dangerous. He's a predator."

Nothing new to Ethan's ears, but hearing them from Angel somehow amplified the awfulness of the words. Yes, Daniel was dangerous. He always had been, even as a teenager. Prison had only made him harder, angrier.

Ethan leaned his guitar against his chair, then gathered Angel's hands in his. "If Daniel hurts you in any way, he'll end up pissing blood for a week. That's a promise, cast or no cast on my damned leg."

Angel's eyes went wide. "Don't say that."

"It's how I feel. I care about you a hell of a lot, and I protect what—" The words caught in his throat. *I protect what I love.* "I protect the people I care about. Right now? That's you and not Daniel."

"He's your brother."

"Blood doesn't make someone family. He's hated me for the last eight years, and there's nothing I can do about that. Wanting to be brothers again? That's on him. I'm not waiting around for his approval, and I sure as hell won't get it when I come out."

Angel's eyes got so wide Ethan was positive his eyeballs would fall out. "You're going to come out?"

"I have to eventually. I mean, I haven't figured out how or when, but soon. And I think I need to tell my Dad first. Then my siblings."

"Promise you won't rush this for me, though, okay? Do it when it's right for you."

Ethan loved that Angel said that to him. "Thank you. We should get to the house."

"I'll help you up."

"Uh uh. Dinner. At the house. You with me. No more hiding from Daniel."

For a moment, Angel seemed poised to argue. Then he rolled his shoulders and straightened his spine. "You're right. Let's go."

* * *

All of the peace that Angel had collected during their music session fled completely by the time he and Ethaniel made it to the main house for supper. A smaller crowd than usual at the table helped a little bit. Ruth and William, Daniel and Sarah, and Caleb.

Ruth's beaming smile when she saw them together cemented his decision to eat with the family. To stay close to Ethaniel. She settled them at her end of the table. Sarah looked longingly at the empty chair on Ethaniel's other side from across the table, but stayed put next to her surly father.

Pork chops again. Angel liked them but Ethaniel couldn't eat them. Too greasy.

"Jillian won't be joining us," Ruth said after William said the blessing. "She's got a fierce migraine."

"It's been a long time since she's had one, hasn't it?" Ethaniel asked.

"A few years, I expect."

Angel wasn't sure if that meant something, so he kept quiet and accepted small servings of everything. Ruth disappeared and returned with a simple plate for Ethaniel. Steamed chicken and veggies and some apple slices.

"Where's Polly?" Ethaniel asked after a few minutes of everyone eating and no one talking.

Caleb grunted. "She's up north visiting her folks for a few days."

"Everything all right with them?"

"Yeah, she was feeling homesick, is all."

Angel wasn't entirely convinced of that. Being a stable hand, he excelled at getting around unnoticed, and more than once he'd overheard Caleb on hushed phone calls. Strange, hushed phone calls. But he and Caleb weren't friends, and Angel didn't like to gossip, so he hadn't said anything to Ethaniel.

Maybe he should.

"Ruth says you asked for your guitar," William said to Ethaniel.

Ethaniel glanced briefly at Angel, then nodded. "Yes, sir. I played for a while in the garage this afternoon."

"Good. It's good to see you doing more than listening to that little contraption all the time. Music is good for the soul."

"That it is."

Angel grinned.

"Guess all his talent didn't get blown away in Afghanistan," Daniel said.

Ethaniel's fork scraped across his plate, and he went visibly stiff all over.

Daniel's smile was cruel and he knew it. "The little fairy has a decent voice, too."

"Daniel Jacob Shockley," Ruth said. "I have told you repeatedly to be respectful at this table, not only to your brother but also to Angel. They're family."

"Angel's not my family."

"Well, he's *my* family. If you can't be respectful, you can eat in the kitchen."

Daniel stared at his mom for a few seconds, then picked up his plate and left. Some of the chill in the air left the room with him, and little Sarah visibly relaxed. Angel bumped Ethaniel's knee with his own and got a soft bump back.

Ruth huffed.

Angel didn't like seeing Ruth upset. He wanted to fix it. "Please don't put yourself out over me. I can eat in the kitchen."

Ruth reached out and took his hand. "It isn't only about you, sweetheart. I know Daniel had a hard time, and I know prison is a terrible place, but we raised him better than this. He needs to learn to keep his temper and watch his tongue."

The rest of the meal was pretty quiet, and before long Caleb and William retired to the living room to watch television. Daniel was gone by the time Angel and Ruth started cleaning up, and they had the dishes stowed away in no time. Ethaniel and Sarah settled together at the kitchen table so she could do homework and he could watch.

Ruth broke out a deck of cards and Angel stayed for a few hands of Gin Rummy with her and Ethaniel. She made all four of them hot chocolate, and for a little while, it was like Angel really was part of the family.

He held on to that lovely feeling for the rest of the night, long after he'd gone back to his apartment, gotten undressed, and said goodnight to Ethaniel over the walkie-talkie.

* * *

The last week of October melted quickly into November. Ethan's days had gathered a much needed routine that started with a light breakfast, followed by a walk around the perimeter of the house. Sometimes, if the ground wasn't moist, he'd hobble down to the barns to visit Angel. Then he'd listen to an audiobook before and after lunch.

Every day at three-thirty he met Angel in the garage to make music. He loved listening to Angel sing, and Ethan's fingers were rediscovering their lost callouses. They played until dinner. Once in a while, if they both got worked up, Angel would lock the door and give him a blow job. He still wouldn't let Ethan reciprocate, and that hesitation, more than anything else, kept him from telling Angel about the supplies he'd purchased.

Every night ended with them on the walkie-talkies. Sometimes they'd jerk off together. Most of the time they simply talked.

The second week in November, almost exactly a month after Daniel's release, Caleb drove Ethan to see his orthopedic surgeon about his leg. He had a good chance of getting the cast removed and replaced by a walking boot. Those things looked evil on the best of days, but he'd do almost anything to finally ditch the crutches.

He would never forget the look of utter joy on Angel's face when he walked into the garage that afternoon and saw the boot on his leg. Or the giant "Whoop!" Angel released. Or the toe-curling blow job he got afterward.

As Angel stood and dusted off his knees, Ethan snagged his hand. Angel was visibly hard in his jeans, and damn it, Ethan wanted to finally see Angel's dick. "Why don't you ever want me to return the favor?" he asked.

Angel frowned. "It isn't a favor that needs to be paid back. I suck you off because I love doing it."

"Well, equally gay guy right here, babe. I kind of love sucking dick, too, and while I appreciate all of the attention mine has gotten this past month, it's beyond time I get at yours." He cupped Angel's erection, pleased when Angel pressed into his hand. "I haven't even seen you yet."

Angel glanced at the door, then rested a hand on top of Ethan's head. "Tonight. I'll sneak into your room again if you can stay up."

Ethan's chest heated. "Oh, I'll be up."

Angel laughed, then stepped away from Ethan's touch. "I have no doubt. Now stop thinking about my dick so we can play music."

Ethan kind of floated through the rest of the evening, now that his night promised Angel naked in his bed. He wanted Angel in his arms, in his mouth, skin on skin while they explored each other. If things went further, he had condoms waiting. If not, he would gladly take what Angel wanted to give him.

* * *

Angel ate dinner in the kitchen, because all of the Shockley siblings were there, along with assorted children. The meal was a mini celebration of Ethaniel's cast removal, and Ruth loved any opportunity to cook for her kids. He didn't want to intrude, though, especially with the Look Daniel threw his way at every opportunity.

The Look that said: *I know you took it up the ass in prison to survive.*

It was the Look that made Angel want to curl into a ball and take up as little space as possible.

Abigail and Lesley cleaned up, because Ruth excused herself to bed early, complaining of a headache, so Angel stayed out of the way. Eventually Ethaniel joined him at the kitchen table with a deck of cards. "Sarah's playing with her cousins," he said.

They played cards for a while, with Abigail and Jillian joining them later. The house slowly began to empty of family, and as the clock pushed closer to nine, everyone at the table began to yawn. Angel's stomach wobbled as he left that night, knowing he'd be back in a little over an hour. He wanted to be with Ethaniel so badly he ached with it, but he was also terrified. Terrified of reacting badly, terrified of the condom breaking, terrified of making an absolute fool out of himself.

No matter what happened, though, Ethaniel would make it okay. He always did. He made the world a better place simply by existing in it.

Angel let himself into his apartment and shucked his coat. Hung it on the hook by the door. He turned, aiming for the small fridge and a few sips of orange soda. A shadow in the corner of the living room moved, and Angel shouted. His pulse raced and adrenaline surged, leaving both hands shaking.

Daniel stood near the couch, hands in his jeans pockets, his fierce glare firmly in place.

Angel swallowed hard and contemplated how fast he could get back out the door. "What are you doing in here?" He hated that his voice wobbled without permission.

"Used to be my place."

"It's mine now." Acid flooded his stomach. "Please leave."

"You should lock your door if you don't want folks to visit." He sauntered over to the fridge and opened it. Grabbed the almost empty bottle of soda and gulped it down.

Anger rippled beneath Angel's skin. He'd never once felt unsafe in this apartment, never felt the need to lock his door or carry a key. No one had ever entered without his permission, not since the day Ruth installed him here. And now Daniel thought he could waltz in to Angel's safe place and drink his soda?

"Get out," Angel snapped.

Daniel laughed, menace coating the sound. "Didn't come all the way up here to get out. Came up here to get off."

"You have a right hand that seems pretty fucking functional."

"Well, listen to the mouth on you. Wasn't sure you had balls, much less a spine."

"I do. I spent years letting assholes like you talk down to me, but I'm done. This is *my fucking place.* Now get the *fuck out.*"

Daniel raised his eyebrows and lifted both hands, palms out, a gesture of surrender. "Fuck, don't get your panties twisted, princess."

He moved toward the door. Angel stepped to the side, giving him all the room he needed. Daniel reached for the knob. Angel should have anticipated it but he didn't, so the backhand that smacked into his cheek snapped his head to the right. Pain blazed through his face and blurred his vision. A fist flashed in his peripheral, and Angel had enough survival instinct left to duck. Daniel shouted when his fist slammed into the wall instead of Angel's face.

He darted around Daniel and grabbed the doorknob. Turned it hard.

"You little shit." Daniel tackled him to the ground, smothering his smaller body face-first into the rough carpet. Panic speared Angel in the gut and he thrashed. "Think you're better than this, prag? Think you're better than me?"

Angel grunted and tried to roll, but Daniel had him pinned. "Don't do this."

His chuckle was pure evil. "Don't worry, bitch, I know better than to dip into an ass like yours without a rubber. But you are going to suck me off, and if I feel teeth you're gonna lose a few."

The old carpet was pinching his face and Daniel's weight made breathing hard. Angel's own tidal wave of fury and terror weren't helping. All he could think about was getting away. Getting Daniel off his body. Getting to the safety of Ethaniel's arms.

Ethan, I need you so bad.

But Ethaniel wouldn't be riding to the rescue. He hadn't even tried the stairs yet with his boot, and Angel was supposed to be going to *him* in a little while.

That might not happen now. The one thing Angel knew deep down was that he was done being anyone's sex toy. Done being abused and taking it.

He was fucking done.

"Won't bite," Angel said, putting enough squeak into his voice to hint at resignation. "Please, just…okay."

"Good girl."

Resenting the use of the word girl, Angel bit back his hate and forced himself to get onto his knees after Daniel stood. Daniel undid his belt buckle and fly and fished out a semi-erect dick. Angel waited for Daniel's hands to fall away, baring himself.

"Suck it."

Angel did one better and punched Daniel in the junk with both barrels. Each fist collided from a different angle over tender flesh. He didn't wait for Daniel's scream. He shot up and yanked open the front door. Cold air hit him in the face.

At the top of the stairs something caught his ankle. Angel grabbed at the banister but his fingers missed the smooth wood.

He stumbled, arms wheeling, and then fell.

CHAPTER TWELVE

Ethan lay awake listening to the house fall silent around him, his walkie-talkie clutched to his chest. Soon Angel would let him know he was on his way, so Ethan could leave the window cracked. Now that he had the boot and was more mobile, he could even get up and help Angel inside.

He couldn't wait for them to finally be alone.

A noise downstairs hinted at movement in the kitchen. A few of the stairs creaked. He hadn't heard anyone go downstairs in the last hour. Maybe someone was going up to bed late. Unless Sarah was sneaking around, but she didn't normally do that.

At quarter to ten, he tried the walkie. "Angel? You there?"

The static didn't break.

Maybe he's in the bathroom.

After five minutes passed, he tried again. The continuing silence wormed its way into Ethan's gut, turning it slowly to ice.

He hobbled to the bedroom window, but he had no view of the apartment or garage. There was no sign of Angel in the yard.

He fell asleep, that's all.

The boot was heavy and he had to walk at a weird gait to move the thing, which made his inner thighs ache, but Ethan left his cane by the bed to save noise. He braved the discomfort and hobbled down the hall to the kitchen. Lights blazed in the apartment windows. The stairs taunted him to try climbing them to see what was going on. He could probably make them in the boot.

Going down would be an entirely new problem.

Something in the shadows engulfing the bottom of the stairs caught his attention. Ethan squinted. The shape was too big to be a raccoon, and the wrong shape for a deer, but what on earth—?

His stomach plummeted to his feet.

He slammed through the kitchen door, one bare foot slapping on the wood deck, his boot thumping loudly across its surface. Cold wrapped around him, seeping right through his flannel pants and t-shirt, but none of that mattered.

Angel lay huddled at the bottom of the stairs, eyes closed, bleeding from several places on his head and face. The sight of him there, so still and pale in the half-moonlight, sent a shock of fear through Ethan so sharp that he doubled over.

"Angel, baby, it's me." He couldn't kneel with any grace, so he flopped onto his hip by Angel's head. Pressed trembling fingers against Angel's throat. A steady pulse did nothing to ease his terror, though. Angel was unconscious and bleeding, and all evidence pointed toward a fall down the stairs.

Had he tripped on his way to see Ethan? He was wearing shoes, but no coat. It was too fucking frigid not to wear a coat in the middle of a November night.

"Come on, Angel, wake up for me."

He touched Angel's cold face, careful of the blood. Nothing.

Before the accident, he would have picked Angel up and carried him into the warm house. Before the accident, he was never without his cell phone, and he could have called for help.

Tonight all he had were his very healthy lungs. "Mom! Dad! I need help!" Over and over, his bellowing voice bouncing off the tree line, until lights began popping on all over the house. The porch lights flooded the side yard with a silver glow.

Dad got there first, his flannel robe cinched tight around his waist. "What happened?"

"I don't know, I found him like this." A shudder tore through Ethan. "He won't wake up."

"Probably hit his head good if he fell down those steps."

Something draped over Ethan's shoulders. A coat. He looked up at Jillian, who was red-faced and close to tears. She handed another coat over to Dad, who tucked it around Angel's limp body.

Mom joined them moments later, the house phone clutched in her hand. "I called for an ambulance. They'll be here in about ten minutes."

"It's freezing out here," Ethan said.

"Can't move him, though," Dad replied. "If he's broken something, moving him could make it worse."

Panic kept trying to seize control of Ethan's reactions. He had to keep it together. He shoved his arms into his coat and zipped it up, but the shivering wouldn't stop. He needed Angel to open his eyes and smile at him. Colorful lights winked behind his eyes, threatening him with both a headache and a potential fainting spell, but he didn't care.

Angel needed him. Nothing else mattered.

Mom went into the garage and quickly reappeared with the space heater on a much longer extension cord. She set it on the ground near them and turned it on full blast. The hot air helped, and Ethan angled so he wasn't blocking any of it from Angel.

Angel's eyelids fluttered.

"Angel?" Dad said. "Matthew? You in there, son?"

"Don't." The single, plaintive word socked Ethan in the heart.

"You're safe," Ethan said. He reached beneath the coat to squeeze Angel's shoulder. "You hear me? You're safe. Can you open your eyes?"

Angel squeezed his eyes tighter, pain pinching his lips. He grunted, gasped, and then peeled his eyelids apart. Those precious brown eyes blinked up at him, swimming in misery and pain so deep Ethan nearly swept him right into his arms.

"What happened, son?" Dad asked.

"Fell." Angel didn't look away from Ethan when he spoke. "Hurts."

"What hurts?" Ethan asked.

"All over."

"Does anything feel broken?"

"Not sure." He twitched beneath the coat, as if testing various extremities. "Don't think so."

"Falling down those steps, you probably got right banged up," Dad said. "Never took you for the clumsy sort."

"Tripped. So stupid."

He tried to sit up. Dad joined Ethan in the effort to keep him down. "You need to hold still until the ambulance gets there," Ethan said. "Please."

Angel's liquid eyes almost spilled over as he nodded, agreeing for Ethan's sake, he was certain. Ethan did his best to keep his shit together while they waited. And then again once the paramedics arrived and began to examine Angel. Dad whispered to one of them, probably informing them of Angel's status without announcing the secret to Jillian, who still hovered nearby with Mom. At some point, a shoe had gotten onto Ethan's left foot. He didn't remember when that happened.

Daniel had chosen not to make an appearance during the commotion, and that was fine by Ethan. He didn't need his brother around making snide comments.

The paramedics got Angel sitting up on a flattened gurney, with one of those metallic emergency blankets wrapped around him. Nothing was broken, only bruised, but they were having a hell of a time getting a cut on his head to stop bleeding.

"I hate to say it, but you're going to need stitches," the elder paramedic said. "Someone can ride with him."

"I'll go," Ethan said without even thinking. "Um, you're both in your robes. I'm at least partly dressed."

"All right." Dad helped him stand, and Ethan blinked those spots away again. "Your mother and I will get dressed and drive over to bring you both home."

"Okay." He liked that plan. It kept him close to Angel. He didn't want to let Angel out of his sight, ever, until the end of time.

Mom squeezed his arm as he passed her. She understood the panic and terror of knowing someone you cared about was hurt.

The second paramedic rode in the back of the ambulance with them, which didn't matter because she was a stranger. He reached for Angel, who slipped a cool hand into his. Something inside of Ethan that had been galloping at full tilt slowed under that simple touch. Angel was alive and safe, and it was all that mattered.

The paramedic offered Ethan gloves, but Angel didn't have blood on his hands. He wouldn't have taken them even if Angel did. Ethan's hands were fine, no cuts, no risk. He held tight on the never-ending ride and didn't let go until they arrived. No one chased him out of Angel's cubicle, not when the nurse took his vitals or the physician's assistant did the stitches. Five along the hairline of his left temple.

"Keep it dry for a few days," the P.A. said. "You can pick up an antibacterial ointment at the hospital pharmacy to guard against infection."

"Thank you," Ethan said.

"You're welcome. Take care of your partner."

He left Ethan open-mouthed. Had he been that obvious? Could anyone look at him and see how much he cared for Angel? Had his dad noticed back at the house?

Angel tugged on his arm. "Don't overthink it."

He barked laughter. "Isn't that my line?" A new sense of relief blasted through Ethan, leaving his knees shaky. He sat on the edge of the exam bed and tucked Angel into his arms. Angel listed into him, face pressed into his armpit. "Fuck, Angel, when I saw you lying there…"

"I'm sorry."

"Don't apologize." Ethan gently kissed his temple near the bandage. "It was an accident."

Angel's entire body flinched. Before Ethan could inquire about that odd reaction, his parents stormed the room. Ethan's heart slipped into his feet, but he didn't pull away from Angel. He didn't do anything except hold him tight while his dad stared at him from a few feet away.

* * *

Angel heard the new sets of footsteps, but assumed it was another nurse or doctor until a comforting hand rubbed across his shoulders. "How are you feeling, sweetheart?"

Ruth.

"All right." He raised his head, tensing when he saw William watching them with a blank expression. Ethaniel hadn't retracted or pushed him away, even with his father there. Uncertain what to do, Angel squirmed until Ethaniel let him go. "I feel better now, Ethan, thank you."

Ethaniel caught on and slid over a bit, giving Angel space. Ruth swooped in with a firm hug. She smelled like lotion and lavender, and he clung to her until she let go. "You gave us all quite the fright," she said.

"I'm sorry." His insides quivered with memories of the truth—the real reason he'd gone ass over heels down those stairs. "It was such a stupid thing to do, and all I did was worry everyone."

"Good thing Ethan there was up and about after we all went to sleep," William said. "Otherwise you might've laid there till morning and frozen to death."

Angel shuddered at the thought. He certainly couldn't tell William that Ethaniel was up and about because they were planning on fucking around in Ethaniel's bed that night, but thank God for best laid plans. They'd probably saved Angel's life.

"I want to go home and not think about it anymore," Angel said.

"Sure, son. You weren't admitted, so springing you shouldn't take too long."

Famous last words. Since hospitals were incapable of releasing people with any sort of speed or efficiency, it was almost an hour before Angel was suffering the indignity of an orderly wheelchair-ing him to the E.R. entrance. William already had the heated car idling in wait. Every one of Angel's muscles hurt, especially in his back and shoulders, and the ride home woke some new aches and pains.

William parked near the side, closer to the garage.

"Angel can sleep in my room tonight," Ethaniel said the moment the car engine went silent. "I'll take the couch."

"What?" Angel shook his head. *Ouch.* "I can't take your bed. Your leg."

"Will survive one night on the couch. You are in too much pain to manage those stairs tonight."

"They're just bruises."

"Bruises still hurt. Take my bed."

William huffed. "Share the bed, boys, you're both grown men."

Ruth's lips twitched hard, as if she was holding back a smile. Ethaniel stared at his father, adorably stunned.

"Okay," Angel said. He needed Ethaniel close to him, and if William was okay with the idea—even if he was oblivious to their relationship—then Angel wasn't going to argue.

The matter seemed decided, so they moved the production into the kitchen. Ruth made him a piece of buttered toast to go with the giant ibuprofen caplets he'd been sent home with.

Ibuprofen and a muscle relaxer for the first few days. As if he
didn't already take enough pills.

William and Ruth retired together, leaving Ethaniel and
Angel alone in the kitchen. Angel wanted to confide the truth to
Ethaniel so badly, to let him know what a monster Daniel was.
But that wasn't the kind of thing you talked about in the middle
of the night, when his body hurt and all he wanted was sleep.
And Ethaniel was still too highly strung from adrenaline and fear
to think rationally. He'd probably race right upstairs and remove
some of Daniel's teeth, and Angel didn't want that.

Tonight he wanted Ethaniel.

"Can we go to bed?" he asked.

"Of course." Ethaniel cleaned up the table and put their water
glasses in the dish drainer.

Angel leaned heavily on him as they both limped down the
hall to Ethaniel's room. The boot was loud and clumpy but it was
better than crutches. Ethaniel helped him out of his stained shirt
and into a clean, too-big sweatshirt that smelled like Ethaniel.
Woodsy and masculine and a little like pine. Comforting scents.

He tucked Angel under the covers, then climbed into bed.
Angel curled up close, grateful for the body heat and the simple
warmth of Ethaniel's arm around his waist. He pressed his ear
against Ethaniel's heart, which was still beating too fast. His entire
body hurt, but it was nothing compared to the way his heart
ached for Ethaniel. Angel had terrified him tonight.

"How are you?" Angel asked. "Tell me honestly."

"My head hurts. I got dizzy a few times but I think it was
from the adrenaline." His fingers sifted through Angel's hair. "I
should have washed your hair for you."

Blood.

Angel raised his head, heart tripping. "Did you get blood on you?"

"No. I think some dried to your hair, but that won't hurt anyone before morning. No one's bringing in a hazmat unit."

"Good." He put his head back down. "Don't ever want to risk you, Ethan."

"A smear of blood isn't a risk unless I'm rubbing it in an open wound."

"I know. It's irrational, I'm sorry."

"It's fine." Ethaniel traced ticklish circles on belly. "Maybe this isn't how I wanted you in my bed tonight, but you're here."

"And with your dad's blessing."

"Hah. True. Honestly? The way I was acting tonight, I'd be surprised if he wasn't wondering about us."

Angel fisted the front of Ethaniel's shirt. "Do you think so?"

"I don't know. He's never asked me if I'm gay, but it's not as if I've ever brought a girlfriend home, either. Even in high school, I didn't date much. After I realized I was gay, I didn't try, and then after being overseas…it's too hard."

"Because the guys you meet don't understand what it's like?"

"Yeah." Ethaniel sighed. "Most of them don't understand what it's like to go through hell and be the only survivor. You didn't go to war, but you understand hell. You understand doing whatever it takes to survive."

Came up here to get off.

Angel shivered and burrowed closer to Ethaniel. He wanted to climb inside the bigger man and stay put until he didn't hurt anymore. Until the big bad monster upstairs had moved on and was no longer a threat.

He dozed in Ethaniel's arms, waking up to every creak of wood or cry of a faraway bird, until sunlight broke through the thick cloud cover and produced a bank of fog so thick Angel wasn't sure he'd be able to see the garage from the kitchen. Ethaniel's curtains were wide open, so Angel studied the fog, unwilling to move his aching body despite his bladder's best efforts to get him up.

Normally he'd be fixing a quick breakfast and preparing to start another day mucking stalls and hauling manure. Not today. Today he'd be lucky to lift a shovel, much less a shovel full of horse shit. No one was knocking on Ethaniel's door looking for him, so he counted that as a win.

At some point the household woke up. Feet creaked down the stairs. Sounds from the kitchen. The rumble of engines as Caleb and Benny arrived for work. They were probably getting the whole story from Ruth over coffee. He could even imagine the rolling eyes and muttered "clumsy kid" comments.

The house quieted again, and the desperate need to pee finally pushed him into action. His neck hurt worse than anything, probably from sleeping in one slightly awkward position all night. He loved Ethaniel's broad chest, but it wasn't the most ergonomic pillow, especially for someone already in pain.

Ethaniel's arm tightened around his waist when Angel tried to crawl away. Angel kissed his cheek and whispered, "I need to pee. I'll come back, I promise."

He mumbled, then relaxed. Angel swallowed a groan as he got to his feet. His back twinged in a few spots, but he made it one door down to the bathroom with little fuss and let out the liquid that had been tormenting him. In the bright glow of the incandescent bulbs, Angel lifted the sweatshirt and took stock.

Bruises on top of bruises, a mish-mash of purple and black and green. His back had taken the brunt. He didn't remember much about the fall, only the desperate need to protect his head, especially from the crash at the bottom. Lying there on the freezing ground, staring blankly at the night sky, unable to process what had happened.

Daniel. Looming over him with a sneer. The boot sailing toward his head.

Angel stumbled back, his hip clipping the side of the sink. He touched the bandage on the left side of his head where the tender, stitched skin throbbed.

Daniel had kicked him in the head.

Dear God, Ethan's going to kill him.

He couldn't tell Ethaniel about Daniel, not now. Ethaniel would do something drastic in his honor, and hurting Daniel would only hurt Jillian and Sarah.

He was very literally going to cheat on his wife last night. He's already hurting her.

And he scared Sarah, that much was clear from the way the little girl avoided him, and when she couldn't, she remained totally silent in his presence. Maybe telling Ethaniel the truth was best for everyone.

Maybe.

Someone knocked. "Angel?"

He dropped the sweatshirt and opened the door. Ethaniel smiled sleepily at him, one hand braced on the jam. "Morning," Angel said.

"You took so long I sent myself as a search party."

"Sorry."

"Counting the bruises?"

Angel flinched. "Something like that. You need the head?"

"Yeah, only be a minute."

He wandered back to Ethaniel's room and perched on the edge of the bed. Someone was moving around upstairs. Probably Jillian getting Sarah ready for school. Angel loved the simple domesticity of that image. His own mother had been a terrible human being, selfish and addicted to drugs for almost as long as he could remember. He couldn't recall a time when she'd told him she loved him. He had no idea who his father was, or if the man was even alive today.

Sarah's father was an asshole, but she had a mother who loved her, grandparents who doted on her, and an uncle who adored her. That was the most important thing.

Ethaniel hobbled back into the room and sank down on the mattress next to him. "I don't know if this boot is better or worse than the crutches. I feel like I'm carrying a toddler around on my leg."

Angel snickered.

Footsteps shuffled down the hall. Ruth appeared in the doorway, dressed and ready for the day, but her eyes betrayed her fatigue. "Morning, boys."

"Morning, ma'am," Angel replied.

Ethaniel lost his "good morning" to a sharp yawn.

"There's a pot of coffee in the kitchen," Ruth said. "And some fresh muffins on the table. Angel, dear, your medications are on the counter, too."

He blinked. "All of them?"

"I didn't imagine you'd be up to running back to the apartment until after you've taken another ibuprofen, so I went up and got them."

"I—thank you, Ruth, you didn't have to do that."

"It was no trouble. I put some Epsom salts in your bathroom, as well. A hot soak will do wonders for your bruises. You boys need anything today, you ring down to the stables, all right?"

Angel's heart swelled with gratitude for a woman who had, in so many ways, been his own personal guardian angel.

"We will, Mom, thank you," Ethaniel said.

She left at the same time two sets of feet descended the stairs. Jillian and Sarah's voices drifted down the hall, along with Ruth's. Before long the front door banged, and the house fell silent around them.

Angel glanced at the ceiling. "Think your brother's still here?"

"Probably. He doesn't usually get up before eleven most days, which is fine by me. The less time I have to spend around him the better I feel."

Ditto.

"You up to a light breakfast?" Ethaniel asked.

"I think so." He needed to eat anyway so he could take his meds. And a shower was definitely in his near future.

Stiff muscles protested so much moving around, but they eventually settled themselves at the kitchen table with coffee, muffins, and a little white dish that held an assortment of tablets and capsules. Ethaniel didn't comment on the drugs that, aside from the addition of the ibuprofen and muscle relaxer, were part of Angel's everyday life.

"I'm still a little fuzzy on what happened last night," Ethaniel said after they'd both silently nibbled on banana nut muffins.

Angel tried not to tense up. "Which part?"

"How you tripped. Were you on your way to see me?"

He didn't want to lie to Ethaniel. Not ever, not even about this. Ethaniel had only ever been kind and truthful to him. He also didn't want to hurt Ethaniel, and the truth was going to hurt. A lot. "Not exactly."

Ethaniel's eyebrows furrowed, etching lines across his forehead. "You didn't have a coat on. Why were you leaving the apartment in such a hurry that you tripped and fell down the stairs?"

Angel sipped at his coffee, mouth dry as a desert. His heart flipped uneasily.

"Hey." A warm hand squeezed his wrist. "Talk to me, babe. What happened?"

"Yeah, *babe*." Daniel's sharp voice broke the silence and sent ice water down Angel's spine. He stepped into the kitchen, arms crossed. "What happened?"

CHAPTER THIRTEEN

Ethan worked hard to keep his expression as neutral as possible after Daniel's unexpected appearance. He hadn't heard anyone on the stairs, which made him wonder if Daniel had snuck up on them on purpose. And his delivery of those repeated words made Ethan's skin crawl. Not because of "babe" but because of the way Angel's face went gray.

Daniel leaned in the kitchen entry, a very distinct challenge in his stance and his steady glare. Not at Ethan, though. He was glaring right at Angel, and Ethan battled against a very real need to stake his claim on Angel. To stand up and piss a metaphorical circle around Angel so Daniel would back off.

Angel, who'd gone stiff as a board and looked like he wanted to bolt.

His initial reaction upon waking last night after the fall came roaring back.

"*Don't.*"

Don't what?

It hit him so hard Ethan got a little dizzy. "You son of a bitch."

Angel's entire body flinched.

Daniel cut his gaze at Ethan. "Look at you, the perfect son dropping language in Mom's kitchen."

Ethan stood, one hand braced on the table for balance. Daniel might have been bulkier, but Ethan was taller. Always had been. "What did you do to him?"

Daniel laughed like he'd told a joke. "I get it. The little fairy there wouldn't put out because he's already getting it from you."

Anger rushed through him like acid, heating his blood. "His name is Angel, asshole. What did you do?"

"Nothing he didn't want."

Ethan stepped to the side, hands curled into fists. Angel grabbed his wrist and held him still with a desperate look on his face. He shook his head, his big doe eyes begging Ethan not to engage. Ethan warred with his need to know the truth versus the itch to punch Daniel in his smug face simply for thinking about touching Angel, and when he finally looked up, Daniel was gone.

Ethan sank back into his chair and clasped Angel's cold hands. "What did he do?"

"He was in the apartment when I got there." Angels voice was broken and almost too soft to hear. "He s-s-said s-s-stuff. I got mad and yelled at him to leave, and I thought he was going to. But he hit me instead."

Fury rippled beneath Ethan's skin. His gaze landed on a bruised cheekbone, and he heard the phantom crack of a palm against skin.

"He knocked me d-d-down and s-s-said I..." Angel shivered. "Said I would blow him, and if he felt teeth he'd kn-n-nock mine out."

Ethan let go of Angel's hands so he didn't accidentally hurt him. The force of anger churning inside him was unlike anything he'd ever felt. Someone precious to him had been threatened and physically hurt, and he started shaking.

Angel touched his knee, so gentle and tentative. "I pretended to play along with it s-s-so he'd get off me. Then I punched him in the junk."

A flicker of pride rose up over the fury, and Ethan covered that still-cool hand with his.

"I tried to get out of the apartment, but he caught my ankle and I fell d-d-down the s-s-stairs. I remember falling and landing at the bottom and most of the pain in between."

"The fall didn't knock you unconscious?"

"No." Angel swallowed hard. "D-d-daniel's boot did."

"I'll kill him." The words tumbled out without censor. Daniel had attacked Angel in his own home, and then again when he was helpless.

Angel could have frozen to death, and Daniel hadn't cared.

"Please d-d-don't s-s-say that," Angel whispered. "He's your brother."

"He's an unforgivable bastard. You could have died last night, Angel. You could have *died* because of him."

Angel started shivering, and Ethan tugged him into his arms. He didn't care who saw. He didn't care who knew anymore. All he understood in that moment was *protect* and *comfort*. Kill was in there, too, but much further down. Base instincts reacting solely out of the feelings he had for Angel.

I love him.

"You need to tell my parents," Ethan said.

Angel made a distressed noise; Ethan held him tighter. Even more than his parents knowing what kind of cruelty Daniel was capable of, he worried for Jillian and Sarah. Two women he loved very much, who used to be so vibrant and full of life, were shadows of themselves ever since Daniel's return. And Daniel had been willing not only to sexually assault someone, he'd been about to cheat on his very devoted wife who'd put her life on hold to wait for him.

For nine years.

"I'm s-s-sorry," Angel said.

Ethan's heart broke a little bit more. "No, stop. You didn't do anything wrong. Nothing."

"I d-d-don't wanna hurt your mother."

"You aren't hurting her, babe. Daniel hurt her the second he entered your apartment without permission. This is on him, not you."

"What if your parents d-d-don't s-s-see it like that? Your brothers won't."

Ethan pulled back enough to see Angel's blotchy face. To look into tear-filled eyes and will Angel to feel his love and support. "What my brothers think doesn't matter. They don't control this house, or who lives here. My parents need to know what kind of person they're letting live under this roof. Near their granddaughter."

Someone knocked on the kitchen door, startling Ethan into protect mode. He angled toward the door, one hand ready to strike.

Russ Hanlon stood behind the glass, his round face a study of worry. Ethan waved him in. Russ brought the cold air with him, then shut the door.

"William told me about your fall last night," he said to Angel. "You all right, son?"

"No, he's not," Ethan replied for him. "Russ, I hate to ask this but can you call down to the office for me and ask my parents to come to the house? It's a minor emergency."

"Sure, sure." Russ regarded them both with a familiar papa bear stare. He'd been on the farm for decades, and he'd watched all of the Shockley kids grow up. If they'd been Catholic, Russ would have probably been named godfather to all of them.

He walked to the handset on the kitchen wall and made the phone call. "Ruth said they'd be up shortly," he reported.

"Thank you," Ethan said.

"Sure thing. Anything else I can do?"

"No, but thanks."

"Sure."

Russ hung around the kitchen until Mom and Dad arrived, both of them clearly worried, and then he headed back down to the stables.

"What's wrong?" Dad asked.

"You guys might want to sit down." Ethan waved at the chairs across from him and Angel.

They did, huddled together and intent on whatever Ethan had to say. Only this wasn't his story to tell.

"Angel falling down the stairs wasn't an accident," Ethan said. "He was deliberately tripped."

Mom's lips parted.

Dad frowned. "What do you mean? By who?"

He squeezed Angel's hands.

Angel didn't lift his gaze from the kitchen table when he said, "By Daniel."

Mom covered her mouth with one hand, eyes wide.

Dad's frown deepened. "Why would he do that?"

Angel inhaled a shaky breath, then launched into a more detailed account of what had happened in the apartment last night, complete with a lot of painful stuttering. Ethan listened to the cruel words and threats with violence in his heart, hating everything Angel had been through and hating the person his brother had become. A brother with whom he'd once been inseparable, and now they couldn't have been further apart.

When Angel reached the boot to the head, Mom started to cry. Dad looped an arm around her waist, his own face strangely blank. "I knew Daniel wouldn't come out of prison the same man he was before," Dad said, "but I never expected this."

"He is the same man," Ethan said. "Prison only intensified the resentment and hate he'd already been stockpiling before he got into the fight that put him there. He could have killed Angel last night and we'd have all figured it to be an accident."

"It can't be true." Mom choked on a sob. "Not one of my boys."

"I'm s-s-so s-s-sorry," Angel said. "I d-d-didn't want to tell you, Ruth, I d-d-don't ever want to be the reason you cry."

"I'm not crying because of you, sweetheart. You aren't breaking my heart." She opened her arms and Angel went to her. The hug was strong and fierce, and it made Ethan's heart swell with pride.

"What's with the sob-fest?" Daniel asked, his broad form suddenly looming in the kitchen entryway. "Someone die?"

"Someone almost did," Ethan snapped back.

Daniel's near-permanent sneer went black. "What did your little butt buddy tell them?"

Ethan stood so fast his leg screamed at him, and his vision went spotty. He grabbed the edge of the table so he didn't fall over.

Dad had stood, too, and he was in Daniel's personal space, as angry and intimidating as Ethan had ever seen him. "Is what Angel told us true? Did you assault that boy?"

"So what if I did? You gonna call the cops? Put your own son back in prison for a cell block whore that shovels horse shit for a living?"

Dad's hand flew so fast only the clap of the blow and the snap of Daniel's head to the side registered. The sound hung in the air.

"Damn you, Daniel James Shockley. I told myself I would never raise a hand to one of my children in anger, and for forty-one years I kept that promise."

Daniel smirked. "Hey, at least you're finally paying attention to me."

"What?"

"Oh, come on, I didn't give a shit about the horses, so you didn't have time for me. Not one baseball game, not one parents' night at school. Ethan didn't like the horses either, but he was the golden boy, always getting poor, pathetic Danny out of messes."

Dad wasn't cowed. "Maybe I wasn't always the most attentive father, but your mother and I raised all five of our children to be respectful, loving human beings. What you did to Angel is beyond reprehensible."

"Oh please. Do you know how many dicks that prag probably sucked in prison? He's already sucking Ethan's, what's one more?"

Mom gasped. Ethan's stomach twisted up tight.

Angel surprised him by tearing away from Mom and planting himself next to Dad. "Shut up. *Shut up!* I am s-s-sick and tired of that kind of bullshit. I've put up with it for years, and I'm *done*. I'm not some toy to be picked up and used whenever you want. I am a human being, damn it!"

Ethan gaped at the back of Angel's head, shocked as hell by the outburst, but also overwhelmed with pride. Despite the pain he must have been in, both physically and emotionally, Angel was standing up for himself. He was finally standing up against someone who had treated him as less than human and staking a claim on his own life. Ethan couldn't imagine how freeing that must be.

Daniel huffed, but otherwise didn't respond. Probably a good thing, because Angel was so wound up, he looked one more snide comment from attacking. Ethan had never seen Angel so assertive, and it was kind of a turn-on.

Dad put a firm hand on the back of Angel's neck. "Yes, you are, son. You are a human being, and you're a member of this family. You deserve a spot at our supper table. You." He stared pointedly at Daniel. "You do not."

Daniel blinked hard. "What?"

"I want you out of this house by lunchtime."

"But my parole—"

"You aren't violating your parole by living down the road at Caleb's house. I won't have you near Sarah and Jillian, not until your mother and I decide what to do."

Daniel's eyes narrowed. "You can't take my wife and kid away from me."

"They can visit you if they wish to do so. At Caleb's. For the time being, you are not welcome in this house."

The glare Daniel leveled first at Ethan, and then at Angel, was venomous and deadly. He turned without a word, and moments later, heavy boots clumped up the stairs.

"William?" Mom said.

"I'm sorry, Ruth." He tucked his wife into his arms. "It's for the best."

Ethan limped to the other side of the table, where Angel stood, staring at the floor. His shoulders had slumped, and he still looked kind of gray. "Hey." He used a finger to tip Angel's head up. "You did good."

Angel's lips twitched into a faint smile. "Your brother got kicked out of the house. How d-d-do you not hate me right now?"

Emotions rose up so strongly he had to let them out or risk suffocating. "Because I love you too much to hate you."

Those big eyes went wide. "You do?"

"Yes." Ethan never wanted Angel to doubt that, or doubt his sincerity, so he kissed him. A gentle kiss in front of God, his father, and anyone else who wandered through. He didn't care because he really was in love with the strong-willed, emotionally battered, but still standing young man in his arms.

Anyone who didn't like it was free to walk away.

Angel kissed him back with raw emotion, hands on the sides of Ethan's neck. When they finally broke apart, they were alone.

"Holy crap." Angel rested his forehead against Ethan's shoulder. "I can't believe that happened."

Ethan laughed. "Which part?"

"All of it." He looked up, his face a study of wonder. "You kissed me in front of your dad."

"Yeah, that happened."

"D-d-do you regret it?"

"No." Ethan was nervous about the fallout, but no more pretending. "I don't want to sneak around anymore, Angel. I hope that's okay."

"Of course. I told you that I'd n-n-never pressure you to come out."

"And you didn't. Part of me wishes I'd kissed you while Daniel was still here, just to say fuck you to the asshole."

"I'm glad you didn't." Angel nosed his chin. "I like the way we did it. Say it again?"

Ethan grinned. "I love you."

"Good, because I love you, too."

* * *

Despite the high drama of the morning, the rest of Angel's day went by in relative peace. Caleb was rounded up to help install Daniel in the little house down the road that was supposed to be for Caleb and Polly after their wedding. Supposed to be—Caleb let it slip that Polly had dumped Caleb the day before, hence the sudden visit to her parents' house. Caleb didn't tell them why, and Angel didn't care a whole lot.

William didn't address the witnessed kiss. He and Ruth returned to the stables after Daniel was gone, and the house was suddenly his and Ethaniel's. Angel went back to the apartment for about an hour to soak in hot, salty water, and to wash the last of the blood out of his hair. The bath helped some of his aching muscles, and it wasn't as much of a production to go back down to the house.

He and Ethaniel spent the rest of the day watching TV in the living room, with Ethaniel's leg up on a footstool. Ethaniel barely managed some broth and crackers for lunch, complaining that his stomach was a mess, likely because of the stress of the last twenty-odd hours.

Relaxing the day away wasn't something Angel had done in…well, probably ever. He liked to be doing something, to keep his mind occupied, but being near Ethaniel settled him. He could let his guard down with Ethaniel, and that meant everything to him.

Sarah burst inside at three-thirty, backpack falling off one shoulder, her cheeks bright red from the cold. She practically jumped onto Ethan's lap, and his already bad color got a little greener.

"Hey, sprout," he said.

"Is my daddy really gone?" she asked in a hushed tone.

"He isn't gone, but he isn't living here right now. He's going to live with Uncle Caleb for a while."

"Good. He's scary and he makes Mommy sad."

"Well, he made a lot of people sad this time, which is why Paps asked him to move out."

She studied her uncle with a child's unflinching honesty. "Did he make you sad, Uncle Ethan?"

"Yes, he did. He also made Angel and Gram sad."

"That's awful."

Ethaniel nodded. "Yes, it is. But I think we'll all be happier this way."

"Okay." She raced upstairs with her backpack.

"She's taking this well," Angel said.

"She was always scared of him coming home, and he wasn't patient enough with her." Ethaniel dropped his head onto Angel's shoulder. "When she used to spend weekends with me in Pennsylvania, I'd tell anyone who asked that she was my daughter, instead of my niece."

"How come?" Lying to people, even strangers, wasn't something Angel would expect from Ethaniel.

"Sometimes I wished she was, because I knew what a prick Daniel was. Is. I told one guy the truth about Sarah and Daniel, and I probably did it because I was pretty sure we were about to hook up. Only that never happened."

"Because you lied?"

"No. Owen was in a complicated place with his ex-boyfriend. Turned out he wasn't as over his ex as he thought, and they're together now. Happy, from what Owen tells me."

"That's good." Angel laced his fingers through Ethaniel's, because he wasn't holding his hand for some reason. He didn't want to be the needy one in their relationship, but he couldn't stop himself from asking, "Are you happy?"

"Honestly? Yes and no." Ethaniel tried to burrow in closer, and Angel liked knowing that he could give comfort for a change. "I'm insanely happy to be here with you. I'm happy *with* you, Angel. But…"

"But Daniel."

"Yeah. I hate how much he hurt our parents today, especially our mother. I've never seen her this upset, not even when she was facing cancer. Daniel broke her heart, and I hate him for that. I hate him for what he did and said to you. What he said about you."

Angel swallowed down rising bile. "Some of what he said about me was true."

"I don't care. It's your past. This is your fresh start, and you don't deserve to have your past thrown in your face over and over, especially by someone who's done worse."

"Worse than taking a life?"

"You reacted to a situation that had spiraled out of control. You wanted to protect your mother. Daniel lashes out in anger and he hurts people on purpose. There is a huge difference between the two of you. At your core, Matthew 'Angel' Garrett? You're a genuine, loving person. Prison didn't take that away from you and that's everything."

Angel smiled at the television program he wasn't even watching. His heart filled to bursting with gratitude and love for Ethaniel, and he didn't know what to do with those feelings. "I never expected this."

Ethaniel lifted his head, green eyes wide and curious, and a little bit pained. "Expected what?"

"You. Finding someone who could look past me being a convicted felon, being positive, being a basket case with a stutter.

I never used to dream past my next sip of orange soda, or think about the world outside of Shockley Stables."

"You ever think about leaving the farm?"

The idea of leaving filled Angel with intense dread, but also awoke his curiosity. He'd never traveled beyond the state. He'd never done anything remarkable with his life. He'd never seen any reason to go anywhere else.

Ethaniel gave him a reason.

"I don't know," Angel replied. "But it feels more possible."

It felt more possible every single day. The life he'd never dreamed of having was finally within his grasp—as long as Angel was brave enough to reach for it.

CHAPTER FOURTEEN

Despite the quiet peace of spending the afternoon with Angel, Ethan's mounting nerves over his father's return from the stables had his stomach doing back flips. Sarah's lap mount hadn't helped, and by the time four o'clock rolled around, Ethan's head was pounding and he was a few scant minutes from vomiting when Angel launched off the sofa.

Ethan looked up, expecting to see Daniel or someone threatening nearby. The living room was empty, and moments later, Angel returned with the basin from the bathroom. Ethan didn't have time to be grateful or ashamed, because liquid and crackers came back up in a violent heave that left him dizzy and shaking.

Once he had nothing left, Angel disappeared and came back with a damp washcloth and two glasses. Ethan swished his mouth with water from one glass, then spit into the second. Angel washed his face.

"What do you need?" Angel asked. "How can I help?"

"Bed." He needed to lie down and rest. He definitely needed a pill.

"Okay, lean on me, Ethan."

Getting off the couch took most of Ethan's remaining energy, and he nearly toppled them both twice on the long shuffle to his bedroom. The boot kept tripping him up and unbalancing his center, until he wanted to give up and sleep in the hallway. Eventually he felt the mattress beneath him and a blanket over him. A pillow under his head.

Footsteps left and returned. "The blue tablet, right?"

Ethan grunted. Angel helped him sit up long enough to swallow the pill with a sip of water, then back down he went. He hated that Angel had to baby him after the awful night Angel had had, but he'd lost control of his body when he plummeted through that roof. He hated that stress had him laid up in bed like some kind of invalid, stomach a mess, head throbbing so hard he wanted to cry from the pain.

He dozed for a while, vaguely aware of whispered voices and the creaking of floorboards. The intensity of his headache fell by degrees until the faint light spilling in from his half-open bedroom door didn't feel like needles stabbing at his eyeballs. Soft sounds from the television drifted down the hall. The alarm clock told him it was after eight o'clock.

Angel.

Angel wasn't there. Had he gone back to his apartment? They ought to be at the kitchen table playing cards with Mom and Jillian, as had become their tradition.

Goddamn PCS.

His bladder gave a kick, somehow full when Ethan clearly remembered barfing up lunch. He twisted so both feet were hanging over the bed, the boot a much-hated obstacle in doing this with any sort of grace. Thankfully his cane was leaning against the table. He sat up as slowly as possible, but the world still got fuzzy for a few seconds. The actual headache was mostly gone, so that was a plus.

Before he could test standing up, Mom appeared in the doorway. "Ethan?"

"Need to pee." Saying that to his mother had stopped feeling childish and stupid after the first dozen or so times during his first month home. Before he'd really gotten used to the cast and how to move around in it.

Mom handed him the cane, then stood on his other side, helping Ethan lever to his feet. He blinked back a few spots, but otherwise he was okay as they made it to the next room. Mom closed the door for him, and Ethan sat to do his business because he didn't trust his body tonight. She was waiting for him when he finished.

"Feel like any broth?" she asked.

"Probably a good idea."

"Go back to bed. I'll bring it to you."

"Thanks, Mom." He glanced down the hall at the flickering lights from the TV. "Where's Angel?"

"He went back to his apartment for the night."

Disappointment clawed at his gut. "Did Dad say something?"

"No, sweetheart, your father hasn't said a word to me or anyone else that I know of about this morning. I think Angel was nervous about being around until after you and your father talk. He doesn't want to intrude."

"He doesn't intrude. I love him."

Mom's eyes got shiny. "I know. I'm glad. You deserve someone special, and Angel is very special."

"I know he is."

She patted his cheek with a cool, dry hand. "Go to bed. I'll have your broth in a little while."

"Thanks, Mom."

He limped back to his room and propped up a few pillows so he could sit upright. Dragging his heavy boot onto the bed used up the last of his energy reserves, and he sat there for a while, doing nothing more taxing than staring at Mom's sewing supplies. When the tray of broth and crackers finally arrived, the person carrying it surprised Ethan into sitting up straighter.

Dad put the tray on the side table, then turned on the bedside lamp. A soft orange glow chased away some of the shadows, highlighting fatigue and stress on his already age-worn face. Skin leathery from decades in the sunshine, but those Shockley green eyes bright and alert.

"Head better?" he asked.

Ethan nodded slowly. "I think I worried myself into that one."

"Expect so." Dad sat on the edge of the bed, hands clasped tight in his lap. "You made me real proud today, Ethaniel."

"I did?"

"Couldn't have been easy telling us what Daniel did, but it was best we know. Daniel's behavior affects this entire family, and you did right in telling your mother and me."

Ethan relaxed a bit more under the unexpected praise. They still hadn't addressed the Angel-shaped elephant in the room, though, and Ethan needed it out in the open. He lobbed the grenade and braced for the explosion. "Dad, I'm gay."

"I know. Have to admit, I think I knew before this morning."

"You did? How did you know?"

Dad chuckled, a raspy and welcome sound. "You didn't date in high school, and I tried to chalk that up to being too busy with sports and studying. You're thirty years old, and you've never once brought a girl home to meet your parents, or even mentioned anyone you're seeing. I always sensed you were running from something but I couldn't put a finger on it until recently."

"Until I came home."

"Until you came home and started getting friendly with Angel. This last month you've been happier than I've ever seen you. This morning…said it all without saying."

Ethan studied his dad's face, but couldn't see any hint of his feelings on the matter. "I love him. He loves me back, and I've never been in love before, Dad."

His dad winced—a short flash of movement but Ethan saw it. And it hurt a little. "Can't say as I understand it, or that I completely like it."

Ouch. "That I'm in love?"

"That you love a man. It's not what's normal."

Double ouch. "It's who I am. I was born this way, and I can't change it."

"I accept that, son. Your mother and I had a long talk this afternoon, and while I don't understand it, I still love you. You're still my son."

Relief punched Ethan in the gut so hard he nearly doubled over. A heavy weight lifted from his shoulders and his soul—the weight of the very real fear that his father wasn't going to accept him or love him anymore. His eyes stung.

Dad's own eyes looked suspiciously wet. "I could have lost you this summer, but I didn't. We could have lost Angel last night, but we didn't. Seems to me you two met for a reason, and if this is God's plan, I won't interfere."

"Thank you. For everything." He swallowed against his tears. "What about Daniel?"

"Your mother and I decided to leave that up to Angel. If he wants to press charges, we won't stop him."

Ethan's heart skipped. "Is he? Pressing charges?"

"He hasn't said."

"He probably won't. Angel won't want to be the reason Daniel goes back to prison."

"Daniel brought this mess onto himself."

"I know." Ethan could hear all of Angel's arguments already. "But he won't see it like that. Prison was Angel's hell, like Afghanistan was my hell. He doesn't want anyone back in hell, even someone who tried to bring a piece of that hell into his safe place."

Dad sighed. "That boy's got too good a soul for what's happened to him."

"Yes, he does. He's a better man than I am."

"Why do you think that?"

"He's never killed an innocent person."

Ethan closed his eyes against the flash of images he'd carry until the day he died. Exploding stone, splatters of blood, dismembered body parts. The scent of scorched earth and flesh. The concussive blast of mortars going off in all directions. Screaming.

A gentle voice broke through the haze of old memories. Hands on his shoulders, grounding him. Muffled words leading him back, until he recognized his dad's voice. Telling Ethan he was safe, he was at home, over and over again.

Ethan opened his eyes to his dad's calm, steady face. Those hands stayed put, and it was the closest they'd come to a hug in years.

"Things happen during war," Dad said. "Things that happen in the moment, because all you can think about is staying alive, and keeping the man next to you alive. And you are alive, Ethaniel. You *are* a good man, because a bad man wouldn't be haunted and a bad man wouldn't have the regrets you do."

A damp track spilled down Ethan's cheek. He had to clear his throat twice to speak around the thick lump in it. "Thanks, Dad."

"You're welcome." Dad patted his cheek, then pulled back. "Now you sip at that broth and eat some crackers before you waste away."

He did, stupidly grateful that Dad stayed and watched him eat. Overjoyed that his relationship with Angel was accepted, instead of rejected. Despite the way the day had begun, Ethan had real hope that things would finally start getting better—for him and Angel, for Sarah and Jillian.

I don't ask for much, God, but I'm asking for this. I'm asking for peace in the family.

Please.

* * *

After a second Epsom salt soak in the tub, Angel was nodding off on the couch while pretending to watch TV when his cell phone rang. The unusual sound startled him into falling off the couch, which did nothing for his still sore body. The phone was mostly for stable-related emergencies, so his heart was already pounding by the time he reached it, on its charger by the front door.

The very much locked and slide-bolted front door.

"Yes, hello?"

"Angel?" Ethaniel's voice. "You okay? You're out of breath."

Okay, so maybe not an emergency after all. "I'm fine, I was dozing. The ringer startled me is all."

"Are you sure?"

"Positive. You've never called on the phone before."

"My walkie battery died. Besides, now that my parents know, there's no sense in hiding."

True enough. Angel took the phone back to the couch and sat. "Are you feeling okay? How's your head?"

"Better. A lot better. I even ate some broth and crackers, and it's staying down."

"I'm glad."

"My dad and I had a good talk, too."

"You did?"

"We did." He could practically hear the smile in Ethaniel's voice. "He isn't totally okay with me being gay, but he's willing to be understanding about it. Open-minded. About us, too."

Angel let out a relieved sigh, and another weight fell away, letting his heart beat a bit freer. "I'm glad. I didn't want things to get awkward."

"They might be a little awkward here for a while, but that's growing pains, right? And he doesn't blame you for Daniel, in case that worried you. No one does. Daniel made his own choices."

More relief flashed through him. "I still feel responsible somehow."

"I know you do, but I need you to hear me and believe me when I say it's not your fault. Nothing you said or did in the present or the past is responsible for Daniel attacking you. That fault lands squarely on my asshole brother's head."

"I believe you. It helps to hear it." Angel turned off the TV he wasn't watching anyway. "I hate remembering how your mom was this morning. I hate that I made her cry."

"She loves you like any of her other kids. She wants you happy and safe, just like I do."

"I want you happy and safe too." The gray-faced, sweating Ethaniel from earlier was an Ethaniel he did not like to see. Helping him through the violent loss of his lunch had been an instinctive thing. He liked taking care of Ethaniel, and he was glad to do it.

"I miss you. Twenty-four hours ago we were planning to get busy in my room, and now we're yards apart in separate beds."

"Technically I'm on the couch."

"What if you got into your bed?" The sexy growl in Ethaniel's voice did funny things to Angel's insides. "With fewer clothes than what you're probably wearing."

Mouth dry and blood quickly changing course, Angel eased his sore body off the couch. They'd jerked off together over the walkies a few times, but usually without the sound of the other person. It was hard to remember to hold the button down while rubbing one out.

"How many clothes are you wearing?" Angel asked.

"Sleep pants. Shirt's already off."

Angel's laughter echoed off his bedroom's walls, the small space containing the sound. "I'm sensing intent here."

"If you're up for it, my intent is for us to jerk off together."

His heart started galloping at the blunt way Ethaniel said that. "Phone sex, huh?"

"Yep. Are you in bed yet?"

"Hold on." Angel put his phone down, double-checked that the front door was locked, then locked himself into his bedroom. He closed the room's only curtain, shucked his clothes, turned off the light, and finally climbed onto the bed. "Okay, I'm here."

"What was all that?"

"I had to make sure all the doors were locked."

Ethaniel was quiet for so long Angel nearly checked to see if the call had ended. "We don't have to if you're still too upset about last night."

"It's not that." As his eyes adjusted the darkness, Angel stared along the length of his body. Too thin. Gangly, even, with nothing he thought was terribly appealing. For a long time he'd been nothing but a mouth and an ass, and now someone as amazing as Ethaniel wanted him. Was waiting so patiently to finally be with him.

"Tell me, Angel."

"Today's the first time since I moved into this place that I needed to lock the door. Before last night I always felt safe here. I was okay alone, but now I want to be with you so badly and I can't be."

"You could be if you want to."

"No. Not tonight, especially. It would feel too weird now that your father knows about us." Angel cringed. "And honestly? I'm not sure I'd make it across the yard without freaking out over every single shadow."

"I'm sorry," Ethaniel whispered in a broken voice that hurt Angel's heart.

"It's not your fault. And it isn't forever. I need to find my balance again, okay?"

"Is it okay if I hate Daniel for breaking your sense of safety?"

"Ethan, don't make me give you that kind of permission. I don't like hate going around on my behalf."

Ethaniel made a soft, surprised sound. "Sometimes your capacity for kindness and generosity stuns me. And I mean that in the best possible way. You're a better man than I'll ever be, Matthew Garrett."

Angel blinked hard, struck dumb by the lovely compliment. He really wanted Ethaniel in the room so he could kiss him for saying such a beautiful thing about such an unworthy person. "You're a better man than you give yourself credit for, Ethan. You were nice to me when you had every reason to avoid me. You have the patience of a saint when it comes to physical stuff. And when you love, you love hard and with your whole heart. I see that whenever you're around your parents, but especially Sarah. She's your daughter in every way except biologically, and even then you're still blood."

"I'd do anything for her. All I want is for her to live a happy life."

"I know. So does Jillian. I spoke with her briefly this evening." Angel had been surprised by the depth of her relief over

Daniel being banned from the house, and it had made him wonder about her reunion with her husband.

"How's she taking this?"

"Honestly? I think she's glad he's gone."

Ethaniel grunted. "Jillian waited nine years and got the worst version of the boy she fell in love with. I wouldn't begrudge her wanting a divorce. It's not as if my parents would turn her out if she did. She's family. She has been for sixteen years."

Cool air chilled Angel's exposed skin, reminding him of what they'd planned on doing and currently were not. He crawled under the cover to warm himself. "Maybe all this was supposed to happen, you know? Daniel showing his true colors so Jillian and Sarah can move on with their lives."

"Maybe. I hate that it came at your expense, though."

"Ditto. My bruises have bruises."

"I'm sorry, I didn't mean for our conversation to get so maudlin. We were supposed to be having phone sex."

"Change your mind?"

Ethaniel didn't reply.

"Talk to me," Angel said. More than anything, he wanted to be able to see Ethaniel's face. To try to gauge what he was thinking.

"I still want to, but only if you do, too. If you aren't relaxed enough to enjoy it then we can talk."

Angel glanced at his locked door, then started to stroke his belly with his free hand. An odd erogenous zone, for sure, but it got blood moving in the right direction again. Arousal prickled his skin and heated his insides. "I'm completely naked in bed right now."

Ethaniel gasped. "Yeah? Are you touching yourself?"

"Only my belly. That flat spot below my navel, but above my pubes. It's so sensitive. Always has been."

"I'll remember that." The soft growl in his voice promised future explorations.

"Are you touching yourself?"

"Do you want me to?"

Angel closed his eyes and tried to imagine Ethaniel in his bed, shirtless, his pants pushed as far down as they could go with the boot in place. Ethaniel had such a pretty dick. "Yes, please. Stroke yourself for me."

"I am. Feels good."

He tugged on his own thickening cock, sending ripples of need across his belly and down his spine. "Play with your balls."

Ethaniel gasped. Angel pictured it in his mind, Ethaniel rolling his sac with those work-roughed fingers that felt so amazing against his bare skin. He imagined Ethaniel was the one stroking his own dick. Ethaniel was spitting on his palm to smooth the way, then giving Angel's dick a hard squeeze around the crown.

Angel didn't have to censor the noise he made, didn't have to hide how good he felt. Imagining Ethaniel with him, urging him higher, and dear God in heaven, he wanted that to happen. He wanted to be naked in bed with Ethaniel, both of them together, bodies pressed close. He wanted Ethaniel's actual hands on him, his mouth on him. He wanted it to be Ethaniel's finger pressing against his hole, dragging him to the brink.

"Ethan!" Angel lost himself to the intensity of his orgasm, both hands working through it until he was a gasping, panting mess.

He stared at the ceiling, dazed by not only how hard he'd come, but from the fantasy that had brought him to it. For all of his fear and nerves, he wanted to be with Ethaniel. He wanted Ethaniel to penetrate him. To finally make love to him.

Something squawked near his ear. Angel wiped himself with the sheet, then pressed his phone to his ear in time to hear Ethaniel's muffled release. He knew the sound well enough by now.

Eventually Ethaniel's side of the line crackled, and then he asked, "You there?"

"Yes." Angel wanted to reach through the phone and kiss Ethaniel, because he adored kissing that man. "How's your head?"

"A little dizzy but in a good way. You?"

"I feel great." His sore muscles had tightened all over when he came, but the pain was worth what they'd done. "I think I'm ready, Ethan."

"Ready?"

Duh, he isn't on your same thought train. "To be with you."

"Yeah?" He could hear the smile in Ethaniel's voice. "You want to make love?"

"Yes. Soon."

Ethaniel laughed. "I think I can handle soon."

"Me too. I love you."

"Love you too. See you tomorrow."

"Definitely." Angel closed his eyes and pretended Ethaniel was lying right next to him, ready for sleep now that they'd sated themselves. Knowing one day in the future, they would be able to fall asleep together. Share their bed and their lives.

Always.

Chapter Fifteen

An unexpected heavy snowfall had Ethan cooped up in the house for three solid days, thanks to ice and his stupid boot. Instead of the garage, he and Angel made music in the living room, with Sarah and Jillian sometimes listening. But all of the unexpected work at the stables to keep the horses exercised and warm left Angel exhausted by dinner. He always excused himself, and Ethan talked to him on the phone until he fell asleep. Usually by eight every night.

No one talked about Daniel, and he hadn't tried to come by the house. Caleb always took leftovers back to him, probably because Daniel didn't know how to heat up canned soup without burning it. Mom might be mad at Daniel, but she'd never let one of her kids starve.

That Saturday afternoon, Mom drove Angel into town for the choir's dress rehearsal. Their performance was the next day, and Ethan was kind of nervous. Not about Angel singing, but about his own promise to attend. He hadn't set foot inside of a church since last year's Christmas Eve service.

Maybe God had let him live this summer, but that didn't mean Ethan forgave Him for letting Butch and Andy die. Andy's newborn baby girl, Alicia Rose, would never know the great man her father had been, and that wasn't fair.

Bored with his current audiobook, Ethan logged online to check his email. A new message from Owen brightened his mood.

Hey man,

Checking in to see how things are on the home front. Your last email teased at the fact that you might be seeing someone. How's that going? Bringing him home for Thanksgiving? Speaking of which, Rey talked David into going to Stratton for Thanksgiving this year. Apparently the owner of a diner there closes up for a few hours and hosts this huge potluck for anyone in town who wants to come. It sounds fun, and Rey swears by something called cracker dressing.

Michael officially has a girlfriend. Allie Holstrom. She's a nice girl. Great at math, which is good, because Michael sucks at it. Michael also thinks I'm parent of the year, because I bought him condoms. Yes, he's barely fifteen, and I don't want to think about my son having sex yet, but I know how I was at that age, and the last thing I need is to be a grandfather at thirty-five.

Later, Owen

Ethan hit reply right away.

Hey, O! It's been an interesting few weeks for sure. The big news is that yes, I'm with someone. His name is Matthew, but everyone calls him Angel. He's amazing and kind and very unexpected. I also came out to my father earlier this week. I'm going to come out to my siblings next week, probably when we're together for Thanksgiving. Then I can do it all at once, and whatever happens, happens. You know?

I don't think I told you that the cast finally came off. I have a walking boot that I usually use a cane with, but I can get around a little more freely. Except when there's eight inches of snow on the ground, like right now. Hopefully it gets back up above freezing again so the damn stuff melts.

As for Michael, tell the kid I said congrats on the girlfriend, and that safe is sexy. Say hi to David for me. Tell me if cracker dressing is any good, I've never heard of it.

Happy Thanksgiving a few days early!

Ethan

He hit send, then closed the laptop. A tiny prickle of pain had settled behind his eyes from focusing on those pixels for too long. He relaxed against his bed pillows and closed his eyes, dozing the headache away until dinner.

Except that when Angel woke him to eat, the prickle intensified into a fierce throbbing. His stomach rolled, and he couldn't hold back a groan.

Angel fed him a tablet with a sip of water, then covered his eyes with a cold washcloth. "The basin is on the bed next to you. I'll be back in a little while, okay?"

Ethan managed a thumbs up, then tried to relax and let the pill do its job. He'd barely done anything all day long, and this was his reward. A debilitating headache and the real possibility of vomiting up the remnants of his lunch.

I hate this so fucking much.

The bad mood stayed with him into the evening. Angel sat with him for a while and having him close helped a little. Sarah even stopped by to give him a kiss on the cheek and tell him she hoped he felt better soon. When his stomach settled, Mom brought broth and crackers, and Angel helped him eat.

For some reason, instead of finding solace in Angel's help this time, it fueled his resentment. Resentment that intensified into anger after a trip to the bathroom left him so dizzy he needed Angel's help to walk back to his bed. After he was settled under the blanket with his stupid leg propped up on a pillow, he said, "Maybe you should go."

Angel froze in the act of sitting down, his eyebrows arched up. "You want me to leave?"

"You shouldn't have to take care of me like this. I have a mother."

"But I thought..." Angel glanced around the room, as confused as Ethan had ever seen him, and it was all his fault. "I've taken care of you before. Isn't that what boyfriends do?"

They'd never used the b-word, and for some reason, Angel's use of it now made Ethan feel worse. "You shouldn't have to hold my dick for me while I take a piss because I'm so fucking dizzy I can barely stand."

Angel took a step backward, arms going tight around his middle like he was protecting himself. "I love you, Ethan, I want to help when you're hurting."

"You shouldn't have to."

"I *want* to."

Ethan's brain took exception to the harsh words and started a fresh set of hammers pounding against the backs of his eyeballs. "Maybe it's not what *I* want. Or is that suddenly irrelevant?"

"Of course it's relevant." Angel backed up another step. "I don't understand why you're mad at me."

"Because I'm a walking disaster that can barely *walk* most days. Because I hardly did shit all day, and that earned me the worst headache ever for no good reason, and I'm so sick of being in pain all the time. I'm sick of being careful with myself and it doing no goddamned good. You deserve someone who can keep the promises he makes to you."

Angel gaped at him. "When have you ever broken a promise?"

He closed his eyes against the light and Angel's pained expression. "I promised you soon."

"Soon? Oh." Something swished, and then the door clicked shut. The bed sank near his hip. "We will make love, Ethan. Soon doesn't have to mean the next day, or even the next week. When it happens, it will be the right time."

He didn't want Angel to make him feel better for not being able to climb icy stairs to get to his apartment, or for having a smashed brain that liked to play tricks on him when he least expected it. He wanted to wallow in his misery for once. He wanted to mourn the freedom he'd lost and the way it made him feel—a loser whose boyfriend needed to baby him, and he hated it.

He also loved Angel more for his unwavering support.

Too bad his awful mood was winning. He blinked his eyes open, despising the colorful dots marring his vision of beautiful

Angel's face. "I should be able to sit up right now and make love to you like a normal human being, but I can't and I hate it. I hate that I'm weak and that my body fights me all the time, and I hate that I couldn't save you from Daniel. Sometimes I hate you too for being so fucking normal."

The words slipped out without thought, and Ethan couldn't take them back. Angel's head snapped like he'd been slapped, and Ethan might as well have hit him for the pain in Angel's eyes. His chin trembled once, and then he stood.

A thousand things flew through Ethan's mind. A thousand ways to apologize and make it better. Nothing made it past his lips, though, because this was what he wanted. He wanted to be alone with his misery, and he'd made it happen.

"Good night, Ethan," Angel said, voice broken and sad.

Ethan stared at the door long after it shut behind Angel, letting the pain of his newly awoken headache drag him under, uncertain if he'd done irreparable harm to their relationship.

* * *

The next morning, Angel dragged his exhausted, sandy-eyed self into the shower. His face hurt from the force of his sobs the night before, and the hot spray helped wake him up a little bit.

At first he'd cried for himself. For his own fear and uncertainty over what he'd done wrong. How he'd messed up so badly that Ethaniel didn't want him around anymore. How he'd driven Ethaniel to hate him, even a little bit.

Until he understood that he hadn't done anything wrong, and then he'd cried for Ethaniel's pain. For a man whose instinct to protect those around him was impeded by his new body. For a man who was used to going after what he wanted and now couldn't get a jostling hug from his niece without throwing up. For keeping all of that bottled up for so long that it had no choice but to come spewing out in one hateful rant.

Ethaniel didn't hate him. Resentment was a better word. He resented Angel's physical ability to climb stairs, walk to the stables, and eat a pork chop without any negative reactions from his body. Except Ethaniel didn't know that every time Angel took his medication, he worried if today was the day he had a bad reaction. Was today the day he cut himself in front of a client?

Bruises aside, Angel's body was outwardly healthy, but he lived with a virus that could turn on him at any moment. They each had a burden to carry, and he needed to remind Ethaniel that it was okay to lean on someone. The life that Ethaniel remembered might be gone forever, and he had to accept his new normal.

And Angel had an idea how.

He finished his shower, then dressed in his usual Sunday clothes: pressed black slacks and a white dress shirt. The choir all wore red robes, anyway, and he'd seen some folks attend church in blue jeans. Not Angel. He'd never show up in church in anything less than nice clothes. Once he was put together, he made a brief phone call to see about his plan—a plan met with genuine support.

Good.

Too nervous about the performance—and seeing Ethaniel again—to eat, Angel sipped water and paced the apartment until it was time to go downstairs. He always met Ruth, Jillian, and Sarah by the car, and when he made it there Jillian was helping Ethaniel into the backseat. William's presence surprised him, as did the idling pickup truck.

Angel was directed into the back of the car with Ethaniel, who wouldn't meet his eyes. He seemed fixated on his clasped hands. Jillian and Ruth got in front, while Sarah skipped over to the pickup to ride with William. William only went to church on holidays, so knowing he was coming to hear the choir sing warmed a little piece of Angel's heart. The piece that hoped one day William might think of him as one of his sons.

The radio station was already playing Christmas music, so Angel hummed along on the ride to Pine Creek Methodist, a squat, white building on the edge of town. Not that Pine Creek was much of a town. One main street supported a grocery store/deli, a gas station and auto shop, and a large stone building housing a tiny post office and government stuff. They didn't even have their own police force. Only infrequent visits by the county sheriff's department.

Angel didn't care how tiny the town was. He loved it for its quiet simplicity.

Ethaniel's appearance at church caused a small stir among the older folks who remembered him, and a few people he'd gone to school with. He endured the welcomes and hug attempts as Ruth led the way toward their regular pew. Angel tried once more to get Ethaniel to look at him, then gave up and headed to the youth room where the choir had been told to assemble.

He tried to ignore a knot of disappointment over Ethaniel ignoring him. It didn't matter. They needed to talk in private, not in front of the family or anyone else. He'd simply corner him at home later.

Right now all he needed to think about was warm-ups, and then getting every single song pitch perfect. Everything else could wait.

* * *

Ethan bowed his head dutifully when Reverend Jameson began the service with a prayer. He listened to the words that asked God to bless their worship time, bless their choir, and to blah, blah. The same opening prayer Ethan remembered from his childhood. The words echoed a little hollow for him that morning. He didn't deserve blessings because he was a jerk.

Waking up to how truly awful he'd been to Angel the night before had settled in his bones like a toxic sludge, leaving him weighed down and gross. He couldn't shower it off, and he couldn't dress it up with nice clothes. He couldn't even look Angel in the eye, afraid Angel would see how horrible he was and end them.

The only thing keeping him seated in the pew and not screaming his failure to the skies was Sarah's firm hold on his hand.

After a few announcements, Reverend Jameson called the choir to the stage. Two dozen people in billowing red robes walked through a side door and arranged themselves on three rows of elevated platforms. Angel stood dead center, a little pale under the stage lights, but straight-backed and chin up.

Love and pride collided in Ethan's chest, squeezing his heart so hard he almost couldn't breathe. His Angel was going to wow the crowd today, he was sure of it.

The program he'd been handed on the way in was a mix of hymns and Christmas carols, and they started out strong with an a cappella version of "Carol of the Bells" that left the audience in a brief stunned silence after they finished. Then Ethan's palms hurt for his clapping, but music swelled over the sound system, and the choir launched directly into "Angels We Have Heard on High."

Song after song was sung with perfect grace, the music washing over Ethan's soul and calming the self-hatred that had dogged him since yesterday. His fingers twitched, picking with an invisible guitar. After he followed along to "O Holy Night," the music changed to something slightly heavier. Moodier but still lovely.

Angel and an older woman stepped out of line and walked to a pair of microphones. Ethan's heart hammered.

His Angel had a solo.

The choir hummed an opening, and then Angel's beautiful tenor began to sing. *"Mary did you know…?"*

Ethan wanted to close his eyes and let Angel's voice wash over him, but he couldn't look away from the joy radiating from Angel's face as he sang. "Mary Did You Know?" was his mother's favorite song, and the first time he'd heard it on the radio, Ethan had gotten chills. He got chills again that morning, because the performance was stunning. The woman backed Angel up several times, the choir never stopped humming, and Ethan had never heard a more perfect thing in his life.

He didn't care that he had tears in his eyes when it was over. Mom dabbed at hers with a tissue. Ethan longed to race onto that stage and sweep Angel into his arms. To hug him and kiss him and tell him how amazing he was, audience or not. He stayed seated and clapped until his hands ached. For a moment, Angel's eyes met his, and Ethan's heart flipped. Angel's shy smile imprinted itself on his memory and did something funny to his insides.

The pair returned to their spots on the risers, and the choir ended the performance with a brilliant mash-up of so many different carols that Ethan had trouble catching them all. They finished with a powerful final verse from "Do You Hear What I Hear?" that had the audience standing for an ovation before the last notes petered out.

Mom helped Ethan stand so he could applaud too, and his height helped him look right at Angel's smiling, red-cheeked face. The choir bowed, and then Reverend Jameson returned to the stage with a folding chair in his hands, which he placed dead center.

That's weird.

Reverend Jameson motioned for everyone to sit, then brought one of the microphones closer to the chair.

Angel stepped away from the others and approached the microphone. His hands were lost to the folds of his robe, but even from a distance, Ethan saw his nerves playing across his expressive face. "This isn't in the program," Angel said, his voice floating across the sanctuary. "But Reverend Jameson said it was okay to add something. And he has no idea this is about to happen, but can Ethan Shockley please join me on stage?"

Surprise jolted through Ethan. Heads turned, seeking him out. He grabbed his cane, curious and a little bit mortified at being the center of attention, but unwilling to leave Angel hanging. Everything in him responded to Angel's call.

Mom helped him get out of the pew, and then he limped down the main aisle to the stage. Angel had produced his guitar from someplace, and Ethan understood immediately.

"Don't be mad," Angel whispered as Ethan settled in the folding chair. He handed over the guitar, using his body to block Ethan from the audience. "This is my way of saying you're worthy, Ethan."

"Making me play off the cuff in front of a hundred people?" Ethan whispered back.

"No. Making you play for me, and for yourself."

Angel moved to the microphone, more confident now than Ethan had ever seen him. "My name is Matthew Garrett, for those who don't know me. I'm an employee at Shockley Farms, and this here is Ethaniel Shockley, Ruth and William's youngest son. Back in August he was in an awful work accident, and he's been home these last few months recuperating. We became friends through our love of music, and I don't think most folks realize what a powerful source of healing music can be."

Ethan stared at his boyfriend's profile, his chest filled to bursting with pride. Angel hadn't stuttered once during that speech. He glanced at Ethan and mouthed, "'Cleanse Me.'"

Without hesitation, Ethan began to play.

* * *

The first time they'd performed this song together, in the quiet of the garage, Angel had sung the lyrics for himself. He'd wanted to share this piece of himself with Ethaniel, the part that had come to terms with prison, and the part that believed he was worthy of living a full, happy life.

Today he sang it for Ethaniel, and for all of the pain he still carried deep inside. Pain that had overwhelmed him the night before and made him lash out. Pain that could be forgiven if Ethaniel allowed himself to believe he was worthy.

Ethaniel played it through twice, and at the end of the second round, he eased into another song. Slower, more powerful for the simple chords he urged from the guitar, and he mouthed the name of the song to Angel.

"*When peace, like a river, attendeth my soul,*" he sang, falling into the simple beauty of "It Is Well" and the personal meaning behind Ethaniel's choice. On the chorus, Angel urged the audience to join them. "*It is well, with my soul….*"

The words settled in Angel's heart, and when he saw the tears sparkling in Ethaniel's eyes, it took everything in him to finish the hymn. He wanted to hug him, to tell him it would be all right, because they could work through anything together. He put all of that into his singing, charging the simple words with the love in his heart and the unfettered joy bursting out of his soul.

"*It is well, it is well, with my soul!*"

This time, along with the applause came several shouted "Amen's" and "Hallelujah's." Reverend Jameson joined them. Ethaniel put his guitar on the chair so he could stand for a firm hug from him. Angel, too.

Instead of to their pew, Angel guided Ethaniel off the side of the stage, and out the door that led to the practice room. He didn't stop there, though, because the emotions churning inside him were too big. Ethaniel limped along until they reached the rarely used kitchen tucked away in the back of the building.

In the privacy of that musty room, Ethaniel wrapped him up in his bigger, rangier body and held tight. Angel buried his face in Ethaniel's shoulder, breathing in the man he loved so much, eyes stinging with emotion. Ethaniel's own breathing was labored, his chest heaving. Hands stroked lightly up and down Angel's back.

"Thank you," Ethaniel said. "Thank you. Thank you."

"Don't thank me."

"How can I not? I'm so sorry about last night."

"Forgiven. I know where it came from." Angel pulled back so he could cup Ethaniel's cheeks in his palms. The wetness in his eyes made Angel's chest tighten. "You are so strong, Ethan. Stronger than you let yourself believe, and that has nothing to do with what your body can or cannot do. You have a strength of spirit I've never seen before, to have survived what you survived and come out of it a loving human being. Please, don't ever doubt again that you're strong."

"You're right." Ethaniel's voice cracked. "I've spent so much time resenting what I've lost that I can't clearly see what I have. I don't want to lose sight of that again." He pressed a chaste kiss to Angel's forehead. "I don't want to lose you."

"You won't. In case you missed it, I'm too stubborn to be scared off for long."

"I noticed. How long have you been planning that?"

"About two hours." Angel grinned. "I called Reverend Jameson this morning and asked about it." Ethaniel tensed, so he clarified. "I didn't tell him about us or our fight. I told him how you've helped me with my stuttering, and about how we'd been playing together, and how that was helping your depression over the accident. He thought it was a great idea for us to play today."

Ethaniel relaxed, his lips twitching into an amused smile. "I never figured you for a schemer."

"I have my moments. Especially when I want something."

"And what is it that you want?"

"Exactly what I have." Angel pressed his palm against Ethaniel's heart. "You."

"I'm all yours."

"Yes, you are." He rested his head over his hand and enjoyed the steady sound of Ethaniel's heartbeat. "And I'm yours."

They held each other a few minutes longer, until Ethaniel's leg ached too much to remain standing. Angel helped him limp out to the vestibule, where his parents, Jillian, and Sarah waited for them. Jillian held his guitar case, and William smiled proudly at both of them. Ruth hugged them soundly, and Angel realized in his heart what the Shockleys had been telling him for months.

This was his family.

They were home.

CHAPTER SIXTEEN

After a light lunch of chicken noodle soup, and a quick stop in his bedroom, Ethan allowed Angel to help him traverse the long stairs to Angel's apartment. He hadn't felt so settled in years. Something about letting go on that stage, giving up his fears and regrets in worship, had freed him of so many things he couldn't even name. His soul felt lighter, more free to live and be happy.

He would never stop missing Andy and Butch, but he let go of some of his survivor's guilt. They wouldn't have wanted him to spend his life regretting the fact that he'd lived while his friends had died. He couldn't love Angel the way Angel deserved if he couldn't start loving himself again.

Angel locked the door behind them, and Ethan's heart gave a funny twist at the new automatic action. Even in broad daylight with someone else there, Angel needed the safety net of a locked door.

Ethan hobbled over to the couch and sank into the squishy cushions. Angel curled up next to him, his head in Ethan's lap. Ethan stroked his hair and neck, enjoying something as simple as existing together in a quiet moment, with absolutely nothing important to do.

"It was a needle prick," Angel said, apropos of nothing.

Ethan stared at his profile, his confusion lasting only a moment before he realized what Angel was confessing. Answering a question Ethan had never been able to make himself ask.

Angel rolled onto his back so he was looking at Ethan. His face was relaxed, but his eyes were stormy. "I managed to get to my third day in prison before I was assaulted the first time. It landed me in the infirmary for a day, and I got talking with one of the inmate volunteers. He gave me advice on how to survive, and I was so scared of it happening again I did what he suggested. I became exactly what Daniel said I was. A bitch to a big guy who could protect me in exchange for sex. And he did. Problem was Kane also had enemies, not only inmates but guards, too."

Ethan forced himself to remain quiet and relaxed while his insides were burning with rage. Imagining what Angel had experienced and hearing it firsthand were two entirely different animals, and he silently hated the men who'd hurt Angel. He wanted to cut their dicks off and shove them up their own predatory asses. Instead, he listened to Angel's truth.

"Since killing got a life sentence tacked on to whatever you're serving, guys got real creative when they wanted someone gone. One of the guards got involved in a plan to get Kane out of gen pop and into the HIV ward by stabbing him with a needle that had infected blood in it. Only when it was supposed to go down, a fight broke out and I got stabbed instead."

Angel's left hand drifted to his lower back. "Here. I didn't know what poked me at first, not until everything got sorted. Then I got transferred to segregation, and because a guard was involved and my lawyer was lawsuit happy, I got my parole eligibility reduced from five years to three."

Small favors.

"It's a weird, complicated, could-only-happen-in-prison sort of story," Angel continued, "which is why I'm glad few people know. I hate explaining it all. It's so stupid, you know? A needle jab during a fight."

"It's better than some of the alternatives," Ethan said, surprised at how rough his voice was. He cleared his throat hard, not wanting to think about the other, more violent ways Angel could have been infected.

Angel nodded. "I know. I'm not proud of myself for needing someone else to protect me, but it helped me survive with more pieces of my soul intact. I know that for certain."

"Good. I'm glad you survived, Angel. I don't blame you for anything you did back then. It got you here to me." He tugged Angel into a hug. Angel shifted so he was sitting in Ethan's lap, their arms wrapped firmly around each other.

Ethan closed his eyes and relaxed into the heat of the body pressed so tightly to his, the heart beating wildly against his chest.

"I don't blame you for anything you did in the past, either," Angel whispered. "And neither should you, because it brought *you* here to *me*."

The scent of scorched stone and smoke tried to fill his nostrils, but Ethan clung to Angel, using him to stay grounded and out of the flashback poking at the edges of his consciousness. He had to say it. He hadn't said it out loud to anyone since his discharge interview, and he could tell Angel. Angel wouldn't look at him like the monster he saw in the mirror every day.

"I killed a woman for running toward us carrying what I thought was an explosive." His throat tightened with the emotion he'd felt when he had looked at the thing in the dead woman's hands. "It was a camera, not a bomb. She was trying to get out of the line of fire, away from the fighting, and I killed her."

The bright red of arterial blood filled his vision, pumping out of the bullet holes he'd put in her neck and face. He started shaking. Angel held him tighter, whispering words he couldn't hear, stroking his back and hair. Keeping him together while the emotions bubbled up and out like toxic lava, scorching his skin and his heart and leaving ash behind.

"You were protecting your unit, babe, you were in a war," Angel said. "You saved your friends and yourself."

Ethan choked, tasting copper. "She wasn't a threat."

"You didn't know that."

"Doesn't absolve me."

"It also doesn't incriminate you. I know this haunts you. I know you hate yourself for killing her, but what if she *had* been carrying an explosive? It could have easily gone the other way, and you'd be dead."

Some of that ash blew away, leaving a little bit of himself intact. Intact and listening, hearing the words for the first time. Therapists had told him the same thing, over and over, and Ethan hadn't wanted to listen. He hadn't been ready to accept that innocent people died during war, and it wasn't necessarily his fault.

Hearing Angel say it stirred the possibility that maybe, just maybe, he could forgive himself for killing that nameless women in a back alley during the worst few years of his life.

"Thank you for telling me," Angel said. "It won't make it better all at once, but sharing the burden with someone willing to help you carry it? It helps."

"Yes, it does." Ethan hugged Angel so tightly he feared hurting him, but Angel simply clung to him. His guardian Angel. "Thank you."

The first hints of a headache poked behind his eyes. Ethan rested his forehead on Angel's shoulder, willing it to go away. And because he was amazing, Angel said, "You want to go lie down? You have to be exhausted after everything."

"Good idea."

Angel helped him to the bedroom, and Ethan didn't care that he needed the support. He unbuttoned his dress shirt and shrugged out of it. Once Angel had him settled under the covers, Angel took off his own shirt and slacks, then curled up next to him in only his boxers. Ethan curled an arm around his shoulders and held tight, while his head continued to pound. Sleep stole in quickly, and he lost himself to pleasant thoughts of the nearly naked man next to him.

* * *

Angel lay awake long after he felt Ethaniel go under, contemplating the things they'd said to each other and marveling at all they'd managed to overcome. He ached for Ethaniel's pain while celebrating the progress he'd made tonight. They'd shared their worst truths and come out the other side stronger than ever.

By some fortuitous sequence of events, he and Ethaniel had found each other in the most unexpected place, when neither of them was even looking for a relationship, and that was the biggest miracle of all.

He pressed harder against Ethaniel, enjoying the heat of his resting body. Something poked into his hip. Curious, he investigated the pocket of Ethaniel's pants and discovered two condoms and a small bottle of lubricant. The sight of those items sent a blast of need through Angel's body so intense he actually moaned and started getting hard.

His erection rode Ethaniel's hip and upper thigh, and it took all of his self-control not to start humping Ethaniel like an over-eager pup. Except he *was* eager. For the first time in six years he *wanted* to have sex, and he wanted it to be with Ethaniel. He wanted it to be Ethaniel for always.

He pressed gentle kisses along Ethaniel's neck and collarbone, tasting the skin, exploring with his tongue. Ethaniel made a soft, breathy sound, still asleep. Angel skimmed fingers across Ethaniel's chest, drawing nonsensical patterns along his pecs, around his dusky nipples. Little buds he longed to lick and suck on. He didn't want to take too many liberties while Ethaniel was sleeping, so he limited his actions to those simple things.

Ethaniel huffed and shifted, and then his eyes opened. "Mmm, feels good."

"Yeah?" Angel boldly pinched his left nipple, and Ethaniel gasped.

The hand on his hip slid down to squeeze Angel's ass, pressing his erection harder into Ethaniel's thigh. "Oh yeah."

"Your head hurt?"

"Not much." His free hand drew Angel's head up for a firm kiss. "I brought stuff if you're ready."

Angel's heart tripped at the gentle way Ethaniel was taking care of him with words. "I found it, and I'm definitely ready." He skated a hand down Ethaniel's belly, into the waist of his pants, under the elastic of his briefs, and clasped the waiting erection. "Feels like you are too."

Ethaniel laughed. "Oh baby, I am so ready. But only if you're sure."

"I've never been more sure." He licked the nipple closest to his mouth, enjoying the way Ethaniel gasped and pushed against his hand. Angel stroked his dick lightly, a teasing motion hindered by the layers of fabric still covering him.

The hand on his ass dipped below his boxers to cup skin, and Angel's belly wobbled. He couldn't explain the hesitation he'd carried for so long, the unwillingness to be totally naked for Ethaniel. To let Ethaniel take care of him the way Angel enjoyed taking care of Ethaniel. That stopped today. Today Angel wanted everything.

He sat up and shoved the covers away so he could wrangle Ethaniel out of his pants. He'd put the boot on over his dress slacks so it took some careful maneuvering to get him naked and the boot back on to protect his weak leg. Once that task was done and Ethaniel was splayed out for him in his bed, Angel swung a leg over his hip and sat on his lower belly. The same position from their first time together—his hard cock on Ethaniel's stomach, and Ethaniel's wood poking his ass.

Ethaniel gazed up at him with so much emotion in his eyes, trusting in whatever Angel did next. Angel stretched out across his chest and kissed his way into Ethaniel's mouth. Lips and tongues and wet heat, and it was everything Angel had ever wanted. Ethaniel's hands kneaded his ass, urging him to thrust gently against Ethaniel's stomach, and that was good. So good.

They kissed for a long time, because they had all the time in the world. Time to explore and exist and taste. Angel breathed Ethaniel in until they were the same person, moving together, making Angel dizzy with it. He licked a path across Ethaniel's jaw to his neck, where he took his time exploring the lightly whiskered skin under his chin.

"Angel."

He lifted his head, and the desperation in Ethaniel's eyes rocketed down his spine.

"I want to suck you," Ethaniel said. "Please."

Anxiety flashed hot and cold through his chest, but Angel couldn't say no. He could, however, protect his lover. Angel climbed off, then shimmied out of his boxers, baring himself for the first time. Ethaniel's expression went dark and lust-filled, and Angel's fingers trembled as he opened the condom and rolled it onto himself.

Ethaniel shifted higher, sitting straight up against the pillows. Angel wasn't tall enough to kneel so he stood and bent his knees enough to bring himself to the right height. Hands braced on the wall, thighs trembling with anticipation, Angel offered himself to his lover.

The first press of lips and heat nearly sent Angel out of his skin. He had to stop himself from giving in and thrusting into Ethaniel's mouth. A hot, seductive mouth that worked him like a man deprived of something precious for far too long. Ethaniel cupped his ass, kneading both cheeks, while he sucked him in deeper. Angel groaned and closed his eyes, unable to keep them open as his nerve endings buzzed with pleasure and need.

Why did I deny him this for so long?

He braced one forearm on the wall and grabbed Ethaniel's head with his free hand, fingers threading into his thick hair. Needing that contact. Ethaniel made a sound like a purr and it vibrated through Angel's dick, into his balls.

"Oh God," he gasped.

Ethaniel did it again, and Angel cried out, unable to stop himself because it felt so damned amazing. The hands on his ass urged him forward and back, helping Angel slowly fuck Ethaniel's mouth, and he'd never seen a sexier sight than Ethaniel peering up at him from beneath a fan of dark eyelashes, lips stretched tight around Angel's cock.

Hands fell away from his ass. Angel thrust gently, watching Ethaniel's face for any signal that he was uncomfortable. All he saw was lust and adoration and tenderness. Little things that Angel had never seen before from a sex partner, and he treasured every single second of this. Then a slick finger pressed between his cheeks, down to his entrance, and Angel gasped.

Ethaniel's gaze went utterly wicked, and that finger pressed harder. Angel tried to relax, and the duel sensations of a mouth on his dick and a finger pushing into his ass made the task seem impossible. Ethaniel pulled back so he could suck hard on the crown, and Angel wasn't entirely sure what kind of sound he made then. The single digit worked its way inside to the first knuckle, a familiar pressure he needed more of. He pushed against Ethaniel's hand, urging him to go deeper, to stretch him wider.

Yes.

"Oh fuck," Angel said.

"Soon, baby." Ethaniel licked the length of him. "Want two?"

"Yeah. Oh God, yes."

Two was almost too much, the burn so harsh Angel couldn't breathe—until Ethaniel curled them and brushed his spot, and Angel might have screamed. He didn't know, didn't care. All he knew was Ethaniel's fingers and mouth, and the loving, tender care Ethaniel was taking with him. His senses were alive, buzzing with pleasure, and too soon his balls drew up, warning him.

"Stop."

Ethaniel ceased touching him immediately, his concern clear. Angel squatted over him, putting them at eye level. "Too close," he said. Ethaniel smiled, that concern melting into need. "Want you in me when I come."

"So do I." Ethaniel stole his breath with a long, lingering kiss.

"Just like this." Missionary would be too hard on Ethaniel's leg, and Angel needed to see his face.

He opened the second condom and rolled it down Ethaniel's length. He used applying more lube as a good excuse to stroke him a few times, slow and steady, enjoying the way Ethaniel's nostrils flared and his breath hitched from something as simple as Angel's touch. A touch he'd felt before but that was different this time.

Different because they were finally making love.

Angel rose up and edged backward a few inches. Ethaniel steadied him with a firm grip on his hips. Relying on touch, because no way could he break eye contact now, Angel notched Ethaniel's cock at his entrance and bore down. The pressure made him gasp, and then groan long and low as Ethaniel breached him.

"Ethan, fuck."

"I've got you."

Angel had no doubts about that. He lowered himself, taking in more of Ethaniel's cock, and the gentle ache became an unrelenting burn that sent anxiety fluttering beneath his breastbone. He fought against the need to pull away, to get free, because he wasn't being forced. He wasn't giving anything up that he didn't want to. He was with Ethaniel, a man who'd cut his own dick off before hurting Angel.

He was safe.

A rough palm cupped his cheek, and Angel opened his eyes, uncertain when he'd closed them. Ethaniel's green eyes shone with love and that was enough to shatter Angel's hesitation. He sank down onto Ethaniel's erection, seating him fully, and then pulled up again. Down. The burn settled into the sweetest sense of pressure and fullness, and Angel let out a half-laugh, half-gasp of pure joy.

"You are so beautiful," Ethaniel said.

Angel kissed him hard. "Love you."

"Love you too."

They rocked together, setting a slow, sensual pace. Angel's still-covered dick and balls rubbed across Ethaniel's abs, enough pressure to keep him toeing the edge without going over. He took his time exploring every inch of Ethaniel's mouth with his tongue, tasting his skin, occasionally plucking at a nipple. They moved as one, creating something so perfect Angel wanted to exist there always.

His orgasm came quickly and unexpectedly, the condom catching his release, and Ethaniel kissed him through it until it all became too much. His sensitized body trembled, and he barely had the strength to scoot down Ethaniel's body so he could peel off the condom and suck him to completion. Ethaniel shouted. Hands tangled in his hair. It only took a few solid pulls before Ethaniel was pumping into his mouth.

Angel swallowed it all.

"Fuck, that was amazing," Ethaniel said. He slid farther down the bed, and Angel climbed up, flopping onto his chest. Boneless and sated and so happy he didn't have the words.

His body hummed with contentment and joy, and Angel had never been happier in his life. Everything felt right, from the gentle aches in his body to the scents of sweat and musk all around them. The rise and fall of Ethaniel's breathing. The hand lazily stroking his back.

"Angel?"

"Hmm?"

"You okay?"

Angel lifted his head, smiling so hard his cheeks hurt. "I'm perfect."

Ethaniel's green eyes glittered. "Yeah?"

"Yes. So much yes."

"Good." He sifted his fingers through Angel's hair. "You make me so happy."

"Same." Angel kissed his chin, then settled his head over Ethaniel's heart, listening to the steady beat beneath his ear. "Can we stay like this forever?"

"Definitely."

Forever could be five minutes or five hours, but it didn't matter. They'd do this again and again, and Angel had never been happier in his life.

CHAPTER SEVENTEEN

Four weeks and a lot of physical therapy later, Ethan said goodbye to the goddamn boot and hello to real shoes again. He still needed the cane, thanks to a limp and a leg that was a lot of PT appointments away from being fully healed. The doctors all warned him he might always have a limp, but Ethan remained optimistic.

Wasn't a positive attitude part of the healing process?

He also spent more nights in Angel's apartment than in his own bed, something that no one commented on, not even his parents. Daniel had been on his best behavior during Thanksgiving dinner, but their father hadn't lifted the ban on living there again. Caleb said Daniel was drinking a lot at night and keeping him up when he needed to sleep, and the strain was beginning to show. Ethan had overheard Dad tell Caleb he could move into the main house, but Caleb had refused. He was too concerned about what Daniel might do if he was left on his own.

They all worried. Daniel made his appointments with his parole officer, and Russ verified Daniel worked at the stables—despite the fact that the most Daniel ever managed, according to Angel, was to polish a few saddles. Russ kept him away from the horses and for good reason. The man was too angry all the time, and animals sensed those things.

Ethan's thirtieth birthday passed with a simple cake and ice cream celebration in Angel's apartment, followed by several long, sensual hours making love, and it was perfect.

Another heavy snow fell the week before Christmas, giving Sarah a handful of snow days before the official winter break. Ethan enjoyed having her home as a distraction. His leg was healing, but his reading and computer time hadn't improved much. He could eat a few more things than before, but his stomach was still crazy sensitive to motion and smells.

Almost five months since he fell through that roof and he was still a mess. His depression got the best of him now and again, but Angel helped him through it with tender patience Ethaniel didn't always think he deserved. Angel knew he didn't want to try anti-depressants because of his body's tendency to hate medications and react badly, and he worked Ethaniel through the bad spells with love and support.

The Sunday before Christmas, Mom invited Daniel to dinner. He threw a few nasty looks Ethan and Angel's way, but kept his rude mouth shut for most of the meal. Dad even invited him to stay and watch TV afterward with him and Caleb. Jillian asked to speak with Daniel privately before he watched TV, and the pair went upstairs.

Sarah didn't have homework so she stayed in the kitchen and played UNO with him and Angel. The kid was a shark at that game, and Ethan couldn't wait teach her how to play poker.

Something thudded directly overhead. Ethan looked up, as if that would tell him what had been dropped. A muffled, angry voice had him up and charging for the stairs, cane forgotten, his leg protesting the sudden use.

All he needed to hear was "cheating whore" to make his blood boil. He shoved Jillian's bedroom door open, pausing long enough to take in Jillian on the floor, hands covering her face, and then he launched himself at Daniel.

Training took over, and he had Daniel flat on the ground, one arm twisted up tight, his face in the carpet and a knee in his back. "You son of a bitch."

"Ethan, what—crap, Jillian?" Angel's voice, somewhere in the room.

Daniel bucked. "Get the fuck off me."

"What did you do?" Ethan snapped.

"Nothing she didn't deserve, the cunt."

He pressed harder into the small of Daniel's back, enjoying the pained grunt that got. "Try again, asshole."

"Ethan, that's enough." Dad, his voice shaky with anger. "Let him go."

Ethan tightened his grip once, then backed off. He nearly fell over trying to stand, because of his damned leg, but Angel was there to hold him upright.

Jillian was sobbing in Mom's arms. Dad and Caleb stood near the women, both ready to do battle if necessary.

"This is why," Jillian said. "This is why, right here. I can't do this anymore."

"Do what, honey?" Mom asked.

"She wants to fucking divorce me," Daniel snarled. "Sixteen years together, and she wants to leave me."

"Can you fucking blame her?" Ethan's temper was soaring to nuclear levels, and only Angel's touch kept him from knocking his brother senseless.

"No but I can fucking blame you! Did you tell her to do this, huh? My kid already loves you more than me, so why not take my wife away, too?"

"It wasn't Jillian's idea," Mom said. "It was mine."

Daniel turned his furious glare to the women in the room. "How dare you?"

Mom passed Jillian over to Caleb, then stood, shoulders back. "Jillian is as much my daughter as Abigail or Lesley, and she always will be. She waited for you, Daniel, but you aren't the man she married. You aren't the man I raised, either."

"Yeah? Then who am I?"

Grief flashed briefly on her face. "I don't know anymore."

"You're unwelcome in this house," Dad said. "Get out before I call the police."

Daniel looked at each of them in turn, his anger becoming something thick and heavy in the room. Ethan watched him carefully in case he lashed out again. He didn't, choosing to shove his way past him and Angel, and to storm down the stairs.

Ethan sat on the bed before he collapsed, limbs shaking now that the adrenaline rush that had carried him upstairs began to wane. Angel stayed close, his own body trembling a little.

"I knew he'd be angry," Jillian said as her sobs subsided. "But he said such awful things to me." She lifted her head from Caleb's shoulder, and the dark spot on her cheekbone made Ethan's temper flare. "He's never hit me before."

"You did nothing wrong," Dad said. "That boy's got so much anger inside of him. I don't understand it."

"Sarah." She glanced around the room. "Where's Sarah?"

"I told her to stay in the kitchen," Angel said. "She didn't need to see this."

Something dark slithered in Ethan's gut. "Can you go check on her? Please."

"Sure."

Mom went with Angel, and Ethan sent up a silent prayer that his gut was wrong. Dad helped Ethan limp his way to the top of the stairs. Going down was not going to be fun.

"Sarah?" Mom's voice carried clearly from the living room, and then Angel's from the kitchen.

No.

"Ruth?" Dad called. They started down the stairs, pausing when Jillian shoved past them, shouting her daughter's name.

At the bottom, Ethan clutched at the wall, leg throbbing, while everyone else scrambled around the house. Caleb and Dad grabbed their coats and went outside. Ethan watched helplessly as his unspoken fear came true in the frantic shouts of his family, and the fear chilling the air around him.

Sarah was missing.

* * *

Angel did his best to keep Ethaniel distracted while he was banned to the living room sofa with an ice pack on his swollen leg. He'd done too much, but even his obvious pain didn't stop Ethaniel from trying to get up and help. Not that either of them could do much at the moment.

The state police were there, assisting in the search of the vast property, but the fact that Daniel was missing, too, along with Caleb's truck, pointed at the very real possibility of kidnapping.

Because of Daniel's violent behavior and being on parole, an Amber Alert was issued for Sarah, and an APB put out on Daniel for possible parole violations.

Benny's wife Lesley came to sit vigil with the women, while Benny joined in the land search. Eventually Abigail arrived, too, her normally perfect hair and makeup messy, like she'd rolled herself out of bed. Ruth started baking things to keep herself busy, and soon the house filled with scents of cinnamon and apples.

As one hour turned to four, and then six, with no sign of Sarah or Daniel, a heavy blanket of responsibility settled on Angel's shoulders. Grief struck him all at once, and he sagged to the floor near Ethaniel. A hand ruffled his hair, and he pulled away from the touch, not wanting to be comforted.

"Angel?" Ethaniel said.

"I told her to stay in the kitchen."

"So?"

"So it made her vulnerable to Daniel."

"Asking her to stay put was the right thing to do. She didn't need to see her parents like that."

"But—"

"No buts. Look at me."

Angel twisted his neck to look at him sideways. Ethaniel's eyes burned with a lot of things, mostly fear and anger, but also determination.

"This isn't your fault," Ethaniel said. "All of this is Daniel. All of it."

"If I'd pressed charges last month, he'd be in jail now. Sarah would be home safe."

"Doesn't matter. If I don't get to what-if myself about the past, then you don't either. We can't change it. All we can do is live with it. You hear me?"

Angel wanted to argue but he couldn't. Ethaniel was right. There was no changing what he did or didn't do, and Daniel alone was responsible for Sarah being missing. No one believed she'd run away, or that Daniel taking Caleb's truck was a coincidence. They were together, heading God knew where.

The amazing part of the entire drama was the way the Shockley family pulled together. All of the siblings were involved, and their spouses were either helping or at home watching over their own kids. Someone was on the phone with someone else all the time. Even Russ returned to the farm to do nothing more than be there for the family he'd worked for most of his life.

I'm part of this family.

The realization hit him in the heart so hard he couldn't breathe for a moment. Looking at Ethaniel, so handsome and strong and *his*, made Angel incredibly grateful for his life. No matter what he'd done to get here, this was where he was meant to be.

The clock inched past two in the morning, and they still had no news. Jillian had been installed in William's recliner with a glass of brandy to calm her nerves a little. Abigail had offered a Xanax, which Jillian turned down. Angel was pretty sure Abigail slipped one into Ruth's coffee mug, because as the hour wore closer to three, Ruth seemed less highly strung.

Everyone was exhausted from worry and stress, and a few times Angel's head fell backward against Ethaniel's leg. Each time,

Ethaniel finger-combed his hair, as if reminding himself they were both still there. Together.

"Some of you might as well go to bed," Ruth announced at quarter after three. "We can't all stay up and expect to function in the morning. Jillian?"

"I can't." Jillian had downed the brandy, but tears still leaked from both eyes. "Not while my baby is out there with that lunatic."

Ruth frowned. "Ethan? Angel? You boys should go get some rest."

"I can rest right here," Ethaniel said.

"Yes, well, you can, but Angel can't unless he climbs on top of you."

Angel's face burned and he ducked his head.

Ethaniel's hand rested on his shoulder. "You should go lie down for a bit in the downstairs bed."

He pressed his chin against Ethaniel's fingers. "Only if you come. You're going to stress yourself into a migraine."

"Already have."

Angel sat up straighter and turned around on his knees. All the little signs were there—the crinkles at the corners of his eyes, the flat press of his lips, the deeper shadows under his eyes. "Why didn't you say something?"

"This isn't about me."

"Shut up. Ruth?"

"I'll get his pills," she said. "And an ice pack."

Angel pressed a palm against Ethaniel's clammy cheek. "You don't have to suffer because of this, you know. It's not brave."

His lips twitched up. "Sorry." Then down again. "I'm such a mess."

"Maybe, but I still love you. You need to tell me when you're in pain, okay? I know you don't like it, but *I* like helping you. It's part of the job description."

"I don't think I got a copy of that."

"Well, right at the top it says 'thou shalt allow thy partner to help thee in moments of pain and crisis'."

Ethaniel's mouth broke into a full-on smile. "Partners, huh?"

He leaned in so he could whisper the words meant only for Ethaniel. "I'm in this for the long haul, if you are."

Those green eyes he loved so much softened. "I am too."

With Ruth's help, they got Ethaniel down the hall and tucked into bed, a fresh ice pack on his leg and two pills down his throat. Angel shucked his shoes, but left his jeans on in case of emergency, and climbed into bed. He snuggled up close to Ethaniel, soaking in his body heat, warm under the blankets in a winter-chilled room.

Ethaniel looped an arm around him, a familiar weight. In the dark of the night, he asked what had probably been on his mind all night. "Why?"

Angel knew but asked anyway. "Why what?"

"Why did Daniel take her? What does he hope to accomplish? She's already scared of him, and this is only going to make it worse. The family is going to hate him."

"Maybe that's what he wants."

Ethaniel tensed. "What do you mean?"

Angel struggled for the right words. He didn't want this to come out wrong and upset Ethaniel. "From what you've told me about Daniel from high school onward, he's always felt like a victim. Like he's been given a raw deal, therefore everyone else is responsible for his behavior. Does that sound right?"

"Yes."

"Prison made all those feelings worse. He blames you for him being there, even though it wasn't your fault. He blames you for Sarah not liking him which is, again, not your fault. Hell, he blamed you for Jillian wanting a divorce, even though it was Ruth's idea."

"Okay, but that doesn't explain kidnapping his kid."

"My guess is he's proving he's the bad seed everyone thinks he is. He's imploding his life on purpose so he can play the victim and blame his family for his bad behavior. He'll blame it on Jillian for wanting a divorce, I guarantee it, and he'll probably still find a way to blame you."

Ethaniel let out a long, angry breath. "I don't know what I did to make him hate me so much. I really don't."

"You left. He said it to your dad, he didn't want anything to do with the horses, just like you. But instead of joining the Army or moving to another state, he got married too young, ended up strapped down here, and meanwhile his little brother is off to see the world."

"Some world."

"You two were inseparable for a while, and then you left, Ethan. He couldn't."

"Well damn. That...actually makes a lot of sense."

Angel pinched his nipple through his shirt. "Gee, thanks."

"Ow, don't do that, my head hurts too much to play. And I really don't feel like vomiting tonight."

"I'll behave, promise."

Ethaniel was quiet for a while. "It really does make sense, what you said. Daniel and Jillian got married when they were eighteen because she got pregnant. She miscarried, but the deed was done, and then she was pregnant with Sarah, and then Daniel was in jail."

"Meanwhile you were out there living your life. Daniel had no way of knowing how awful things were in Afghanistan, or how much you struggled when you came home, because he didn't want to know. He was content hating you, and it hurts me to think he might never stop hating you."

"Why does that hurt?"

Angel flattened his palm over Ethaniel's heart. "Because I love you, and when you're upset, I'm upset. He's your brother."

"He hasn't been my brother for a long, long time. I'm finally seeing that."

"I'm sorry."

Ethaniel stroked his hair, a comforting touch. "Don't be. Be sorry for my parents. This is killing them."

"I know. I hate seeing them both in so much pain."

"So do I. They'll get through it, though. They always do."

Angel rubbed his cheek against Ethaniel's chest. "Because they have each other."

Ethaniel made a rusty sound, like a laugh but not. "Point taken. I don't like to think what shape I'd be in if I hadn't come home and found you here. You gave me something to get better for, Angel. You make me want to think past the next few minutes and have a real future."

Something warm and wonderful curled around Angel's heart. "Same. We'll get through this, Ethan. All of us."

Tangled together, they dozed until the first edges of dawn brightened the room and awareness stole back over Angel. He listened to Ethaniel's steady breathing until other sounds hinted that daylight wasn't what woke him. A commotion downstairs had him sitting up, fast enough to startle Ethaniel awake.

"Wassup?" he mumbled.

"I'm not sure." Angel threw back the covers, but before he could get out of bed the bedroom door swung open.

Abigail grinned so brightly at them that Angel didn't have to ask. "The police found Daniel and Sarah up near Wilmington. She's not hurt. They're bringing her home."

"Thank Christ," Ethaniel said. "Daniel?"

"Jail." Her smile turned grim. "And he's gonna stay there, too. No way is anyone in this family ponying up for bail, even if he's granted it." Someone called Abigail's name. "Sorry, one of the kids needs me."

Ethaniel waved her off.

Angel curled around him in a gentle hug, unsure of Ethaniel's current state and unwilling to risk a jostling hug, despite the fact that his insides were doing happy somersaults over the news. Ethaniel held him so tightly Angel briefly feared for his oxygen supply, but Ethaniel gentled his hold. Angel lifted his head, unsurprised to see tears in Ethaniel's eyes.

"My girl's coming home," Ethaniel said, voice hoarse with emotion.

"Yes, she is." Angel pressed a soft kiss to his lips. "She's coming home to her family."

"And my brother is going away again."

"I wouldn't wish prison on anyone, but Daniel is too angry to be anywhere else right now. He's angry and dangerous, and your family doesn't need that around."

Ethaniel cupped the back of his neck. "Our family. Our family doesn't need that around."

Angel smiled. "Our family."

He really, really loved the sound of that.

Chapter Eighteen

Christmas Day - One Year Later

Ethan held the kitchen door for Angel, who bore the brunt of the gifts they'd brought down from the apartment to lavish upon the family. Ethan had a few gift bags in his left hand, his cane in his right, and the door by his hip, and the entire production got them both inside and out of the freezing cold.

The familiar scents of cinnamon and bacon greeted him, a caress of memories following along. Ghostly images of Mom at the stove, preparing Christmas morning brunch for the family, who all ended up filling the house by ten a.m., after the grandkids had opened gifts at their respective homes. It was only a few minutes past nine, and from the relative quiet—and lack of cars outside—he and Angel were the first to arrive.

Jillian looked up from the stove where she was frying bacon to keep warm in the oven for later. She wore a silly Christmas sweater with a stitched cartoon reindeer on it—a gift from Sarah last Christmas. She'd given Ethan a similar one, which he'd worn last night to the Christmas Eve service at church.

Mom would have loved it.

"Uncle Ethan!" Sarah bounced in from the living room and carefully hugged his waist. "Uncle Angel! Merry Christmas!"

"Merry Christmas, sprout," Ethan replied. "Can you help Uncle Angel with some of those presents."

She eyeballed the precarious stack in Angel's arms. "Are any of them for me?"

"A couple might be."

"Yay!" She unburdened Angel of two small boxes and ran off to the living room.

Angel laughed as he followed her. Oh, to the have energy of a nine year-old again. Ethan hobbled after the pair of them so he could deposit his gift bags. Dad was in his recliner clutching a mug of coffee. When Ethan leaned down for a quick hug, he caught a whiff of bourbon with the dark roast.

He didn't begrudge his dad a drink on the man's first Christmas without Mom in forty-three years.

The tree, which Sarah had helped pick out from the woods around the property, had been decorated to the hilt with ornaments, garlands, and lights—a lifetime's collection of memories in each bauble hung with a wire hook. After putting his gifts under the tree, Ethan sought out his Baby's First Christmas ornament. The blue teddy bear was hugging a rattle, and on his white belly were the words "Ethaniel Ezekiel" and the year he was born.

All five baby ornaments hung in a cluster, even Daniel's. Despite the additional years in prison last winter's stunt with Sarah had given him, Mom had still loved her wayward son, and she'd continued to visit until she too sick to make the trip. She'd kept the return of her cancer a secret for months, its aggressive appearance in her brain and lungs a death sentence she hadn't wanted to burden her children with.

Ethan, Angel, Jillian, and Dad had been with her when she passed in September, the pain and grief still fresh for them all.

Angel's hand slipped into his and squeezed. "You doing okay?"

"So far." Ethan touched the silver glass angel ornament he'd given Mom last year. She loved angel figurines at Christmas. Dozens were strewn throughout the downstairs. His heart seized with grief, and he blinked back the tears stinging his eyes. Getting through today without breaking down was probably not happening.

"Uncle Angel, look what Santa brought me." Sarah tugged Angel away, which had the simultaneous effect of pulling Ethan back from the tree because Angel didn't let go of his hand.

"What did he bring?" Angel asked.

Sarah held up a complicated Play-Doh contraption that looked like it was quite the mess maker. "See? It's exactly the one I asked for."

"Looks like Santa did good, then." Angel released Ethan's hand so he could squat over the pile of presents. "What's that one there?"

Ethan watched them for a few moments, admiring how at ease Angel was with Sarah. The two had become good friends in the last year, and it warmed Ethan a bit to know that even though her father was a raving asshole, she had another honorary uncle who loved her to bits. Jillian had even approached Ethan a few months ago, asking if it was okay to name Ethan as Sarah's guardian, should anything ever happen to her.

He might have shed a few tears of joy before saying yes.

Jillian and Sarah still lived in the main house. Sarah maintained her room upstairs, while Jillian had moved into the downstairs room after Ethan abandoned it to live in the apartment with Angel. Having Jillian's room farther from Sarah would help in the future, now that Jillian was easing into the world of adult dating. Newly divorced, she hadn't yet brought anyone home to meet Sarah or the family, but Ethan knew she'd find love one day. Jillian was too special, and Sarah deserved a stepfather who would adore her the way she deserved.

The front door banged open. Ethan went into the front hall to greet Caleb and his current girlfriend Susan, and help them add their load of presents to the pile under the tree. Caleb had been cheating on Polly the previous fall with Susan, which had caused Caleb and Polly's breakup. Susan had endured a meal full of stink eye from Mom the first time she joined the family for dinner. Susan had charmed Mom, though, more than Polly ever had.

At least Caleb was happy again, and far less stressed out than when he'd been maintaining an engagement while falling in love with another woman.

Ethan wandered into the kitchen where Jillian was doing her best to fill in for Mom, cooking and getting the formal table set. All of the food would be placed on the counter and kitchen table buffet-style, so the family could eat as they pleased. She already had one end of the table piled high with muffins and Christmas cookies.

He helped himself to a lemon cookie, one of the few sugary treats that his stomach could handle—probably because of the lemon. Not even his doctor could explain why lemon didn't upset him, but eating an orange was playing Russian roulette with his insides. Angel and Jillian shared daily dinner duties, and neither one had ever complained about Ethan's slowly widening but still very restricted diet.

Russ and his wife Helen arrived next with gifts for the various kids, and right after came Abigail and her brood. Always the last to arrive, Benny and Lesley rounded their hellion sons into the living room. The tree had exploded with gifts, wrapped in all colors and styles of paper, gift bags overflowing with tissue. Gift-giving was usually contained to the kids, with the siblings drawing names and swapping a single gift.

Everyone was feeling extra sentimental this year, and no one had stuck to the tradition. Ruth's unexpected passing in September had left a big hole in the Shockley family dynamic. No amount of Christmas presents would fill it, but the thrill of opening a gift and finding something unexpected and wonderful could help them forget for a little while.

His assorted nieces and nephews wanted presents, but brunch was always first. Ethan tempted fate by adding a single piece of bacon to his dry pancake. He took a corner of the sofa, instead of the formal table, so the concentrated food smells didn't bother his stomach, which was playing along so far. Headaches were fewer and farther between now, and his neurologist was optimistic about his continued improvement.

He'd escaped that fall with a slight limp, the occasional migraine, and a healthy awareness of exactly what sort of food he put into his body. He'd also fallen in love with the best person he'd ever known, and he'd never been happier. One day he wanted to leave the farm again, to live somewhere else, but not until Angel was ready. Not until Ethan's eyes allowed him more than an hour at a time on the computer, so he could a stable work-from-home job and earn a decent living.

Besides, Angel still needed to find his passion. He was twenty-five, with so many possibilities open to him. If that meant college, then Ethan would wait for him. If Angel one day decided he wanted to stay on at the stables...well, they'd talk about it. They'd figure it all out together.

Angel settled next to him with a simple plate of scrambled eggs and toast, with a corn muffin on the side. Coming out to his family last year hadn't been easy, but no one had been outright rude. Revealing his relationship with Angel had ruffled more than a few feathers, especially from his brothers, but his siblings had taken their lead from their parents. Ruth and William accepted it unconditionally, and so did their kids.

Even if Benny still gave him funny looks once in a while.

Ethan's brothers could believe whatever they wanted about gay people, as long as they continued treating Angel with respect.

Family members came and went from the living room, bringing food and beverages in and out. Ethan worked on his pancake, alternating bites of the bacon slice. By the time Angel took both of their plates to the sink and returned with glasses of iced tea, Ethan was pretty sure his stomach was going to cooperate. Eventually the family amassed in the living room and the present explosion began. Angel stuck close to Ethan's side of the sofa, still distinctly uncomfortable being in such a noisy crowd, and Ethan did his best to keep him centered. A hand on his knee or a squeeze to his shoulder. Small touches to remind Angel that he wasn't alone, no matter what.

All of the kids made out like bandits, with toys and clothes and money from Paps. Ethan gave everyone bags of candy, mostly to annoy their parents. Abigail kept a healthy kitchen, save the occasional holiday indulgence. She even made a teasing "I'll get you" gesture at him over her youngest's head.

Angel had fretted over the need to buy gifts, and in the end he simply signed his name to all of Ethan's. Angel didn't have to prove anything to anyone. Abigail gifted Angel a new pair of work boots, insulated for winter, and Angel blushed so red Ethan feared he would spontaneously combust. Caleb and Benny didn't bother, but they'd joined forces with Abigail to buy Ethan a Northface jacket in a nice navy blue.

"Since your ass doesn't move as fast as it used to," Benny said, "and we can't have it freezing off before you get where you're going."

Ethan flipped them off while he continued to admire the coat. He adored it.

The kids began migrating to other rooms to play once their supply of gifts ran out, until it was only the adults. Benny and Lindsey. Abigail and Mark. Caleb and Susan. Ethan and Angel. Jillian sat alone, smiling, seemingly un-haunted by the ghost of her absent husband. Daniel hadn't been home for Christmas in over a decade. Ethan barely remembered what it was like to have him there for the holiday.

Dad finally got up from his rocker, a little stiffer and more slowly than in months past. A small pile of gifts wrapped in simple red paper was stacked by his chair. "I'm not much of a shopper, never have been," he said. "And your mother, bless her soul, knew it too. I found these things tucked away in our closet after she passed. She'd gone ahead and made up presents for you kids, so I didn't have to think much about it. Some place called Shutterbug or something like it."

Abigail gasped softly. Ethan's throat ached.

Dad slowly started passing the boxes out to the clusters of couples, and one to Jillian. Ethan clasped the small, grapefruit-sized box in both hands, trying not to let them shake. He glanced at Angel, whose round eyes were wide and curious. Mom had ordered Christmas presents months ago, when she knew she wouldn't be with them. She'd thought ahead to make it easier on Dad, and to make sure her kids had something meaningful. When Angel finally met his gaze, it was full of wonder and love, tempered by grief.

He tried to limit public displays of affection in front of his family, mostly because it made Angel uncomfortable, thinking their making out might make his family uncomfortable. But today Ethan needed the soft kiss he pressed to Angel's lips. It gave him the strength to begin peeling away the red wrapping paper.

The paper gave way to a white cardboard box. He ignored exclamations from his siblings and their mates as they dug into their gifts. His fingers trembled as he popped open the box lid and pushed aside a layer of white tissue.

A flat white disc the size of a peach lay in the tissue, a red ribbon looped through a hole on top. He lifted the simple ornament which had the year printed in gold lettering. The image on the opposite side made his breath catch and his heart gallop away.

He had no idea who'd taken the photo, but they'd captured him and Angel on stage at the church. At Easter they'd played

"The Old Rugged Cross" together, and in this photo they were gazing right at each other with the kind of total adoration that was next to impossible to capture in a snapshot. But someone had, and the beautiful photo expressed all of the love he felt for Angel —and the love Angel felt right back.

They hadn't made any sort of official announcement, but they also didn't hide their relationship when they were in church, or while doing the occasional errand around town. Some folks grumbled and turned away, a few shot them dirty looks, but most respected Ethan's parents enough to be quiet and let them live their lives.

"Oh, wow," Angel whispered.

Ethan held the ornament closer so he could study the nuances of the photo, everything from the round shape of Angel's lips as he sang some lyric, to the genuine smile on Ethan's face as he played. He loved performing with Angel. They'd played Christmas carols last night until Ethan's fingers ached. They played almost every single day.

Something warm and wet tracked down Ethan's cheek. Angel wiped it away for him, then wrapped an arm around his shoulders. "It's beautiful."

Ethan could only nod, unable to dislodge the lump in his throat.

"Your mother," Dad said, "she knew how to do right by her kids."

"Yes, she did," Benny replied.

Ethan looked up. All of his siblings had tears in their eyes, and Abigail was openly crying, her face pressed into her husband's shoulder. It looked like they'd all received an ornament of some kind—one last special gift from their mother.

"Can you grab my guitar for me?" Ethan asked.

"Of course." Angel scrambled off the sofa, then returned a few moments later. They'd left the guitar in the house last night.

Ethan arranged the strap and settled the guitar on his lap. "Mom's favorite Christmas song seems appropriate, wouldn't you say?"

Dad nodded, his own face blotchy and sad.

He'd been practicing using online YouTube videos, needing the fingering to be exactly right for today. For the day his private family performance would serve as the greatest of hymns—an offering to God as thanks for the amazing woman who had a smile for everyone, a hug for those in need, and the most generous heart of anyone Ethan had ever known.

Ethan's fingers danced across the strings, plucking the opening chords, giving Angel the signal to begin singing.

"*Mary, did you know that your baby boy...?*" Angel sang clear and bright, capturing the lilting melody of a song that, in its own way, sounded like a prayer. Lesley hummed along, and Caleb sang some of the lines, too. "*...the deaf will hear, the dead will live again, the lame will leap....*"

Ethan didn't try to stop his tears as the power of the lyrics hit him like a jolt to the solar plexus. He was a long way from leaping any real distance, but he had his mobility, and that was something. His life hadn't gone according to any of his own plans, and that was okay. He believed now that God had a plan of His own, and all Ethan could do was make the best of what he had, and to love the people in his life.

If heaven was real and the song was true, one day he'd see his mom again. Maybe one day Ethan himself would walk without a limp, alongside the people he cared for most in the world.

But he wasn't ready to go to that place yet, and not for the first time in the past year and a half, he was grateful that he'd survived that fall through the roof. It only proved God wasn't done with him yet.

At the end of the song, Ethan set aside his guitar and gathered Angel up in his arms. Angel's heart beat rapidly against his as they clung to each other, happy and sad and everything in between. "I couldn't imagine my life without you in it," Ethan whispered.

"Me either." Angel kissed his temple. "All of this because your mom smiled at a nervous new churchgoer and decided to start a conversation."

Thank God for her.

Angel pulled back, then took Ethan's right hand in his left. "I was going to wait and give you your present in private, but this feels like the right moment."

Ethan tilted his head, intrigued—especially when he became aware of the whole adult portion of his family watching them. And it wasn't like Angel to make a show, or even make himself noticeable around his siblings. "Okay."

He dug into the pocket of his slacks and produced a square black box.

Ethan's heart galloped away like a startled colt, and he squeezed the back of the sofa with his free hand.

"I love you, Ethaniel Ezekiel Shockley," Angel said, his voice as shaky as his hands. He snapped back the box lid, showing off two stainless steel bands. He swallowed hard, and Ethan nearly melted into the floor. "Will you marry me?"

He stared at the bands, stunned stupid by Angel beating him to the punch. He'd planned to propose on Valentine's Day so he could make the occasion ridiculously romantic, and now Angel had gone and stolen his thunder. His kind, sweet, loving Angel, who'd only ever been the perfect partner.

Ethan giggled—a full-on, actual giggle that sounded a little maniacal, and then said, "Yes. Of course, yes."

"Oh, thank God." Angel's goofy grin made Ethan laugh again.

Abigail and Jillian both squealed. "My baby brother's finally getting hitched," Abigail said.

Angel plucked the wider of the two bands from the box and carefully slid it down Ethan's left ring finger. Ethan admired its shine, then did the same for Angel. He loved the idea of spending the rest of his life with Angel, not only as lovers and partners, but as husbands.

Ethan drew his fiancé into a kiss, sparing nothing in its intensity and the promise he put into every sweep of his tongue and press of his lips. Angel pulled away first, his cheeks bright red, embarrassed but happy.

"I was going to ask you, you know," Ethan said.

"I know." Angel grinned, so impish and charming. "I'm not sure why it was so important for me to be the one to ask."

"I love that you did. It tells me I'm not the only one who wants forever."

"I want all of it. The good times, the hard times, and everything in between. And I want it with you, Ethan."

"You've got me."

"Good."

They both laughed and hugged, and then endured hugs and back slaps from the rest of the family. Dad's hug lingered, and Ethan enjoyed the rare embrace. He memorized the husky, work-roughened body, the scent of his dad's cologne and shaving soap, and the ever-present smell of leather. "Wasn't what I always dreamed for you," Dad said once they broke apart. "But you're happy, and that's all your mother and I ever did want."

"I am happy, Dad." Ethan reached for Angel's hand and squeezed tight. "So happy."

"Good. Takes hard work to stay that way, but you're made of stern stuff. You'll be okay." He winked, then followed Jillian into the kitchen.

Angel pulled Ethan down the hallway a bit. "So when do I get my present?"

Ethan cupped his cheek, thumb stroking the soft skin below his eye. "You want your present, huh?"

"Hmm. Depends. Will it scandalize your siblings?"

"Absolutely."

Angel's smile shifted into something feral. "Do tell."

"I'd rather show you. Alone in the apartment."

"In bed?"

"Most definitely in bed. Naked."

Angel put a hand on his hip. "This isn't the usual stuff we do while naked in bed, is it?"

Ethan leaned in closer, enjoy the sugary scent of Angel's skin. "That will be involved, yes, but the present is in a wrapped box beneath our bed."

"Do I get three guesses?"

"No, but I'll give you hints." Ethan loved the game they were playing, even though Angel probably had guessed based on last month's very revealing conversation revolving around sex toys and things Angel wanted to try. "It requires both batteries and lube."

Angel's eyes went wide. "You got it?"

"Maybe."

"Will your family miss us for an hour or two?"

"I honestly don't care." And he didn't. Ethan dragged his newly-minted fiancé through the kitchen and out the back door. No one asked where they were going, which was good, because Ethan didn't trust himself not to blurt out the truth—that he was taking Angel back to their place to fuck him with an eight-inch vibrating dildo.

Some things were better left private.

At the top of the stairs, Angel stopped him with a firm tug on his hand. Ethan froze with his fingers curled around the knob, curious.

"Were you really going to ask me?" Angel said.

"Yes. On Valentine's Day."

Angel laughed. "That is so you. Are you sorry I beat you to it?"

"Not at all." Ethan turned and wrapped Angel up in his arms, barely feeling the cold air swirling around them. "The only thing that would have made your proposal more perfect was if Mom had been here to see it. She'd have loved it."

"She told me to do it."

"She what?"

Angel ducked his head. "The last time I saw her alone in the hospital, she told me I should make an honest man out of you. But not until I knew it was right."

"Sounds like her." Ethan's heart ached for his mom, even while it celebrated the life he was about to begin with Angel. "She saw what we could be before you or I did."

"I expect Ruth saw two lost and lonely souls who could potentially be the best of friends," Angel said.

"Our guardian angel."

"Yes. And I think this?" Angel joined their ringed hands together. "Is the answer to a prayer none of us dared voice out loud."

"I know I didn't. But now that I have you, I will spend the rest of my life proving I'm worthy of the love you've given me, Matthew 'Angel' Garrett. I promise."

"Me too."

They sealed the promise on a kiss, and then moved the show indoors. As Ethan made love to his fiancé that afternoon, he swore to himself to never take for granted the blessings in his life —be they physical, emotional, or the people he loved. He was still a little bit broken, and that was okay. Everyone was, in some way or another. And despite their jagged edges, he and Angel fit in the most perfect of ways.

Ethan would cherish that, because they both deserved to be happy.

Always.

About the Author

A.M. Arthur was born and raised in the same kind of small town that she likes to write about, a stone's throw from both beach resorts and generational farmland. She's been creating stories in her head since she was a child and scribbling them down nearly as long, in a losing battle to make the fictional voices stop. She credits an early fascination with male friendships (bromance hadn't been coined yet back then) with her later discovery of and subsequent love affair with m/m romance stories. A.M. Arthur's work is available from Carina Press, Dreamspinner Press, and SMP Swerve.

When not exorcising the voices in her head, she toils away in a retail job that tests her patience and gives her lots of story fodder. She can also be found in her kitchen, pretending she's an amateur chef and trying to not poison herself or others with her cuisine experiments.

Contact her at am_arthur@yahoo.com with your cooking tips (or book comments). You can also find her online (http://amarthur.blogspot.com/), as well as on
Twitter (http://twitter.com/am_arthur),
Tumblr (http://www.tumblr.com/blog/am-arthur), and
Facebook (https://www.facebook.com/A.M.Arthur.M.A).

ALSO BY A.M. ARTHUR

All Saints
Come What May
Say It Right
As I Am

Off Beat
Body Rocks
Steady Stroke
Hot Licks

Discovering Me
Unearthing Cole
Understanding Jeremy

What You Own

Us
Here For Us
Sound of Us (coming soon)